PRISONERS OF THORNBRILL

PRISONERS OF THORNBRILL

Hannah Pennington

May It Happen Press

For information contact:
Hannah Pennington
www.hannahpenningtonauthor.com

Paperback: 979-8-9869831-0-3
Hardcover: 979-8-9869831-2-7
Ebook: 979-8-9869831-1-0

May It Happen Press

Second Edition

Developmental edits by Victoria Lynn, Glory Writers
Copyedit and line edit by Addison Horner, Avocado Tree Press
Proofread by Renee Dugan
Formatting by Hannah Pennington
Cover Art by Hannah Pennington © 2023
Cover Design by Hannah Pennington © 2023
Map by Hannah Pennington © 2023
Typefaces: *Aegean* by Matt Frost and *Luminari* by Philip Bouwsma

To the readers who miss the tales and adventures of their childhood. I hope this brings back some of the magic.

<3

Praise for Prisoners of Thornbrill

"*Prisoners of Thornbrill* is an exciting YA adventure that takes you from the depths of the Grand Canyon to an entirely new world! The book is an engaging, wholesome, page turner; the perfect story for young readers and those who miss the whimsy and wonder of Narnia."
- CHARITY A. LAND, AUTHOR OF THE LEGACY OF CHEVOLTA series

"I laughed. I cried. I cheered. *Prisoners of Thornbrill* is a triumph from start to finish!"
- JESSICA FLORY, AWARD-WINNING AUTHOR OF *OCEANS OF SAND*

"What a ride! A daring dragon adventure with swords, shapeshifters, and sibling bonds that will transport you to a new world. Hannah Pennington delivers with an action-packed tale that's great for kids and teens alike. Brother-and-sister duo Jason and Melanie are so relatable, and their determination in the midst of adversity is admirable. A truly hope-filled story with an emphasis on faith and perseverance!"
- ANGELA KNOTTS MORSE, AUTHOR OF THE SON OF AVARIA TRILOGY

"*Prisoners of Thornbrill* charts the epic adventures of Melanie and her brother Jason after they stumble across a dragon egg from another realm. It combines adventure and excitement in perfect doses and will have fantasy fans gripped from the outset!"
- C. L. LAUDER, AUTHOR OF *THE QUELLING*

"Dragons, portals, and battles, oh my! This book kicks off what promises to be an amazing trilogy, reminiscent of the Chronicles of Narnia, Adventures in Odyssey, and the legends of King Arthur. Imaginative, daring, and witty, *Prisoners of Thornbrill* contrasts the darkest of hearts with the most valiant of heroes."
- CYDNIE TRENHOLM, AUTHOR OF *BY MY OWN BETRAYAL*

"A sweeping, adventure story perfect for dragon lovers! Filled with spunky, memorable characters, Melanie and Jason's story is one that won't soon be forgotten!"
- SABRINA LOZIER, AUTHOR OF *BROKEN CROWN*

Pronunciation Guide

Characters
Aleth: a-lith
Baraden: bear-uh-den
Bareth: bear-ith
Boliver: bah-lih-ver
Brefiüll: breh-fee-yull
Briefur: bree-fur
Eldrain: el-drain
Elethýna: el-uh-thee-nuh
Elkarim: el-kuh-rim
Elken: el-kin
Elthar: el-thar
Fallon: fal-lun
Helketh: hel-kith
Helmir: hel-meer
Helnah: hel-nuh
Keth: keth
Laena: lay-nuh
Latthias: luh-thigh-iss
Lingolm: ling-golm
Scalaed: skuh-laid
Thendrell: then-jrull
Waldens: wall-dinz

Locations
Allendia: a-len-dee-uh
Anguill: ang-gwill
Arfire: ar-fire
Endlewood: en-dull-wood
Endrial: en-jree-yull
Flüm Allarway: floom a-lar-way
Flüm Thrae: floom thray
Hvitria: hvit-tree-uh

Lakéthion: la-kay-thee-on
Lethios: lee-thee-os
Rhydrah: rye-jruh
Tharretill: ther-i-till
Thornbrill: thorn-brill
Tildain's Chasm: till-dain
Tindoria: tin-dor-ee-uh
Yolderain: yole-duh-rain

Creatures & Races
Anguison: ang-gwis-on
Azeur: a-zuer
Byrn: birn
Froxil: frox-ill
Hündr: hŏon der
Lythoras: lith-or-us
Silvedus: sil-vi-dus
Starlark: star-lark
Tarothyl: tare-uh-thill
Trarewolf: trare-wolf
Ziyar: zai-yar

Items
Abrielstone: ay-bree-ul-stone
Clavnir: klav-neer
Ilvir: ill-veer
Mastrónias: mas-troh-nee-us
Thardenveil: thar-din-vail
Tharlyps: thar-lips
Yelnight: yell-night

The Realm of
Tindoria
Endlewood
Drian Forest
Greenfields Road
Flúm Elsfar
(Emerald
Flúm Aldeyin
Lakéthion
Sea of Starlight
The Deltas of Aldeyin
Great South Road
Flúm Lurta
The White Coasts
Sea of Starstone
Flúm Luster
Flúm Helfar
N
W
E
S
Miles
25   50   75   100

(Golden Mountains)
Castle of Ascenya
Goldwood
The Black Coasts
ALLEZ PIADZ
(Ruby Mountains)
Arfire Maze
Tildain's Chasm
Thornbrill
Flüm Castyl
Flüm Yennas
Sunguld Lake
ld Mountains)
Anguill Swamps
Spire of Tavnir
Flüm Vardin
Fog of Tordin
Flüm Thrae
Tharlyps Forest
CHARRETILL
Flüm Athek
Flüm Kilnath
Trellin Forest
Great River
Rainwood
THE DEPLORABLE WASTE
RHYLDRAH
Flüm Dhyr
(Diamond Mountains)
(Sapphire Mountains)
Diamond Pass
Flüm Ebyr
Great South Road
KLICRIVA
The White Village
...llth Forest
Yolderain
Bay of Rholdir

Contents

Prologue

They would *not* have this one.

The green-mantled figure fled with amazing speed on a shimmering unicorn. Their breath misted in the crisp morning air. Shouts echoed throughout the forest behind them, and the green rider leaned forward just as an arrow whizzed passed them. After whispering in the unicorn's ear, the rider straightened and adjusted the reins in a pair of white-knuckled hands. With a determined shake of its mane, the unicorn lurched forward, streaking through the wood on hooves aglow with golden sparks.

The screams ceased as the pursuers fell far behind, unable to keep pace with the unicorn.

Safe for the moment, the rider pulled the reins, drawing the unicorn to a halt. Dismounting, the rider entered a glade still asleep in the morning hush. This place would shield them. The hood fell to reveal the face of a regal woman. She raised an alabaster arm, waving it in a graceful arc, and the trees bowed low about them. Branches and limbs creaked and groaned and held one another in an impenetrable wall. The rustle of leaves stilled, as if the forest held its breath to watch what happened next.

Unclasping her mantle, the woman cradled a large black stone in its green folds. Her eyes, though filled with heavy sadness, shimmered like emeralds. Freed from the hood, her hair tumbled like a golden waterfall past her waist and touched the diamond-studded hem of her chartreuse gown.

Hunted by the barbarians of the Fortress of Thornbrill, she had managed to smuggle one dragon egg to safety. Undefeated and unchallenged, Thornbrill's dragon army grew with every passing day, but this was the one dragon she refused to let them have.

Beyond the barricade of trees, the distant thunder of hooves rumbled, growing louder with every passing second. Her enemies were near. Holding the egg out before her, the woman blew softly over it. A glittering puff of gold washed over it, and the egg vanished in a flash of light, setting in motion her world's deliverance.

CHAPTER 1

A Strange Finding

Melanie Waldens was determined to enjoy her last weekend before beginning her sophomore year of high school. She trekked through the woods surrounding the campground, listening to the sounds of Kaibab National Forest. Her family had moved to Arizona and decided a vacation would be a great start to their life in the new state.

Melanie was beginning to agree. The faint rustling of the trees grew louder as a pine-scented breeze zipped past her, whipping her brown hair across her face, and faded into the woods. Melanie ran her hands through her hair, combing it back and out of her brown eyes. The bright shades of green shimmered around her, birds sang in harmony, with the occasional woodpecker interrupting the symphony.

She smiled. It was a perfect afternoon.

Melanie longed to stay here forever. Trees didn't bully, flowers didn't form cliques, and the great boulders hadn't grown braindead from social media use. Stopping to smell the pinewood air, she drank in the scents of the forest. Wild oxygen cleared her mind, and Melanie started to think she just might forget the imminent gloom of cold, concrete classrooms.

She'd spent the last ten years in six different schools,

every one of them the same. Frequent moving was the lot of a Marine Corps sergeant's family, but with her dad's retirement in April, this move would be their last. No matter the town, Melanie had lacked in the making-friends department. To her, it made little sense to form attachments when moving so often. That could change now that she could finally plant roots, but she didn't know where to start. It had been too long since she trusted in a lasting friendship; those had faded with distance and time, and those she had thought were friends never bothered to keep in touch.

She shook the thoughts from her head. This was a time for peace and unwinding. Unhappy thoughts were unwelcome here.

Picking up the pace, she jogged farther into the forest and its soothing serenity. The trail narrowed, leading Melanie around a bend, but she carried on until something sparkled brightly in the corner of her eye. Melanie stopped, backed up, and stared into the ferns.

"What's that?" she muttered as she crouched down to investigate. She shifted her weight from side to side, wondering if changing her angle would reveal anything. A quick flash appeared in the darkness, a glimpse of red in the shadows.

"Ugh," Melanie frowned at the thought of littering. *Bet it's a soda can.* She reached into the shrubbery to grab it. It didn't feel like aluminum, and she needed two hands to grab hold of it. With a groan, Melanie dragged out a round, football-sized stone. She plopped back on her butt, confused.

"I thought I saw you sparkle," she told it, rolling it around in her hands. Wiping off the soil, Melanie began to see veins and splotches of red, a rich color that swirled in layers with a holographic sheen. Dust had dulled the stone's sleek black surface, but Melanie still could not determine its material. She bounced it gently to feel its weight. Though it was roughly the size of a football, it felt lighter than it should have. Melanie arched an eyebrow, curious and captivated.

"What are you?" she whispered.

She wanted to show Jason. Tucking the stone under her arm, Melanie stood up and headed back towards the campgrounds.

Jason searched hungrily for his family's cooler. Dinner time had finally arrived, and he had done his best to wait patiently, but this thirteen-year-old boy had had food on his mind for hours now. He grabbed the blue-and-white container and hauled it out of the tent, practically tasting the juicy, charbroiled burger that would soon grace his palette. Melty cheese, dripping with ketchup and mayonnaise, at least four slices of bacon, toasted bun—

"Oof!" Jason's daydream was dashed as he collided with his sister, who seemingly appeared out of nowhere.

"Geez, Jason, watch it!" Melanie scoffed. "You okay?"

"Famished," Jason replied, his hazel eyes wide. "Whatcha

got there?" He jabbed a finger at her finding.

Melanie hefted the rock to one side, cocked her head back at Jason, and said with a smile, "I have absolutely no idea."

Jason nodded uncertainly. "Right…So why do you have it? I mean it looks pretty neat, but…" He shrugged in confusion, still staring at the stone.

"I thought it could be worth something, who knows? Maybe we can take it to the Antique Road Show to find out," she joked. "Think these could be rubies?"

Jason scratched his head, ruffling his brown hair. "Rock questions are for Cousin Kyle." He shuddered. "What a *nerd!* Anyway, my brain is running on fumes, and I need burger fuel." He gestured to the cooler. "I also heard s'mores are on the menu, and I was gonna steal one before dinner. Coming?"

"Pfft! One does not simply have *one* s'more." Melanie smiled conspiratorially. She dumped the rock into her backpack at the tent's entrance and wheeled around to chase after her brother.

Jason ran to his dad, who was setting a grill grate over a freshly made campfire, and confiscated the marshmallow bag sitting next to him. Mr. Waldens jumped to his feet and said, "You only get the whole bag if your intention is to challenge the Chubby Bunny King!" He grappled his son and used the ever-reliable tickle-him-till-he-can't-breathe technique until Jason weakly surrendered the bag through squeaky breathing.

"I was waiting for you to get socked in the face there, Hon," Mrs. Waldens told her husband from her seat at the picnic table as she unwrapped a burger patty.

Melanie stifled her laughter, but Mr. Waldens shrugged it off with a knowing smirk and placed the marshmallows on the table.

"Injustice!" Jason giggled as he reached dramatically for the picnic table. "To reconcile my violation, I demand triple the marshmallows!"

Melanie threw a graham cracker at his face. "You're not gonna get squat if you lie there in a puddle of self-pity."

Jason finally composed himself and joined his family, attempting to stuff a record of seventeen marshmallows on his stick.

Within those few minutes, Melanie had quite forgotten about her strange discovery.

CHAPTER 2

"Leave It!"

M elanie!" Mrs. Waldens's echoing voice made its way to her room. "I want you to clean your room. I don't even remember the color of your carpet anymore; I haven't seen it in eons!"

Melanie lay on her bed, flipping through an outdoor sports catalog, and ignored her mom's request.

"I want it finished before I get back from the store," Mrs. Waldens added. "I got to grab paper towels. I'll be back in fifteen minutes."

Draping the catalog over her face, Melanie flopped her head on her pillow and groaned. Peeking from under the pages, she looked at her room with disgust. It really *was* a disaster, but the chance of the mess disappearing by sheer force of will was zero percent.

A pile of books sat stacked in the far corner of Melanie's room, and clothes lay strewn everywhere but the hamper. Her catalogs, full of expired deals and discounts she likely never would have used, littered another corner. Her school supplies had overtaken the desk and surrounding floor over the summer, and her carpet, wherever it was, desperately needed vacuuming.

She waddled through the mess to her window and opened

the curtains, desperate to find any excuse to procrastinate.

The Waldenses lived in Page, Arizona, a small town flanked by the Colorado River and red sandy vastness in every other direction. Their house was part of a development on the western side of town. Framed by a low picket fence, their front lawn desperately tried to stay pretty and green in the ruthless summer, while the backyard had given up all hope and sat unkempt with wild, parched shrubbery. A wall of evergreen spires gave them privacy from neighbors, and palm trees along the sidewalks wove green fronds in the dry air.

Taking a deep breath, Melanie turned to face her room and said, "Operation: Cleanup." She dug her phone out of her pocket and queued up a motivational playlist.

After seven songs, Melanie cleared away the disaster, placing the last of the books on her shelf. Spinning around to the song as it neared the end, Melanie saw her backpack slumped against the closet.

She still hadn't unpacked since returning from camping yesterday evening. She would have to, though, to use the bag for school tomorrow. *Ugh, I'll do it later,* she reasoned. *I cleaned enough today already.* Sidestepping towards the backpack, Melanie kicked it into her closet in perfect sync to the music. "Done!" She threw her hands up triumphantly.

The mysterious stone rolled out of her backpack.

Melanie picked it up. "Guess I brought it home." After a pause, she placed it on her shelf with a shrug, then turned her attention to the carpet, a glare growing on her face. "And now for you." Melanie marched out of her room to fetch the vacuum, never noticing the rock wiggle and begin to crack.

Whistling happily, Jason skipped up the stairs on the way to his room for a video game session. As he passed Melanie's doorway, he spotted the rock. After a quick glance around, he waltzed in and inspected the rock with an impish grin. His hazel eyes twinkled with mischief.

"Pfft, like she'll miss it for five minutes," he scoffed. His fingers grasped the rock, fluidly slipping it behind his back. "And the master thief escapes," Jason whispered, dashing out of Melanie's room into his own. In his haste, he didn't notice the cracks grow and spread.

Plopping onto the floor with crossed legs, Jason tilted the rock in his hands. The falling beam of afternoon light streamed from his window and illuminated the red splotches on the rock.

"Maybe they *are* rubies," Jason mused and fished out his multi-tool from his pocket. Flipping out the knife blade, he carefully tried to scrape out a red splotch. He froze when a web of cracks rippled from the back and into view. The red splotch twitched and peeled off.

Jason backed away, eyes locked on the rock that now wiggled of its own accord. Something smoky leaked from the cracks before evaporating in steam.

"Melanie?" Jason fumbled for the doorknob. "Your rock is—!"

That was when the rock exploded.

"Okay, let's get this over with," Melanie mumbled as she plugged the vacuum in. Her foot went towards the power pedal, when a shriek vibrated through the entire house, followed by more terrible screams.

"Jason!" Melanie shouted, adrenaline surging through every muscle as she ran down the hallway. "What happened?"

The screams pierced the air again once she reached Jason's room and saw the doorknob rattling. Melanie whipped open the door and collided with Jason, who was white as a sheet as he slammed the door shut behind him. Melanie braced his shoulders to stop him from running away and asked, "Are you okay, Jason? Are you hurt?"

"It's in my room!" Jason squeaked.

"What is?"

"You know exactly what!" Jason yelled. "You're the one who brought it home!"

"What?"

Jason pointed to his room with his knife. "Just open it, you'll see!" His voice shook with fear.

Opening the door a crack, Melanie strained her eyes to

see anything unusual in Jason's room. Nothing was there.

"Bro, I don't see anything," she said in a low voice.

Jason pursed his lips together. "It's in there, probably waiting to ambush and eat us!"

"I don't see anything," Melanie repeated. "If it's another scorpion—" She cried out and took a mighty leap from the door as something hissed by her feet.

Jason pointed frantically at the ground. "*There!*" he yelled and took off running.

Melanie held her breath, petrified. Staring up at her with eyes of red fire was a small black reptile with a crown of crimson horns. A spine of dark red spikes ran down its back to its tail. It flapped leathery wings menacingly, snarling through its needle-sharp white teeth.

"It's gonna kill us!" Jason yelled from the security of the staircase.

"Jason, shut up, don't scare it!" Melanie held her hand out to signal silence, not breaking eye contact with the creature.

"What the heck is it?" Jason asked, a little less loudly.

"It's...a dragon," Melanie whispered.

"Are you there? Melanie!" Jason thundered up the steps. "Did you get eaten?"

"Shhh!"

Jason froze when he looked at the dragon for the first time. "Holy shiitake mushrooms," he breathed.

After an eternal second of silence, the dragon stopped growling at Melanie. Both held eye contact. The dragon's pupils dilated, and it began to purr calmly. It seemed comfortable so close to Melanie, and its eyes sparkled with curiosity. Melanie became aware of her heart thumping faster, and the room around them faded from focus. She and the dragon searched each other's eyes, brown on red, and a warmth bloomed in Melanie's chest, thumping in a separate rhythm. Then, just as quickly as it had come, the sensation receded, and the dragon skittered back into Jason's room.

Melanie released her breath and followed the dragon with Jason close behind.

"Where did he come from?" Melanie wondered as they watched.

Creeping over to a stack of books, the dragon set its tiny teeth into a book's spine and began to pull with all its might.

Melanie watched the rest of the stack come crashing down on it with a chorus of thumps followed by a muffled squeal.

"Whoa, what are you doing?" Jason asked as Melanie crawled over and shifted the books off the poor creature. With no hesitation, she picked the dragon up with gentle hands. It didn't appear to be hurt.

"Okay, cool," Jason hissed, panic seeping back into his voice. "It's got strong scales, it's fine, now *please put it down!*"

Sitting cross-legged on Jason's carpet, Melanie placed the dragon back on its feet. It shook itself off and snorted happily. Wisps of smoke curled from its nostrils and mouth. Melanie and Jason stared, wide-eyed.

When Jason spoke, the pitch of his voice had raised an octave. "Oh heck, it *is* a dragon."

Melanie nodded, unsure what to say.

"A real live dragon in my bedroom!" Jason said. "It could burn the whole house down!"

"Then let's not provoke him, and I think we'll be fine."

"Oh, it's a 'him' now? How do you know?"

When Melanie looked down at the dragon, the strange heartbeat returned for a moment. "It's just a strong feeling."

"Get rid of it," Jason demanded.

The dragon purred innocently.

"I don't think we should," Melanie said.

"What, so you're saying we should keep it?" Jason cried. "Are you insane? Hello? The FBI or CIA might find out, then they'd be hopping all over us."

"Well, I don't think he would survive on his own. He doesn't have the slightest clue of how to fend for himself."

"Animals have survival instincts hardwired into their brains," Jason said. "It's a well-known fact!"

"But he's just a baby! He could be eaten by a coyote."

"It's got freakin' *fire-breath!*"

Melanie looked at the dragon. He was gazing up at her now and placed a tentative paw on her knee. Sniffing her legs and giving her face another glance, he hopped into Melanie's lap.

"Oh, great," Jason flung his hand at her. "It's imprinted on you. Now it'll never leave."

Imprinted? Melanie found herself smiling at the notion. And she could have sworn the dragon looked just as happy. "Looks like he gets to stay here."

Jason rubbed his forehead. "Or we drop it off in the middle of the desert."

"Jason!"

"Alright, alright," he said in a quieter tone. "We'll do it your way...for now. But if 'barbecue' ever crosses its mind, game over."

Melanie stroked the dragon's neck. A faint peaceful heartbeat thudded in time with her own. As crazy as it sounded, she was quickly growing attached to him.

Jason crept closer to get a better look. The reality of a living mythical creature sitting with them began to sink in.

"I guess it's kind of cool," he admitted. "I mean, it is an actual dragon for crying out loud!" He let out a nervous chuckle. "So what do we tell Mom and Dad?"

"We can't!" Melanie looked up. "If they knew, and someone found out, we could all get in trouble. The authorities might take the dragon away for experimenting. We could get arrested. We need to keep this a secret to protect them."

"But where are you going to hide it? What is it going to eat?"

Melanie sighed. "I don't know—not right now, at least."

"Leave it in the desert."

"No!"

CHAPTER
3
Scalaed

Melanie's eyes widened when she heard the hum of the garage door. Mrs. Waldens had returned from the store.

Jason opened his mouth to speak, but Melanie interjected, "We're *not* ditching the dragon."

"I was gonna say 'chuck the lizard,' but okay."

"Help me hide him," Melanie panicked and began tossing things aside in the room. "And get rid of these eggshells!"

Jason hunted down the black and red pieces of egg scattered by the explosion. They were still warm, and any remaining fluid had been boiled off. Dumping them into his trash can, Jason dove into his closet in search of a hiding place for the dragon, who watched the commotion with calm, curious eyes.

Melanie rummaged blindly through old toys under Jason's bed. "Come on," she muttered. "There's got to be something."

"Eureka!" shouted Jason as he held up a bird cage that had belonged to his deceased parakeet Pikachu. He slammed the cage on the carpet and tried shooing the dragon inside. The creature didn't budge. In desperation, Jason gave him a little spank. With a yelp, the shocked dragon hopped inside the cage.

"I'm home!" Mrs. Waldens called from the stairs. "Everything okay?"

Lifting the cage, Melanie shoved it in Jason's closet and shut the door. She turned to see her mom standing in the doorway, studying her daughter's terrified expression.

"What on earth is going on in here?" Mrs. Waldens asked, befuddled. She scanned the room with her hands on her hips. "Looks like the disaster just moved from your sister's room to yours. Melanie, help him clean. I want this room spotless by dinner. Is that clear, you two?"

"Crystal." Jason flashed a huge smile with two thumbs up.

As soon as Mrs. Waldens left the room, the siblings looked at each other and opened the closet. The dragon was sleeping.

"Guess we can clean while he naps," Jason said with a sigh. He shoved the small, unimportant items under his bed. He was a strong believer in the mantra "Outta sight; outta mind." Normally Melanie would reprimand him, but she wanted the room clean just as fast as he did. They had to convince their mom everything was normal.

Once finished, Jason took the bird cage from his closet and placed it on the floor between them.

"I guess we'll have to raise him," Melanie said.

"I'm sorry," Jason said in disbelief, "did you say, 'raise him?' How on earth is that a good idea?"

"You said so yourself," Melanie said, growing defensive. "He's imprinted on me, so now he thinks I'm his mother. He'll expect me to provide for him, so casting him out would be a death sentence."

"I didn't use *all* those words, but—"

"Come on, Jason!" Melanie pleaded. "This is a *dragon!* If anyone finds out, we're doomed. I have to protect him."

Protect him? What's gotten into her? Jason had no idea what to do. Scenarios cycled through his mind. Abandoning the dragon to the elements might lead it to burn down the house in revenge.

He held up his hands. "Fine, we'll keep it. But we need a plan."

"Thank you." The tension in Melanie's shoulders eased. *How hard could this be?*

"So how do we keep Mom and Dad from finding out?" Jason asked.

Melanie shrugged. "We'll keep him outside somewhere…"

"So I don't have to change his newspapers. Good."

"…but I don't want another creature to eat him."

Jason groaned. "He's got fire breath, Melanie."

"We've only seen smoke," Melanie pointed out. "Maybe he's not old enough to shoot fire yet."

Jason glanced out his window, which overlooked the backyard. "What about the shed? We don't use it anyway."

"That works," Melanie said. "We also have to feed him somehow. I could sneak him some of my food from tonight's dinner."

"Yeah, but isn't that kind of a waste? I mean, maybe you could try and find something else that's, well, free."

"Yeah," Melanie agreed. "But where in this town am I

going to get free food?"

"The dumpster?"

Melanie glared. "Yeah, right. That's a perfectly healthy diet—" Her mouth hung open. "Oh my gosh, that's it! Jason, you're a genius."

Jason was utterly confused. "What did I say?"

"I can go to Bert's Butts & Cuts and ask them for cuts of meat no one buys."

"That butcher shop?" Jason clarified.

"Yes! Okay, okay, now we have to plan out a schedule. School starts tomorrow. Should I bring the dragon?"

Jason did not even hesitate before he said, "No way! Leave the lizard home. Come on, is that even a question? He'll be fine in the shed."

"But if I can't keep an eye on him, Mom or Dad will see him for sure."

Jason scrunched his mouth in thought. "Well, it's not like you can stuff him in your desk. Just face it, Melanie, this is going to be the toughest thing you've ever done. Though it might be a close second to my AI trashcan science project..."

Melanie nodded as she thought of all the tasks and burdens that lay in her future. To keep the dragon a secret would mean she could not let anyone get close to her. She'd have to seal off connections. Trust no one.

However, the inexplicably strong bond between her and the dragon would not allow her to let him go. What was this feeling that drew her close to the dragon? This pulsing, beating, warmth? It was a string of emotion that tied them together—their hearts speaking to each other. And it told her she was now responsible for his life.

Melanie grabbed an empty food container and crept into the kitchen. She raided the fridge for bacon, then flew up the stairs to her room, where Jason had moved the cage. Walking over to it, she tapped the little reptile's forehead.

His red eyes blinked, but he immediately sat up when he smelled the bacon.

"Here you go, boy," Melanie said as she placed the container in front of the open cage door. "This should hold you over until I get more."

"If you're sure it *is* a boy," Jason said with his arms crossed. "I might not remember everything from zoology class, but I didn't see you check him for femoral pores or anything."

"He's a boy," Melanie assured him.

Jason watched the dragon skeptically as he devoured the bacon. "Dang!" Jason exclaimed. "He couldn't wait to say Grace? What a pig!"

"Yeah, kinda reminds me of a brother of mine," Melanie said with a smirk.

"Hey!"

The dragon yawned. Jason backed out of blast range but sighed in relief when the baby curled around and went to sleep.

"We should name him," Melanie finally said.

"Yeah? Like what?" Jason asked. "How about Torch."

"Boring."

"Scalasaurus."

"Pfft, what?"

"Barney."

"Oh, heck no."

"Just throwing out random options here." Jason shrugged.

Melanie sorted through possibilities in her mind. "I want something original. Something cool..." She thought for a moment. "Scalaed!"

"Skuh-laid?" Jason made a face as he tried to say the word.

"Yeah!"

"Like, Kool-Aid?"

"No, goof, like his strong scales." Seeing how her brother was completely uninterested, Melanie said, "Never mind. I'm going to bike down to Bert's and ask about the meat. Tell Mom I went for a bike ride if she asks."

"Well, what do you want *me* to do?" asked Jason.

Melanie rose to her feet. "Move Scalaed to the shed and find him some old toys or something. I'll be back in fifteen minutes."

Then she was gone, leaving Jason alone with Scalaed. He blew through puffed cheeks at the thought of his task. "Alrighty, little mister." He wrung his hands anxiously. "How are we gonna do this?"

Scalaed lay his head on his front claws, tracking Jason with his large red eyes.

"Mom is in the kitchen, so we'll steer clear of there," Jason explained. Talking through it out loud made him feel more competent. "Dad's gonna be home in about an hour… and I still haven't moved you."

Scalaed licked his lips, listening.

Jason stilled his hands, then lowered himself to the dragon's level. "Let's just start over, okay?"

Scalaed moved forward, sniffing Jason's outstretched hand.

"I'm Jason. You're Scalaed, a dragon, which of course you know."

A small yip.

"I'm going to pick you up in this cage, okay? Then we're going to go outside where it's nice and sunny and warm… and then lock you in a dark, stuffy shed, which doesn't sound nice at all." Jason trailed off, exasperated. He needed to stop stalling. He could handle one simple task. "Okay, listen. I'm taking you now. And you are going to sit nicely and not torch me. Capeesh?"

Snort.

"Excellent."

Psyched up, Jason grabbed the bird cage and crept down the stairs. He peered his head into the kitchen archway. Mrs. Waldens was hunched over her phone, back to Jason, watching the news as sizzling chicken on the nearby stove filled the air with spice.

Scalaed loosed a mesmerized growl, at which Jason frantically retreated. Out the back door he ran and toward the shed.

The shed had come with the house when the Waldenses moved in five months ago. The once-red walls had cracked and peeled from the harsh sun, and the white trim lay hidden under a dusty orange film. They didn't need the extra storage, so the shed sat empty. Jason opened the door and slipped inside. He breathed in the hot, stale air as his heart continued pounding against his ribcage. Jason placed the cage on the ground and searched the dusty haze of the shed. Its windows cast beams that sparkled with dust particles, and the baby dragon pawed at them with tiny, tender claws.

Jason opened the cage door. Scalaed stepped out, drinking in his new surroundings.

Old, tattered tarps from the previous owners lay in a faded heap in the corner alongside planks from some abandoned project. Scalaed scratched at one of the nearest tarps, tugging and sniffing it like a cat would do with a sofa.

"Glad to see you find this place more interesting than I do." Jason smirked. "I'll be right back. I've got something I think you'll like."

While the dragon was distracted by the tarp, Jason ran back to the house, propelled himself up the stairs, and ran to his closet. Shoving aside clothes that had fallen off their hangers, he hauled out a box of his miscellaneous belongings. He opened the taped flaps with a swift slice of his multi-tool, checked the contents, and rushed back outside before anyone saw him.

"Hey, lookie here!" Jason announced breathlessly as he

closed the shed door with his foot.

Scalaed craned his neck around and watched Jason drop the box with a thud. The first thing Jason pulled out was a green fleece blanket displaying a monkey in a jungle. "This oughta be more comfortable than the tarp, yeah?"

Scalaed tracked the blanket as Jason set it next to him. Next was a ball that lit up in rainbow colors, which entranced Scalaed.

"Here's my pal from toddlerhood." Jason lifted up a well-loved stuffed T-Rex. "He's a lizard-y guy like you." Jason walked the toy towards Scalaed, who locked eyes on it. "He's gonna babysit you while I run to the bathroom. All this stress has shrunk my bladder." Jason started towards the door to leave, but not before he warned, "You play nice, okay? I won't be *that* long." Then he was gone.

The shed suddenly seemed twice its size and equally empty. Scalaed mewled sadly and pawed the door. The latch wasn't the most secure thing, as he discovered when it opened a crack. A sliver of bright light beckoned to him.

A new yearning swelled in him. A primal desire to be one with his instincts. And his instincts said to hunt.

Scalaed straightened. *Hunt.* As tasty as the bacon had been, it didn't fill him for long. He was sniffing the edge of the door when a shudder wracked his body. He backed away and squirmed as his muscles flexed and rippled in a wave from head to tail. Scales flew off and hit the window with loud pings, and before Scalaed knew what had happened, he found himself stepping out of a sheet of black skin and scales. He had grown several pounds heavier.

Now, he was *really* hungry. He bumped his head against the door, and it creaked open.

The sun blazed from a sky of brilliant blue. The outside felt warmer and smelled fresher as Scalaed took a tentative step out of the shed. The sandy ground welcomed his paws, and the parched grass tickled him as he passed through.

Scalaed sat and pondered his next move. Then a faint rustling sounded from the other side of the shed. He crept closer to the sound.

His eyes locked onto the rummaging form in the shrubs. This was a strange creature. Its pink nose and paws rooted the ground, making small pits wherever it went, and it wore a mottled, pleated shell, similar in texture to Scalaed's own scales.

Scalaed promptly labeled it "dinner."

With level, calculated movements, the dragon stalked the armadillo. One claw in front of the other. He was poised to strike when his prey caught a whiff and bolted. At least, its version of bolting—more of a wobbly, clunky bouncing.

Instinct overtook Scalaed. Heat swirled in his core—fire waiting to be released. Inhaling for a blast, Scalaed rolled his tongue tightly then funneled a concentrated white-hot thread that seared right through the armadillo, ending the chase and its life. Impressed with himself, Scalaed scampered over and tore into the animal. The smell of smoke broke the spell of his warm, fresh meal, and Scalaed realized it wasn't coming from his dinner.

His little hunting technique had shot through the animal like a flaming laser and lit up a patch of dry vegetation. The fire was catching fast.

Panic shocked Scalaed's insides, and he ran to the fire to try stomping it out. Though he was fireproof, this fire was too fast, too hungry for his paws. It licked higher up the shed.

Scalaed slunk out of sight into the shrubs. What should he do? Melanie and Jason were going to be so mad at him. He had promised he would be a good boy.

The flames reflected in his wide eyes as they engulfed the shed.

Scalaed had to leave. He was in big trouble, and he was too dangerous to stay. He dragged his kill further out of sight and turned to the horizon.

With the sound of crackling flames behind him, Scalaed tentatively spread his wings. Cautious fluttering evolved to effective beating, and Scalaed's wings lifted him off the ground. Adjusting his grip on his meal, he gave one last sorrowful look at his destruction, then flew away. Away from the house and shed, away from home, and into the wilderness where he belonged. Alone, with no one to hurt.

CHAPTER 4

The Little Arsonist

Jason was running past the kitchen when Mrs. Waldens's voice stopped him.

"What are you doing out there?" Mrs. Waldens asked as she sifted through her spice drawer. "That shed is filthy and probably full of mold and bugs. I don't want you playing in it, okay?" She turned and gestured with the paprika jar. "The last thing I want is a trip to the hospital for tetanus."

Jason rolled his eyes. "Oh, come on, I'm just—" He saw the shed out the window, ablaze. His mouth hung open. *Oh, my gosh…* Thankfully, the hanging cabinets above the half bar blocked Mrs. Waldens's view, and Jason intended to keep it that way. "You know what, Mom?" He slid towards the pantry, hoping she didn't detect the shakiness in his voice. "You're right. That shed's a health hazard." *Where's the fire extinguisher?*

"Yes it is, and who knows what nasty little animals it's hiding?" Mrs. Waldens added as she tried to remember what spice she was looking for.

Jason found the extinguisher in the corner, pulled it out, and spun out of sight behind the bar. "It'd almost be better if it burned down, am I right?" He laughed awkwardly.

"Uh-huh," Mrs. Waldens said, her voice muffled by a

cabinet. "Jason, honey, I'm trying to make dinner, and I'm getting distracted from my measurements. Just keep out of the shed and the kitchen. I actually think you have some laundry on your bed you need to fold."

But Jason was long gone.

Melanie sped down the road on her purple mountain bike as the late afternoon air kissed her cheeks.

The road took Melanie east, past the hospital, small shops, restaurants, and towards a red stucco building. The name "Bert's Butts & Cuts" had brought a chuckle to her family when they passed it one day. Its sign—a sandwich-holding pig with an…ample derriere—stood above the black-and-white awning that rippled in the weak breeze.

Melanie parked her bike outside and took a deep breath. Reminding herself of the importance of her visit, she entered.

Varieties of meat artfully lined the glass counter display, each nestled on beds of crushed ice. A second counter, flanked by small tables, mirrored it on the other end of the shop, but with a display of gourmet deli sandwiches. The menu made Melanie's mouth water, especially after seeing the sign proudly stating the shop partnered with the local bakery for fresh bread. She would have been tempted to buy one, but the sandwich bar had closed a couple hours ago. With a rustic aesthetic of dark-stained wood, black iron, and Edison lights, the butcher shop was nothing like Melanie was expecting.

Neither customers nor employees were anywhere to be seen. Melanie stuffed her hands in her pockets, wondering if this had been a good idea.

"Ed!" a voice boomed from the back. "Ed, help me close up, it's almost six o'clock."

A muscular man in his forties walked behind the cash register with a belt full of evil-looking knives.

"Um, hi." Melanie waved meekly as she moved to the front desk.

The man looked up, his blue eyes crinkling as he smiled. "Evenin'! How can I help you, Miss? We're just about to call it a day."

Melanie smiled and asked, "Are you Bert?"

The man laughed heartily and said, "No, I'm Gus. Bert was my granddad. What can I do for you?"

Melanie replied, "I was curious if you have any cuts of meat that no one will ever buy?"

Gus scratched his salt-and-pepper crew cut and asked in a confused tone, "Like the scraps?"

"Yeah, anything that might otherwise go bad." Melanie kept her hands clasped closely to her middle, a subconscious habit she formed during conversations.

Gus said, "Well, we have some chicken heads in the back, some bones, organ meats, and slabs of pig fat. Plus I think we have some whole pig heads. I don't get requests for these cuts all that often, but they are available for reasonable prices. I can help you make a selection if you tell me what you're planning on cooking."

"It's for…my pet, actually." Melanie shifted her weight, squeezing her hands more tightly.

Gus furrowed his brow in confusion.

"Special diet." Melanie smiled sheepishly. "Vet's orders."

Gus shrugged. "So just a little bit of everything?"

"That works!"

"Alright then, I'll just get Ed and have him bag it for you." He turned to the back of the store. "Ed! Come out here, please."

A boy around sixteen with black hair scampered through the door, peeling his plastic gloves off.

"Sorry, Dad." He faced Gus. "That pig was a challenge."

Gus nudged his son's shoulder. "Tell me about it when we get home." He nodded his head at Melanie. "We have a customer."

Ed turned red. "Oh, sorry, Miss. What can I get you?"

"Just two pounds of the scrap cuts, please." Melanie answered.

Ed tried to say something to Melanie, but all that came out was, "Problem, no sure." Horrified at his lack of communication skills, he retreated to the back of the store.

Melanie couldn't help but smirk. "Aw, he's charming."

Gus sighed and cracked a grin. "The boy's gone twitterpated."

Compelled to avoid awkward silence at all costs, but hating small talk, Melanie rocked on the balls of her feet before finally deciding to speak. "So…butts and cuts?"

Gus hung his head guiltily with a laugh. "Granddad was a hoot. He founded the place back in sixty-five. By the way…" he slipped a hand next to his mouth and leaned forward. "Despite the name and cheeky logo, pork butts are actually the shoulder." With a wink, he continued, "But Granddad had a killer recipe—divinely smoked pork butts so tender that the meat just falls apart, mmm! Hence the name. Then the shop was passed down to my dad, who added the sandwich bar, then down to me where I partnered with the local bakeries. I'm trying to get Ed to understand the basics of the art, but…he might feel fulfilled elsewhere."

"Here we go." Ed returned with a large bag tied with a white string bow. "A little of everything as requested."

Melanie received the bag. "Thank you…Ed, is it?"

"Call me Edmund." He tousled his black hair. "My mom has a thing for romantic names."

Melanie laughed and nodded politely. "Well, thank you, Edmund, you're a lifesaver!"

"My pleasure." Edmund hadn't stopped smiling at her.

"Why don't you ring her up at the register, son?" Gus instructed. "I'm going to close up the back."

"Sure," Edmund said, and Melanie followed him to the register.

Cracking open her wallet, Melanie handed him a few bills. "How often do you have these kinds of cuts?" She asked before pocketing the change.

"Well, we don't really keep the offcuts in the shop for very long," Edmund replied. "They end up in our terrines or stocks. About every week we clear them out."

"Oh, perfect!" Melanie sighed. "I'll be back next week then."

Heat engulfed her chest, but it wasn't that calm rhythm she knew; it was a rapid, panicked thumping.

Scalaed!

"You okay?" Edmund asked, noticing her sudden paleness.

Scalaed's in trouble! "I have to get home!" Melanie said aloud as she ran for the door.

"What's wrong?" Edmund worried over her sudden change.

"I need to go," Melanie said once she reached her bike and kicked her kickstand. "Sorry, I can't explain it, but I have a strong feeling something's wrong."

"If it's an emergency, you'll need faster wheels than those." Edmund crossed his arms. "I've got a 4Runner. Let me help; we'll mount your bike."

Melanie could not trust this boy. *I can't bring this guy to my house, can I? He'll see Scalaed.* But the dragon's panic forced her to accept his offer.

"Thanks," was all she said as they ran into the parking lot.

The back door of the house whipped open, and Jason

cursed as he rushed out, armed with the fire extinguisher.

With a groan, the shed collapsed with a fiery crackle. Sparks rocketed from the debris and ignited the dry vegetation around it.

Jason coughed as he aimed. White plumes blasted from the nozzle and hit the base of the fire with a loud hiss. A cloud of smoke pummeled Jason, but he kept spraying. Between the blackout and the stinging in his eyes, he was surprised he put out the fire at all.

The wind eventually carried away most of the smoke, revealing an extinguished, smoldering heap, and Jason dropped to his knees, swallowing gulps of air. He rubbed the burning from his eyes, then froze.

"Scalaed!" he called for the dragon.

There was no answer.

"Oh, I am so dead."

Seeing smoke swirling in the distance sucked the breath from Melanie's lungs.

"I hope that's not for you." Edmund squeezed the steering wheel. "How much farther?"

Melanie had no air to speak. Her heart thudded as fast as the pulse that linked her to Scalaed.

The 4Runner barreled down the road and screeched to a

halt in front of the Waldens's house. Edmund hardly parked when Melanie leaped from the vehicle to the backyard, plastic bag squeezed in an iron grip.

"What happened?" Melanie demanded, her voice shaking as she scanned the backyard for her dragon.

"What does it look like?" Jason yelled, clutching the scorched remains of his plush dinosaur. He didn't realize he was *that* attached to Tyrone S. Orr, until he saw his old pal staring back at him, sad and charred.

"Where's Scalaed?" Melanie cried.

Jason shrugged haplessly as he glossed over the rubble. "I found paw prints when I was sifting through the mess, and it looks like he ran away toward the canyons."

"We have to find him!" She began to pace. "He could get eaten or—"

"Melanie!" Jason snapped.

Melanie stopped and turned to face him, nearly getting a face full of sooty fur.

Jason lowered Tyrone. "He can defend himself no problem. Look what he did!"

"Now you're upset over that old thing?"

"Hey!" Jason curled the toy away from her, offended. "Tyrone was my childhood," he whimpered.

"Is everything okay?" Edmund entered, walking Melanie's bike back to her.

"Um, yes." Melanie ran fingers through her hair, eyes darting around.

Edmund wasn't convinced. She looked frazzled. "You

sure? Is there anything I can do to help?"

"Who are you?" Jason scrunched his face in confusion.

"I drove your sister here. She said there was some kind of emergency?"

"It's under control now," Jason assured as he began to lead Edmund away. "Thank you very much for driving her back and checking in, but we got it from here, have a great evening, goodbye!"

Edmund was back in his vehicle before he knew it, and he opened his mouth to say something but Jason spoke first. "You saw nothing, buddy. Got it?"

"Geez, man, chill!" Edmund raised a calming hand as he turned the ignition. "I tipped over my dad's smoker once and lit up the whole deck. Accidents happen, I get it."

"Precisely," Jason finished. He made a shooing motion with his hand.

Melanie appeared behind him, squeezing her hands together again. "It's fine, Ed. Thank you."

"You know..." Edmund hung an elbow out his window, ignoring Jason's glare. "I never got your name."

"I'll tell you next week." Melanie smiled sheepishly. It was easier to forget someone with no name, and the longer she could keep it that way, the better.

Edmund scoffed, amused. "Okay, then."

Melanie waved him off, and as soon as he was out of sight, she grabbed Jason's arm. "Let's go find Scalaed."

CHAPTER 5

Heartlink

Scalaed left his guilt behind in the clouds. The wonders of the sky flooded him with joy as he flew. The white fluff of clouds condensed on his black scales, and he purred happily at the coolness. His stomach also purred, and he remembered the armadillo in his clutches. He began his descent, hoping to find a hidden spot to eat.

A flock of starlings met him. Thousands of them, seemingly flying with one mind in a swirling living cloud. Scalaed had never seen such a thing, and he flew among the starlings, who morphed and changed around him, keeping him in a bird-less pocket. Excited to be involved, he roared along with the cacophony of chirps and tweets. Having had his fun, he parted ways with the aerial ballet and landed in a slot canyon on the banks of a riverlet from the Colorado River.

He would be safe here. He couldn't hurt anyone here. Cacti and wildflowers and grasses grew around him like a shield, and the towering rock walls shrouded him in cool shadow. Backing further into a rocky overpass that resembled a shallow cave, he chewed into his meal.

An abnormally cool breeze washed over him, and Scalaed stopped eating. His nostrils twitched at the sudden scent of flowers. Not like the wild ones that surrounded him, but richer, fuller. It smelled like nothing he had ever known…or did it? As fleeting as a blink, an image wiped across his vision. A forest. A unicorn. Why did it feel familiar? Then, like a wave on the beach, the scent and memory receded into oblivion, leaving Scalaed wondering what it was.

Melanie and Jason biked behind the neighborhood, following the nearby golf course trail down the shallow cliffs towards the highway.

Melanie placed a hand over her heart, feeling for the pulse that tugged at her, guiding her to Scalaed. The plastic bag of meat swung from her handlebars, affecting her balance, and she quickly regained her hold with both hands.

"I hope he's not too far," Jason said as they wound down the trail. "Mom is making enchiladas, which I do *not* want to miss."

Melanie only replied, "We're getting closer."

They forked off the golf trail onto a narrow, cracked road that allowed them to pass through a tunnel under the highway. The summer heat continued to beat down as Melanie navigated a faint dirt trail into the wilderness. The only sign of life was a lone restaurant behind them. Red sand and rock dotted with cacti blew past them as Melanie picked up speed.

Jason pedaled harder to keep up. His hands felt funny from the rough terrain vibrating his handlebars, and he asked again how much farther.

Melanie's heartbeat weighed heavier and heavier. "Very close." She began calling for Scalaed.

Jason groaned. "Well, he has to be, because we can't go any farther than this."

They skidded to a halt, spraying gravel down the towering cliff to the river below.

Scalaed hadn't noticed he dozed off until he heard faint voices. The sun had lowered in the sky, and the feathery colors of dusk brushed the horizon. He heard the voices again, closer but still distant.

"Scalaed!"

It was Melanie and Jason. How did they find him?

Footsteps crunched far overhead, and he heard Melanie say, "He's so close. I feel him."

Scalaed's own heart began thumping in tune with a separate rhythm, and he realized that was how Melanie found him. Her heartbeat didn't sound angry. It was worried. Could she forgive him after all?

Scalaed tentatively stepped out into the light and looked up behind him.

Melanie and Jason stood at the top of the cliff, and Melanie exclaimed, "There you are! I was so worried about you, buddy." Her voice echoed off the rocky walls.

The tip of the canyon leveled out enough to allow the siblings a way to the bottom, albeit a narrow and treacherous one. To free her hands for holding onto the cliff, Melanie had looped the plastic bag around her wrist. Its weight dug into her skin, and she made a note to get rope and an anchor system for a safer descent if there was a next time.

They finally made it to the bottom, but stopped short of reaching Scalaed.

"Was he always this big?" Melanie asked timidly.

Jason's eyes widened. "I don't think so."

"How did he grow so fast?"

"Sis, you're asking for logic in a situation involving a mythical creature. I think it's better not to ask."

Before, Scalaed had been the size of a house cat. Now he was closer in size to their Aunt April's pit bull.

"Well, at this rate, he wouldn't have lasted long in the shed anyway." Melanie walked over and pet Scalaed. "So I guess it's not a big deal that it burned down."

"Speaking of, he should apologize." Jason crossed his arms. "If not for the shed, which I don't care about, then for Tyrone."

Melanie rolled her eyes with a smile, then knelt down in front of Scalaed. He pattered his feet excitedly and trotted up to her, dropping his chin on her lap with an expectant gaze.

Melanie returned Scalaed's gaze, that warm rhythm once

again pumping faintly in her chest.

"Scalaed," Melanie began firmly with a smile.

The dragon blinked at his name.

"Please apologize to Jason for destroying his toy," Melanie spoke with a motherly tone. "He loved it very much." She sent her brother a playful glance.

Jason scowled.

Scalaed lifted his head, his eyes darting to Jason, then back to Melanie.

"I doubt he understands me, you know." Melanie looked over her shoulder at Jason.

When she faced Scalaed again, he searched Melanie's face, his eyes full of wonder. He placed a paw onto her knee, leaning his nose closer to her. A soft trill purred from his throat, and he slipped off, walking over to Jason with a shameful tilt to his head. He looked up at Jason and bonked his head against his legs, then sank to the ground with a sad whine.

Jason's jaw gaped as he locked eyes with Melanie. "Did he…?"

Melanie smiled in disbelief. "Well, forgive the poor thing!" She laughed. "Look how sorry he is!"

"Fine." Jason squatted to pet the remorseful dragon. "I'm still salty, but I forgive you, Kool-Aid."

Scalaed sniffed and ran back to Melanie's arms. As she coddled him, he warbled a mournful tone, and the bond between them pulsed. Melanie widened her eyes. She didn't hear words in his sound, but the sentence still glowed clearly in her mind. Short though it was, she understood what Scalaed had said: "I'm sorry."

Melanie held Scalaed under his face with a newfound wonder, her voice no more than a stunned whisper. "I understand you, too!"

Scalaed lit up, his tail swishing excitedly and mouth open in what Melanie assumed was a smile. She hugged him tightly.

"Okay, as cool as this is," Jason said, "what do we do with the little arsonist now?"

"Looks like he's got a nice setup here. He's hidden from any rafters, can clearly handle himself, and he's barely a mile from home," Melanie said. "Oh! Scalaed, I got you something." She lifted up the plastic bag and unwrapped the meat. Scalaed's heartbeat quickened in her chest as he snatched up the cuts. "I don't know how much game there is around here for you to hunt, but I'll bring meat like this every week, okay?"

Scalaed approved with a nod as he continued gnawing on a fish head.

"You know," Jason said, "at the rate he's growing, he'll be big enough to ride in no time."

Melanie shot her brother a stunned look.

"Seriously?" Jason put his hands on his hips. "The possibility of riding Scalaed hasn't even occurred to you?"

"No, it's just...wow, that..." Melanie's voice trailed off.

"Sounds awesome?" Jason finished for her. "But you know what sounds even awesomer? Enchiladas."

"That's true; we need to get back to Mom." Melanie thinned her lips. "Hopefully she hasn't missed us." She stroked Scalaed's back. "We gotta go home, now, Scalaed."

The dragon straightened and snuggled up against her chest, his head resting over her shoulder.

"Ohh, you're making it even harder to leave, you stinker."

She felt Scalaed grunt rhythmically. *Is he laughing?*

"Alright, down, you." Melanie smiled as she pulled him off. "I'll see you tomorrow."

Scalaed curled into his cave and puffed a goodbye, a ribeye bone in mouth.

Melanie and Jason returned the goodbye and left for home. They climbed out of the canyon, mounted their bikes, and pedaled back to the house, whose shadow stretched out toward them. The lights turned on, anticipating the oncoming dusk.

Mrs. Waldens was waiting for them in the kitchen, arms crossed and face tense. She flung out a hand towards the window. "What happened to the shed?"

The siblings exchanged looks. Then Jason shrugged meekly. "Um, no more tetanus?"

School began the next day, and Melanie expected to be filled with anxiety. But with the heartlink—as she now called it—connecting her to Scalaed, she knew that he was safe.

But the bond still proved distracting. Melanie constantly honed in on the warm rhythm to check on Scalaed. Lectures blurred together in distant ramblings amidst the beating heartlink. Not a single lesson was absorbed that day. Her imagination drew pictures of what she thought Scalaed was up to as she autonomously walked from class to class.

As Melanie merged into the next hall, adjusting her backpack, she collided with a student. A stack of books tumbled to the floor.

"Sorry!" Melanie winced and helped to pick up the books. "Oh! Edmund?"

The butcher's son smiled. "Hi!" His ears turned bright red.

"I'm so sorry, I've got a lot on my mind, but I should have paid more attention." Melanie's hands moved as nervously as she rambled.

"Nah, no harm done." Edmund shrugged stiffly, still smiling.

"That meat was perfect, by the way," Melanie said as they continued down the hall.

"Oh, cool!" Edmund nodded, his voice cracking. He cleared his throat. "What are you using all these offcuts for, anyway?"

Melanie stopped, her heart skipping as she tried to recount her lie. "Uh…my uncle. He's got a horse ranch and his guard dogs are on a weird diet." She tittered, nerves flaring. "That is to say, meat instead of those rabbit pellet-looking things. They need fats, organs, omega-3s…" Melanie's voice died down. *I'm saying too much.*

"You know, I haven't seen you here," Edmund noted, "and

I would have remembered if I did."

Melanie clenched her hands together. "I moved here from San Diego. Dad retired from the Marines and now works as a park ranger for the Grand Canyon National Park. This is my first year attending. I'm Melanie, by the way." The last part left her mouth before she could stop it.

"Nice to finally put a name to the face! I'm Edmund… and you already knew that. Military brat, huh?"

Melanie didn't notice Edmund cringe at himself. "Yeah, we used to move around a ton, but this is the last time." She laughed with a scoff. "Attachment to places and people is somewhat of a foreign concept to me."

"That's gotta be hard." Edmund frowned.

Melanie shrugged. "I'm used to it." *I can't start forming attachments now even if I wanted to.*

"Well, since you're sticking around the area, let's get you some friends." Edmund's voice sounded nervous. "I can be the first on your list, if you want?"

Melanie immediately caught on, remembering their exchange when they first met. *Oh no. Attractions are* not *good. Not now. Of all the times in my life…* Fear erected walls around her heart, while sadness at this lost opportunity slowed her pace. She could not let anyone get close to her. Too dangerous.

"Well, uhh," Edmund stopped at a door. The knob in his hand, damp with sweat from embarrassment, squeaked in his grip. "This is my class."

Melanie realized she had never answered him. "Oh! Sorry, yeah, that sounds great. I'll see you around, Edmund." She bustled off, wanting to forget her awkwardness.

Melanie was glad for Jason's company on the bus ride home. Being in eighth grade, he had been in a separate building.

"I could practically feel your stress from the other side of the campus, Mel." Jason raised an eyebrow. "You holding up okay?"

Melanie shrugged. "This heartlink Scalaed and I share... all I want to do is check on him. And Edmund's here. Thankfully he's a grade above me so we don't share classes, but he's got a crush on me, which makes everything much more... sticky. I can't avoid him because I need to shop at his store to feed Scalaed, and that's gonna burn a hole in my wallet, so now I have to get a job..." Melanie flopped her head against the seat in front of her and moaned.

Jason looked at her down his nose. "Melanie?"

His sister peered back at him through her side-swept bangs.

"I don't vibe with stress, 'kay?" He folded his hands. "So I'm gonna stay by your side through this insanity and make sure you don't crack." Jason had accepted their new reality, and adapted with ease. He had no qualms with avoiding new friendships, as all his real connections were over video game chat rooms anyway.

Jason patted Melanie, who gave a half-smile. "I'm glad I have a brother," she said.

"You don't get much of a choice." Jason smirked. He handed her a candy bar he got from the vending machine. "That sixth sense will become second nature, you'll be able to ignore it better, and getting a job is easy. I saw the county library is hiring."

Melanie nibbled on her bar. "Since when did you always know what to say?"

"Pfft, I've always been this wise. But I've got nothing for your Edmund problem. Guess I'm gonna have to take him out." Jason pumped an imaginary shotgun.

Melanie thinned her lips and narrowed her eyes. "Now you've ruined it."

"You're welcome."

Melanie felt weighed down by her parents' presence at the dinner table. What if they saw right through her or Jason? She looked up from her plate and saw her brother looking cool as ever, effortlessly unworried. She pushed the broccoli around the chicken with her fork, trying to breathe through the anxiety.

"How's Page?" Mr. Waldens asked.

Melanie knew a probing question when she heard one. "I

mean, it's school." She shrugged indifferently. "After attending so many they start to all feel the same."

"How are your teachers?" Mrs. Waldens asked.

"Oh, my history teacher's a harpy," Jason said.

"Jason, that's not very courteous," Mr. Waldens reprimanded him.

"No, it's true! Miss Fathom's got beady eyes and a beaky nose. She's a spindly little woman with a stare like knives. She's hiding wings up those sleeves for sure."

Melanie laughed as Mrs. Waldens shook her head.

"So would you say you're adjusting well?" Mr. Waldens asked, eyes on Melanie.

"Yeah." Melanie nodded, smiling at her dad for assurance. *You don't know the half of it.*

"You have a chance to make some real friends now," Mrs. Waldens added. "I know it hasn't been easy in the past, with so many moves. Have *any* of them stayed in touch?"

Melanie shook her head, eyes on her plate. "*I* tried, but I guess they'd rather cut ties. It's fine."

"Well, how about your classmates?"

Jason smirked. "There's Edmund."

"Oh?" Mrs. Waldens set down her fork. "Is he nice?"

"He's no one." Melanie glared at Jason through her lashes. "Anyway, he's a junior."

"Cool guy, works at Bert's Butts," Jason added, which earned him an angry nudge from Melanie below the table.

"Really?" Mr. Waldens said. "I've been meaning to check that place out. I'll have to say hello."

"That's wonderful that you made a friend already." Mrs. Waldens beamed. "Maybe we'll have him over!"

Melanie pasted on a pleasant smile and hoped her brother felt the daggers she stared at him.

"Well, listen." Mr. Waldens put down his fork and looked between his children. "If anything comes up, if you're struggling, the change is too much, or you need to talk about anything, your mom and I are always here for you."

Every word pounded a stake into Melanie's heart. She wanted to tell them about Scalaed. She wanted their help, their guidance. Her eyes began to mist, and she immediately drew her gaze downward back to her plate to blink the tears away.

"We love you both." Mrs. Waldens smiled. "No matter what happens."

CHAPTER
6
Routines

NEXT SUMMER

Jason was right about the heartlink. Over the year, it became a calming sense. The subtle changes in heartbeats told Melanie Scalaed's mood, and vice versa. It grounded Melanie, and she began to better her grades, much to her teachers' delight.

Her English teacher had suggested she attend study groups and make friends, but Melanie had politely declined. Dismissing invites over the past year had gotten easier, and she had a handle on burying the guilt. She would much rather leave school as soon as possible to visit Scalaed.

Melanie smiled as she and Jason boarded the bus on the last day of school, ignoring the other teenagers' chatter and gossip. Today she would get to sit with Scalaed and read him the books she checked out. Her new job at the county library gave her hours of access to find books about dragons, which were Scalaed's favorite. Her latest borrow was titled *The History and Influence of Dragons*.

She and Scalaed spent hours talking at every opportunity, mostly about Melanie's day and what she learned. She joked that Scalaed had become an honorary Page student.

"You joining us, Jason?" she asked.

He shook his head. "I'm playing with Dylan and the boys later. A new map just dropped along with a new weapon update." Melanie may not have had friends, but Jason did. The convenience of video games kept his friendships alive through the moves, and Jason once told Melanie she should get into video games for the sake of making online friendships. She insisted they were a waste of time.

The bus reached her house, and Melanie wished Jason luck in his campaign before hopping into her new car, a sweet-sixteen gift from her parents.

The Arizona sun blazed through Melanie's windshield, so she swung down the visor. Her hands gingerly tested the black leather steering wheel. Too hot. She plopped back in the seat, angled the vents to her face and the wheel, and waited for the cold to kick in.

Because it was Monday, she had to stop at Bert's as soon as the steering wheel cooled off enough to touch without frying her hands.

Her phone pinged—a text from Edmund.

See you soon!

Sighing, Melanie leaned against the headrest. Edmund was a good guy and frankly hard to avoid—especially when her mom kept inviting him over—but Melanie knew he wanted to be something more. In another life, she would not have hesitated, but a romantic relationship would only lead to betrayal and trust issues. Deep down, Melanie wanted to tell him about Scalaed. He deserved to know, but she needed to wait until the time was right, whenever that would be. If ever.

How bad could it really be? Would knowing the truth put him in danger? Melanie closed her eyes, sifting through possible scenarios. What if Scalaed was discovered? Could anyone trace him back to her, let alone her family and friends? Would he be considered a wild beast, albeit a mythical one? Maybe she could tell Edmund after all. She could even tell her parents. Melanie smiled wistfully at the prospect.

But the smile faded when her mind turned to other outcomes. A dragon was no ordinary animal. A hiker was bound to catch him on their phone. A hunter was bound to stumble upon his tracks, and people had a nasty habit of sharing anything and everything online. Virality could land a social media post on a scientist's page, or a news reporter's feed. The sensation would drive them to find Scalaed's origins. Was this creature an extraterrestrial? Did someone create this highly dangerous beast in a lab? Was Scalaed an enemy bio-weapon?

Anyone with the resources to do so could trace him back to Melanie. And anyone involved would be sought for questioning. Who knows where that road would lead? Her family's ruined reputation, investigation and interrogation, a heavy toll on mental health, and it could even cost Scalaed his own life.

No. Melanie deflated in her seat, her brows knitted in defeat. *I can't tell anyone. It's safer this way.*

When she opened her eyes, the clock blinked four forty-five. She had to go before Edmund closed up the shop. Wiping the tears she hadn't realized brimmed on her lids, Melanie sniffed away the last of her emotions, gripped the cool wheel, and put her sedan into reverse.

The bell tinkled upon Melanie's entrance, and the smell of sandwiches greeted her, but the dread in her stomach drained her appetite.

"Hey there, stranger!" Edmund waved from the register, then thanked a patron who was turning to leave.

Stranger, Melanie thought. *If only.*

"We have some good stuff this time," Edmund bragged from the back as he gathered her cuts. He took extra care in packing the cuts and stacked them neatly in the plastic bag. Smiling, he tied a chocolate bar to the bag with a blue ribbon.

When he returned, Melanie stood at the cash register, avoiding his gaze.

"Your parcels, my lady," Edmund said cheerily. He leaned both elbows on the counter.

Melanie smiled, but it was an obvious mask.

"What's wrong, Mellie?" he asked.

There was that nickname again. Melanie eyed the chocolate bar. It was her favorite, but she couldn't recall ever telling Edmund so. This was all too much. So she prepared to say what she had been mentally rehearsing the whole drive up.

"This is my last run," Melanie said.

Edmund straightened. "What? Is it something I did? The meat quality—"

"No, Ed." Melanie closed her eyes, clasping her hands together until her knuckles turned white. "I don't need meat anymore; the dogs are being put down tomorrow morning." A necessary lie.

"Oh dang, I'm so sorry!" Edmund's hand flitted towards hers for a moment, but stopped. "I guess we'll have to find more ways to see each other." He scooted the bag an inch closer, pivoting the chocolate bar into clearer view.

"Look, Ed, you really are a sweet guy, and I like you. But I'm not in a good place to start a relationship. With anyone." She had to be firm, because clearly Edmund hadn't taken her countless hints thus far. "I've got trust issues, so I have to work on myself a lot before subjecting a boyfriend to that, and overall it's just too dangerous—"

"Dangerous?" Edmund interrupted. "What do you mean?"

Crap. Melanie had slipped. She dropped a twenty dollar bill on the counter and grabbed the bag. "It's nothing, forget about it." *I need to go.*

"Melanie, wait," Edmund threw off his apron and followed her out the door. "Talk to me, please!" He grabbed her wrist, and she spun around, her expression stony save for her wide brown eyes.

"Are you in trouble?" Edmund slid his grip from her wrist to her hand. "Is there *anything* I can do to help?"

Melanie sucked in her lip, trying to swallow her emotion. *Why is he making this so hard?* She gently wiggled her hand free, composing herself. "I misspoke. I'm not the girl for you, Edmund. You would only get hurt. Understand?"

"I..." Edmund couldn't find his words. As she walked to her car, he blurted, "I'll wait for you!"

Melanie turned one last time. "Please, don't."

Then she was gone, her car turning down a street and vanishing.

Melanie allowed herself to cry on the drive home. By the time she reached the driveway, she had pulled herself together and mostly made peace with the situation. Besides, she was now off to see Scalaed. Her heart skipped a beat at the thought, and soon Scalaed's own rhythm beat happily in response.

Swapping four wheels for two, she biked the same path she and Jason had mapped nearly a year ago, after Scalaed had burned down the shed. Her legs pumped with adrenaline when she reached her secret spot: a mound of boulders that could conceal her bike and the anchor point bolted into the stone. Being so close to the Grand Canyon meant there were no shortages of places to shop for hiking gear.

After Scalaed established residence in the small canyon cave, Melanie had bought the rope climbing equipment with the last of her allowance. Seeing how expensive rope could be was the conviction she needed to land a job at the county library.

Melanie didn't have a harness. She stowed her bike, grabbed hold of the rope—a speckled tan color to blend in—and carefully rappelled down to the bottom.

"Hey, Scalaed!" Melanie held out her arms to the huge black form that trotted out from the shadows.

Scalaed had grown at such a shocking rate that after ten months and countless scale sheds, he stretched twenty feet from nose to tail with a forty-foot wingspan. And he was still growing.

The dragon huffed hot air into Melanie's face as he greeted her, pulling her into him with his nose. He smelled salt on her face. Had she been crying?

"I'm actually good now," Melanie assured. "I just had to say goodbye to Edmund. You're a proficient hunter now, and he was getting too close, anyway."

Scalaed purred softly.

"No, no, I didn't mean that!" Melanie cried. "You're not preventing anything. I'm sure I wouldn't be ready to date even if you never showed up. And I would never, *ever* wish you to leave!" Melanie kissed his muzzle and smiled. "Hey, I got another dragon book today." She sat against him as she showed him the cover.

A red dragon drawn in various cultural styles grading from top to bottom posed behind a title in bold, calligraphic font: *The History and Influence of Dragons.*

Scalaed snorted in excitement and curled his tail around them as Melanie opened the book.

The first pages were filled with scholars theorizing that dragon legends had been born from ancient speculations in a pre-scientific time. Skeletons now recognized as other creatures, especially dinosaurs, were once believed to be of draconian nature. Other pages showed ancient artifacts and paintings from many cultures depicting dragons.

Melanie trailed her finger along the words as she read. Scalaed followed along, nearly able to read himself.

"'The origin of this reptilian creature of legend is widely debated,'" Melanie read. "'Western culture believed dragons to be demons that needed slaying...symbols of evil.'" Melanie's voice trailed off as she and Scalaed looked at the full-page image of a medieval tapestry. A ghastly dragon lay sprawled in agonizing angles as a knight on a horse speared through its head. Weak flames in faded pigments blended with the red of the blood pouring from the fatal blow.

Scalaed moaned, disturbed.

Melanie quickly shut the book and tried to find something positive to say. "Well...obviously those boneheads never met you."

Scalaed lowered his head onto his claws and rumbled, not comforted.

Drumming her fingers against the book, Melanie put it on the ground and said, "I think that's enough reading for the day. Like the book said, dragon history is all speculation because no one has ever seen one."

Scalaed raised his head and met Melanie's eyes. Her velvet gaze looked gold from the canyon reflection, filled with comfort and love.

She reached out to hug his head. They sat in silence, in the mingling sounds of the rushing river and the synchronization of their heartbeats.

Warmed, and not from the Arizona summer, Scalaed asked Melanie if they would ever find out where he came from. He had told her about the flower smells that visited him more than once. He had also tried describing the forest, but once he brought up the unicorn, their search screeched to a halt.

She sunk backwards into his neck and inhaled deeply. "You know, for the past year I've always thought you came from Earth." She straightened and looked at him directly. "But once you described that unicorn…I don't even know what to think anymore."

Scalaed hummed a series of tones.

"True, it could still be Earth. I mean, I thought dragons were fake once, why not unicorns, too? But how can you smell it?"

Scalaed shrugged. Maybe they were messages.

"From whom?"

Scalaed felt he knew this. A distant tingling in the far reaches of his mind. A name. Someone. Some place.

Scalaed huffed and shook his head.

"Hey." Melanie stood up, changing the subject. "I got you food!" she said in a singsong as she held up the wrapped meat parcels. "Enjoy it, big guy, because this was the last run."

Scalaed nodded, for he had become an experienced hunter. The Grand Canyon with its endless prey and fish had become his domain. Gifted with flight, he had easy access to every part of the massive landmark. He had flown thousands of miles throughout the year without ever leaving. Beyond the national park hotspot he avoided, the canyon hid him in her monolith cliffs. Walls thousands of feet tall dwarfed the dragon to a mere speck in the landscape, his echoing roars lost in the vastness. Undiscovered caves were his rest stops and secondary homes, wild aquifers from the rims fed secret springs that drew larger prey like cougars and mule deer, and the silence of the red world engulfed him.

Scalaed felt a special connection to this place. The Grand Canyon, in her deceptive beauty, harbored unforgiving dangers that repelled the humans beyond the park borders, thus concealing him further from contact. And so the canyon was his guardian. Watching. Silent. Swallowing. But Scalaed dwelt close to her heart, living unknown in her embrace.

CHAPTER
7

Is It a Plane?

Scalaed pranced impatiently as Melanie and Jason kicked off their shoes, laughing. The temperature nearly hit triple digits, and nothing sounded more inviting than a swim in the river. With Wednesday off from work, Melanie visited Scalaed earlier than usual. In Scalaed's home canyon, the water flowed chest-high and more slowly than the main channel where rafting tourists thronged.

Melanie tossed her shirt and pants in a pile and adjusted her yellow floral swimsuit that had been hidden beneath. The strapless neckline rested off her shoulders and fell in a long ruffle that nearly met her high-waisted bottom.

Jason sped past her towards the water. "Last one in has to wash the pots back home!"

"No fair!" Melanie cried.

Excited, Scalaed rushed to her side and told her to get on.

Melanie did so without hesitation, and the dragon galloped past Jason at the last second, splashing into the river as Melanie whooped.

The clear water washed away the sweat, and Melanie floated weightlessly in the refreshing coolness. Jason assaulted her with splashes, and as Melanie sputtered, Scalaed swiped a tidal wave with his tail. Recovering from the wave, the siblings launched themselves at the dragon, pushing him into the water. Scalaed feigned drowning in an overly-dramatic performance, and Melanie splashed him once more.

Cooled off, Melanie and Jason sat on Scalaed's back between his red spikes. The dragon glided like a black swan through the clear water, rocks and pebbles and tiny darting fish rippling beneath.

"How's hunting been?" Melanie's question broke the silence.

Scalaed bobbed his head happily. He had snagged an elk last week. And as he reached adulthood, his appetite and metabolism began to level out where he could eat less often. This allowed more time for adventure and exploring the sights. The beauty and scale of the Grand Canyon were simply beyond description. In fact, there were times Scalaed himself couldn't comprehend what he saw. He wished he could instead show them to her.

"Oh, we've been to nearly all the major canyon hotspots," Melanie said.

"Yeah, thanks to Dad's job," Jason chirped.

Scalaed shook his head. They had never seen the grandeur from the sky. He turned his head to face the siblings, eyes begging to share with them what he had seen.

Melanie and Jason exchanged looks.

"You want us to ride you?" Melanie asked. Secretly, she and Jason had been looking forward to this day for months, but didn't know when Scalaed would be big enough or feel ready. As time went on, it seemed rude to ask.

Scalaed nodded fervently.

Melanie's thoughts suddenly waged war in her mind, freezing her in place. *Wouldn't we be seen?*

Jason however shook in excitement. "Dude, yes!"

"But Jason—"

"Oh, come on, Mel. Scalaed has stayed hidden this long—he knows what he's doing. And so what if some random person sees him? Who's gonna believe a guy claiming he saw a dragon? People have been blabbing about Bigfoot for years and still no one believes them. Even if they *did* manage to get him on camera…with all the stuff on the internet…how would people know it's real? It could be CGI, for all they know."

Melanie bit her lip, feeling the rational side of her mental war losing ground.

"Please?" Jason whined. Beneath them Scalaed gave his own version of puppy-eyes. "It'll dry us off and you wouldn't have to explain your wet hair to Mom."

Closing her eyes, Melanie forced out her answer. "Fine."

"Yes!" Jason grinned as he rubbed his hands hungrily. Scalaed matched his eagerness.

Melanie's mind-battle relinquished its hold over her limbs, and the unexpected relief allowed her to breathe again.

Scalaed thrust out his wings, spraying a mist all around them.

"Please, be careful!" Melanie begged as she grabbed a red spike in front of her.

"Yeah, Kool-Aid." Jason settled in his seat. "Don't drop

me, I am precious to the world."

The siblings held their breath as they braced themselves for Scalaed's leap into the air. The dragon heaved a low preparatory sigh that rumbled ripples in the water. The silent suspense made Melanie squirm.

Her stomach lurched as Scalaed launched into the air with a violent spray of water. She tensed everything to stay mounted—her legs, her jaw, her grip on the spike, her toes.

Scalaed was a little wobbly at first, but he found his balance and soared smoothly through the sky. The red canyon grew distant behind them.

Jason's stomach dropped with every bob of Scalaed's beating wings, but the tumult soon subsided. The flight stole his breath and refused to return it as he soaked in the Grand Canyon. Beneath them, the rocky landscape raced by.

Scalaed was right. Melanie and Jason had never seen the world like this. The evening air billowed through Melanie's swimsuit and hair. She smiled, loosening her grip slightly, and released a laugh. Like a dam unleashed, her breath returned to rush from her lungs in whoops and screams of delight as Scalaed flew through the sky.

"This is amazing!" Jason hollered and risked raising his hands above his head.

Scalaed smiled and dove back down into the canyon, causing Jason to yelp effeminately and latch back on to the spike. Striped walls of reds and oranges streaked past, and the Colorado River below sprayed behind them. Tipping side to side, Scalaed banked hard turns through the winding canyon, much to the siblings' nervous excitement.

The thrill of flying was almost outdone by the fear of falling off. Melanie made a note to look into getting a proper harness system.

Lowering his head, Scalaed launched into a higher speed, causing Melanie and Jason to scream as they careened down the canyon. They whipped around Horseshoe Bend like a slingshot and barreled deeper into the cliffs.

The walls dropped away and spit them out into a wide-open canyon, and Scalaed maintained his incredible speed as they flew south. This place exposed him the most, so he climbed above the northern rim, out of sight from the campgrounds and highway below.

Melanie's heart pounded in her chest. Here she was, flying on a dragon in the Grand Canyon. Her brain refused to believe it, and she even pinched herself.

Scalaed looked back and said they neared one of his favorite spots. His voice rumbled through the siblings' bones.

Kaibab Plateau. A vast green table blooming with ponderosa pines. The year had given Scalaed time to map flight plans whose routes kept him out of sight of tourists, campers, and rangers. Aided by his keen eyes and ears and tremendous sense of smell, he followed this invisible highway over the evergreen forest, avoiding the congestion of the main park and its attractions just south of them. When they descended back into the canyon, the three were swallowed up by ancient monuments and the overwhelming realization of their own insignificant size.

Scalaed slowed, and the roaring wind that had deafened them disappeared. Only the rushing river and the silent depths of the canyon remained. Condors floated above them on updrafts, a herd of bighorn sheep scaled the vertical cliffs with weightless grace, and deer bounded along the river.

"Scalaed," Melanie said, awe stealing most of her voice, "thank you."

"Yeah," Jason agreed as he drank in the world around him. "This is incredible."

The dragon warbled happily, thankful he could share this experience.

The canyon's shadows reached out to them as the sun set, and with reluctance, the three turned towards home. Being out for over two hours had brought dinnertime upon them, and after the day's excitement, the siblings had worked up an appetite.

"I heard the strangest thing today," Mr. Waldens began as he flipped molten, grilled cheese sandwiches.

Melanie and Jason quickly exchanged glances as they set the table with silverware.

Mrs. Waldens was stirring a steaming pot of tomato basil soup. "Oh? What happened?"

Mr. Waldens folded his arms, spatula in one hand as he

leaned against the counter. "Stan came back to the ranger station talking about a commotion near the petroglyphs. Something about a small aircraft zipping down the canyon. Stan says he only caught a glimpse. Said it was fast and black."

The siblings faltered, slowing their progress.

"That sounds so unsafe." Mrs. Waldens shook her head as she ladled soup into bowls.

"Yep, people are stupid." Mr. Waldens laughed as he returned to the stove. "In fact, get this—multiple people swear it was a dragon."

Forks clattered to the floor, and Mr. and Mrs. Waldens saw Melanie scramble to pick them up.

Mrs. Waldens noticed Melanie's fearful expression for only a moment before her daughter cleared it with a suspicious cough. Mr. Waldens continued on about how the number of concerns warranted an official investigation, which could be a nice change of pace for the park rangers.

As the family sat down, Mrs. Waldens continued to study Melanie and Jason. "What have you two been up to? Between long school hours and whatever else you're doing, I hardly see you anymore."

Melanie had no response. Her mind was still whirling over what Mr. Waldens had said.

"We live right next to the Grand Canyon, Mom," Jason said, a string of melted cheese leading from his mouth. "You expect us to stay indoors when there's so much to see?"

"Like dragons." Mr. Waldens wiggled his fingers mysteriously.

Melanie stuffed her sandwich in her mouth to hide her anxiety.

"It's funny," Mr. Waldens said, spooning his soup. "Now that I think about it, there have been a handful of other reports throughout the year from all over the park about dragons."

"What do you think it really is?" Mrs. Waldens asked.

"Not sure, but it's gaining fame among those in the know. How about it, though: our very own celebrity dragon." Mr. Waldens chuckled and said nothing else.

It dawned on Melanie that she would have to move closer to Scalaed to keep an eye on him. Clearly, he wasn't being as careful as he'd said.

"I'm moving out," Melanie told Jason that night.

The siblings sat on the floor in the soft lamplight of Jason's bedroom.

"Wait, why?" Jason blinked.

"You heard what Dad said! I gotta make sure Scalaed doesn't do something stupid. I have to protect him, because…" A strong sense of determination descended on her. She brought her hands close together over her heart. Determination to do what?

"Melanie?" Jason scooted closer. "What is it?"

"Ever wonder where Scalaed came from?" Melanie asked.

"Kaibab National Forest," Jason replied.

"No, that's where I found him. Like…" Melanie leaned in close to whisper, "Where is his mother?"

Jason widened his eyes. "Oh, I never thought of that, but you're right. Either she's super good at hiding or—"

"—Scalaed came from somewhere else."

"Like, another planet?"

Melanie wrestled with her newfound curiosity. "It sounds insane. But think about it: he must be here for a reason." She locked eyes with Jason. "He's got a bigger purpose, I can feel it. And it's my duty to protect him until then."

Jason puffed out his cheeks with an exhale. Eventually, he nodded in acceptance. "Well, if you feel that strongly about it, go for it, but where will you live?"

"I've been saving up." Melanie shrugged meekly. "Living at home really reduces my cost of living, so hopefully I'll have options in a year or two. In the meantime, Scalaed needs to lay low, far away in the deeper canyons, until the rumor here blows over." She sighed. "I won't be able to see him much, but that will give me more hours to maybe work a second job." Melanie leaned against Jason's bed frame and stared at the ceiling.

Her brother put a hand on her shoulder. "You've been awesome this past year, Mel. Can I do anything to help?"

Melanie shook her head. "We should get some sleep."

Jason slapped his knees and shot to his feet. "Yeah, the stress is starting to get to me again."

"Sorry." Melanie smirked as she stood up.

"You got this, okay?" Jason pointed an encouraging finger.

"Everything will work out."

"Thanks, Jason." Melanie smiled, and they both said goodnight.

When Melanie reached her own room, she glanced at the moon glowing brightly through her window. She sighed, leaned on the windowsill with folded hands, and said to the heavens, "I could really use some help. If I could get a place to live by my eighteenth birthday, that would be great. Thank you and goodnight."

CHAPTER
8
Apex Predator

Scalaed rustled, then yawned. His widening maw startled a small flock of wrens near the mouth of his cave. Squinting at the sunlight streaming into his abode, he studied the shadows cast by the world outside. It was afternoon already? Well, the coyote from last night had been delicious…

Scalaed shook off the last of sleep, and a light cloud of red dust settled from his wings. Smaller neighbors scrambled away as the ground rumbled at his exit. A gecko skittered behind a rock, and the wrens hopped higher into their tree, but the red-tailed hawk farther down simply blinked his good morning from his prickly perch. Scalaed nodded in reply. The little raptor was the only one to view him as an equal rather than a terror, and Scalaed had shared many meals with him. He hoped the gecko and wrens would come around in the same way. Still, one friend was better than none.

The last of Scalaed's bulk emerged, his black scales gleaming in the harsh sunlight. Warmth flooded his body, invigorating him for his daily hunt. He prepared to launch, but paused as something caught his eye.

Those flowers hadn't been there before. Scalaed walked closer to the unknown plants growing right outside his cave. Their pink, velvety blooms sparkled at him from their perfect circle patch. Even some of the petals had been cut to stay within the patch.

Scalaed smelled them, then leaned back. They were the flowers from his memories. He had caught whiffs over the years, but he had never seen them. And here they were, in an eerily precise circle where even the black soil stayed in its boundary. Scalaed scanned the patch. It was like someone—or something—had taken a cookie cutter and swapped out a random piece of biome.

His stomach grumbled, and Scalaed decided to check on these alien flowers later. He wondered what menu the canyon prepared for him today. Stretching his wings to welcome the desert breeze, Scalaed swooped from his cliff-face front porch. His passing rumbled like a storm, sending a chipmunk tumbling into the weeds.

The river below sparkled, and Scalaed regarded his soaring reflection. The dragon that looked back at him flew with strength and power. A swell of pride filled his chest, stoking the fire that burned in his core. Inhaling, Scalaed unleashed a pillar of flame—a thick wave of fire that crackled furiously down the canyon. He couldn't help himself; it was too fun.

But risky. He remembered what Melanie told him. She had never been angry with him until that day. Some tourists had begun spreading a rumor about his existence, so he'd had to move far to the west until it blew over. He only saw

Melanie once a month now, but their heartlink seemed to have no limits, for they could still feel each other across the divide. In fact, it only seemed to grow stronger with time. Through it, they had been able to send messages of sorts: brief flashes of a thought accompanied by each other's pulsing heartbeat. If they hadn't been bonded, he could have mistaken them for his own imagination.

His fire could draw unwanted attention if anyone was watching. But his canyon was remote enough to conceal him. Right? He pounced onto the cliff wall, red claws crunching the rock face, and craned his neck to view his home.

His canyon shot off the Colorado River in a private corridor. A waterfall on the north side spilled over and all the way down to a narrow crevasse, where it joined the violent rapids beyond. The canyon towered over his cave by hundreds of feet.

He hadn't seen another human in months. He should be fine.

Continuing his ascent from the canyon, Scalaed flew east towards pine-filled hunting grounds. He shouldn't be this close to Kaibab, but he was really craving elk. He would only be on the outskirts, so that should be fine, right? As the forest neared and the trees thickened, Scalaed tuned into the sounds of wood life. Birdsong silenced upon his approach, and even the pine trees themselves stilled their branches. The hunter had arrived.

Scalaed landed with a thud, the vibration shifting golden pine needles on the ground. He scanned his surroundings with red eyes, his vision sharp as a blade. With a sniff of the air and a swish of his tail, Scalaed prowled the forest.

His coloring did not aid him in camouflage for hunting, but it didn't matter. By the time his prey would see him, he would already have eyes on them. They could run, but Scalaed was faster. They could fight, but Scalaed was stronger. He was a living tank of muscle and flame.

Today's lunch appeared to be a deer. Not as big as elk, but he'd take it. It would fill him up until tomorrow's hunt.

The buck had bounded deeper into the wood after hearing Scalaed's arrival, but the dragon's keen eyes latched onto the swift brown blur.

Zigzag, zigzag fled the panicking deer.

Scalaed rumbled a laugh as he barreled after it. Lunch was giving a good chase. Pine needles swirled up behind him, and a log cracked in half under his weight. He would head the deer off as it crested a hill.

The buck, blinded by fear and running on raw instinct, noticed Scalaed too late. The black dragon leaped down from the top of the hill in front of it, eyes glowing with hungry glee. The deer scrambled to stop and then…white.

Scalaed's concentrated thread of white fire seared straight through the animal's heart, a smoking entry wound the mark of his kill. He shook his head, pleased, and made his approach. The chase had increased his appetite.

But something smelled off.

Scalaed was halfway to his lunch when he caught scents on the air. Sweat. Deodorant. Gunpowder.

A hunter. This far from the campgrounds? Judging by the strong artificial scent of lime and cedar wood, Scalaed concluded he was an amateur. No hunter with a brain would leave his house smelling like that. But the warning gave Scalaed a chance to leap down the hill and out of sight over a brush-rimmed ridge. Through the shrubbery, Scalaed watched a man wearing camouflage and an orange vest emerge from the treeline.

The hunter wasn't alone. A woman followed close behind him and pointed at the fallen deer. "Look!" She jogged over to it. "How many points?"

Scalaed narrowed his eyes.

"Six. Not super impressive." Her partner shrugged. The rifle resting over his shoulder bounced. "We're after twelve or bigger," he added. "Besides, someone's already bagged this one."

Scalaed snarled silently. They needed to back away from his lunch.

The woman knelt down, her eyes roving over the kill until they landed on the fatal wound. She paled.

"Trey…"

He rolled his eyes and squatted next to her. "Now what, Sophie?"

She pointed at the entry wound. A hole the diameter of her fist, wreathed in smoldering fur, leaked faint trails of smoke.

"What made…?" Standing quickly, Trey looked around as he hefted his rifle.

Scalaed's heart skipped as Trey's gaze passed over him. But the hunter's eyes kept moving.

"Whatever it was, it shot clean through the body!" Sophie pressed her hand to her mouth.

Scalaed waited with bated breath for them to leave. If they didn't step away from his food, he might just eat them too. He was certainly hungry enough…his stomach growled ominously.

"We should go." Trey grabbed her shoulder with a grip like a vise.

"You heard that, too?" Sophie clung to his arm.

Scalaed rumbled a low growl, hoping to deter these nuisances. Instead, Trey rolled the bolt of his rifle, loading a round into the chamber as he tentatively approached the ridge. Sophie followed, muttering something under her breath.

What would they do to Scalaed if they found him? Shoot him? Would he have to…dispose of them? Still veiled under the scraggly brush, Scalaed did the only thing he could think of.

A roar—deep, throaty, and otherworldly—blared through the wood.

Terror sent Trey and Sophie diving to the ground, screaming and scrambling to escape. As the last of their fleeting footsteps faded, Scalaed poked his nose out for a confirmation sniff.

Nobody.

That was way too close. Scalaed heaved anxiously as he snatched the deer carcass. He had to get back home immediately. If the rumors had died down at all, he surely just resurrected them.

Melanie sat awkwardly at the dinner table while her family sang happy birthday. There was nothing to do in this cringey moment other than enjoy the pleasure her family took in making her uncomfortable.

Eighteen years old, and she was still ordered to blow out candles. She smiled; she didn't mind. The little flames went out with a puff, and her family cheered.

As Mrs. Waldens served slices of homemade chocolate cake with cream cheese frosting, Jason slid her a gift bag.

"Happy birthday, Sis."

"Aw, for me?" Melanie played coy. "You really shouldn't have."

She pulled out the yellow tissue paper. Beneath was an instant camera.

"Thought you could find some otherworldly subjects to capture with that," Jason hinted. "It's nice because it can't be hacked."

Melanie hadn't thought of that, but Jason had a point. She did have some pictures of Scalaed on her phone; suddenly, she didn't trust her phone's privacy. The device now felt much heavier in her pocket. She needed to print those photos, then delete them, very soon.

Melanie hugged Jason, now sixteen years old and as tall as she. "Thank you so much, Jason. I love it."

Jason squeezed her until she made a strangled squeak. Laughing, Melanie backed away and said quietly, "Remind me to purge my camera roll later." She patted her phone, which began ringing.

"Happy birthday!" Uncle Conrad and his family's voices crackled on the other end.

"Thank you!" Melanie smiled as she wandered into the next room.

After Aunt April and her cousin Kyle wished her a fantastic day, Uncle Conrad took over the call. "Guess what, kid—well actually, no, you're a grown woman now." His contagious laugh made Melanie chuckle. "Listen: so I tried that whole vacation home rental thing, and it wasn't sustainable. So I've got a brand new camper with permanent water and electric hookups on ten acres that were supposed to be for hunting vacationers. It's not far from the ranch. Now, a little bird told me you were looking to move, being an adult and all, so…Would you be interested in renting the place?"

Melanie froze. This was the answer to her prayer! And on her eighteenth birthday, no less. "Oh, my gosh!" Her hands shook as she tried to formulate a response. "Thank you so much, Uncle Conrad, yes! I would love to see it. Today, if possible?"

"Sure thing, kid, it'll be great to see you. Happy Birthday."

When Melanie broke the news to her parents, they were happy for her. She had mentioned moving in the past so as not to shock them when the time came.

"That's so generous of Conrad," Mrs. Waldens said as they all got into the car later that afternoon.

"The ranch business has been really good to him." Mr. Waldens nodded as he pulled out of the driveway, proud of his younger brother.

Uncle Conrad and his family lived on a horse ranch two hours north, but the property Melanie hoped would be hers was near Jacob Lake, a small community on the Kaibab Plateau. The drive from her parents' house was only an hour and a half. Conrad called back later with more details, explaining how he had renovated an old camper park that had fallen into disrepair with electricity, water, and a long-term sewage system. The camper even had a small washer and dryer. It didn't get mail, but Conrad had set up a PO Box in Fredonia, about a thirty-minute drive west.

Melanie could hardly believe it when they arrived. She stepped out of the vehicle with Jason behind her and gaped as she took in her new home. The aluminum hull, shiny and new, glittered in the setting sun.

Conrad had arrived before them, and after giving everyone smothering hugs, panned his arm at the camper.

"Well, this is it! We liked the idea, but it just ended up being too much work in addition to the ranch. Please, take a look around." He handed Melanie a key.

All smiles, Melanie unlocked the door and stepped inside. Outfitted with the latest travel technology, the camper made use of every square inch while not feeling cramped. It had everything she needed, from a stovetop to a closet to satellite Wi-Fi. She squeezed the key a little tighter. Looking heavenward, she whispered, "Thank you!" Her heart fluttered, and she sent a message to Scalaed through the heartlink, "I found it."

Outside, Conrad conversed with her parents while Jason left to investigate the grounds around the camper.

"She seems to love it," Conrad said, folding his arms proudly.

"Is it safe, though?" Mrs. Waldens looked beyond her brother-in-law. "What of bear attacks? I don't know how I feel about Melanie living in…well, not a house."

Melanie waved to them excitedly from the camper window.

Mr. Waldens waved back. "She's happy, though." Despite his reservations, it only made sense to him. Melanie was happiest in nature. For a long while she and Jason had gone exploring after school and seemed to have interest in little else. To live closely in nature's beauty like this suited her.

"And if nothing else, this can be a temporary solution until she finds a more permanent residence," Conrad offered. "Is she interested in college at all?"

Mr. and Mrs. Waldens shook their heads. "She didn't see the sense in going into debt for a degree and classes she could easily take online."

They looked back at Melanie, who gave them two thumbs up as she exited the trailer.

"I wish she would go, though." Mrs. Waldens waved to her daughter. "She has no friends. We've asked her why but she just says—"

"She says most people are stupid," Mr. Waldens chuckled.

"Well, she's right," Conrad scoffed. "If she's the solitary type, then I guess this place is perfect for her," he concluded.

Jason returned from his perimeter check and met with Melanie. "Any thoughts?"

Melanie beamed. "Jason, it's perfect! I'm right where I need to be."

CHAPTER 9

Space Cadet

2 YEARS LATER

The weekend had arrived, and with it came two days off from Coincidence Antiques. Moving from Page meant getting a new job, and Melanie was blessed with an opening at the antique store within weeks of her eighteenth birthday. It was by no means a glamorous position, but it allowed Melanie to provide for herself and her unconventional life. And today looked to be especially beautiful for a day off.

Flinging off her sheets, she rushed to the kitchenette and opened the window. Beautiful weather indeed. Breathing in the pinewood air, she was reminded of the first time she came to this forest. The day she'd found Scalaed and changed her life forever.

Melanie poured a mug of hot chocolate and gently blew the swirling steam from the frothy top. After she took a sip, she pulled out a thick photo album from the black depths of a secret seat compartment.

She wanted a safe way to preserve memories in something that could easily be hidden. Some were prints from her phone, while the rest were pictures taken with her instant camera.

Most were selfies, and she smiled at one of her and Scalaed in his first canyon. That had been five years ago.

Another was Melanie and Jason laughing, trying to put a party hat on Scalaed for his first birthday...another picture of the cake they got him...and yet another of the three of them from Fourth of July. The darkness didn't work well for the photo, but the faintest rainbow glow of fireworks developed their silhouettes enough to show the memory. Melanie's eyes roved over others: one of her birthdays, Jason's birthday, Scalaed's obsession with a rare autumn leaf, and his dumbstruck expression at the first snowfall...getting her license and first car...a photo of Melanie and Scalaed posing in front of her new camper, and countless photos of the trio's wilderness ventures.

The pictures were in no chronological order, with old and new ones mingling on every page: Scalaed holding his first fish in his mouth, a fish nearly as big as he was at the time...Melanie reading books to him...Jason dressing up as a Viking one Halloween...when they discovered Scalaed's disdain for any and all candy...watching movies on her laptop in the old canyon. Interspersed with the memories were many shots of the different skies they had flown—blue, pink, orange, purple—and selfies from those flights.

One year they sneaked all the way to Phoenix. Mrs. Waldens had come down with a cold that New Year's Eve, so she and Mr. Waldens had called it a night long before midnight. Melanie, Jason, and Scalaed took the opportunity to see the fireworks in the city. Perched on a mountaintop overlooking the capital, they sat with popcorn and watched explosions of color ignite the midnight sky.

Five years of fond memories, each one dear to Melanie.

After returning the album to its hiding place, she leaned out the window. "Good morning!" she shouted to the woods and dropped a few Frosted S'mores Pop-Tarts in the toaster. Within moments, the forest shook, and Scalaed ran up to the window. At five years old, he measured thirty-five feet from nose to tail with a sixty-foot wingspan. His crimson horns had doubled in length, and his scales shone like polished obsidian.

"Good morning, buddy!" Melanie leaned out and kissed his nose. "You sleep well?"

Scalaed rumbled. His voice—if one were to call it that— had deepened tremendously from the squeaky purrs it once was. Now Melanie could feel it through the rocks and earth.

"Have any dreams?" she asked before finishing her hot chocolate.

Scalaed began a reenactment, snorting and huffing.

"Wow," Melanie said, laughing, "that sounds crazy!"

Scalaed snickered, then snatched the Pop-Tart Melanie held out to him.

"I thought I'd invite Jason over today," Melanie said as she sat with her plate on the small couch. "We could go for a flight, maybe track down that secret spring we found with the desert willow."

Scalaed barked, and Melanie looked at her watch. "Oh, fine. I don't even know why you like that show." She flipped on the TV and took her plate. "*You* can watch it, but *I'm* leaving."

Scalaed yowled after her.

"I do have good taste in shows! Just not that one," she teased from behind the open closet door. "We both know Bigfoot isn't real!" As Scalaed settled in front of the window, Melanie tapped a number on her phone and waited for it to ring.

"Hey, Sis!" Jason greeted from the other end.

"Morning, Jason!" Melanie replied, putting it on speaker phone so she could pull on her jean shorts. "The weather's gonna be amazing today. Want to come over later?"

"Let me check my insanely packed schedule. Um, gym, gym, *Shadow Ops 4*, lunch, *Shadow Ops 4*…yeah, I'm free today. What time?"

Melanie laughed as she slipped on a white tee and purple tie-front. "Anytime, really, I'm just stuck here watching Scalaed's show."

"Torturous."

"You know it."

"I'll be over after dinner, then."

"Sounds good! Love you, bye."

Finishing her morning routine, Melanie brought her plate out to hand-wash in the sink.

Scalaed stared blankly at the TV.

"Finally see how dumb that show is?" Melanie smirked.

Scalaed gave no response.

"Scalaed, you okay?" Melanie walked over and reached up to pet him.

The dragon blinked a few times and shook his head as he

seemed to reenter reality.

"You cool, buddy?" Melanie asked again. "You were totally zoned out a second ago."

Scalaed looked around, a bit confused, but nodded his head.

"Okay..." Melanie said, eyeing him up and down. "By the way, Jason will be here around dinner."

Melanie rarely had awkward moments of silence with Scalaed, but this one was particularly long. Clicking her tongue, she shrugged. "I'm gonna wash my car. Some raccoon left its nasty little prints all over it. Want to help?"

Without waiting for a reply, she grabbed her yellow-and-pink sport sandals and walked out the door. Scalaed trudged around to the front.

"You're being uncharacteristically quiet, Scalaed," Melanie prompted as she unraveled the hose. "Do you want to talk about it?"

Scalaed shook his head, insisting it wasn't a big deal.

"Well, if you say so," Melanie said. She started spraying down her maroon sedan. Silence ensued again.

"Okay, Mopey, you're gonna help me if you won't talk." Melanie smiled, and spritzed the dragon. "Hold this, while I get the soap."

When she returned, Scalaed had not moved and was staring off into the distance, the hose pouring water out of his mouth.

"Dude!" Melanie cried in exasperation. "You're doing it again."

Scalaed turned around and moaned innocently, dropping the hose.

"Are you sick?" Melanie put down the bucket and soap and stroked his head. "You need to tell me what's going on."

Scalaed stepped back.

"I understand." Melanie nodded. "Take some alone time. We can talk about it when you get back."

Scalaed flew off rather quickly, leaving Melanie with the running hose.

Jason sighed as he heard his phone ping with text messages from his manager Jennifer. He already knew what they'd be about. Gwen was probably hungover again, and Jennifer needed another server. Normally, Jason wouldn't mind covering a shift at The Wynchester, but not today. He was going dragon flying.

So he texted back, saying the shift request was too last minute and he had other plans. Pocketing his phone, he returned to his bowl of cereal.

"What's on your agenda today?" Mrs. Waldens asked from the kitchen as she watched the slow trickle of the espresso machine. "Your Dad was called in early this morning, otherwise I'd suggest we do something as a family."

"Might squeeze in a gym session, then play a few matches

with the boys before hanging out with Melanie today." Jason shrugged before finishing off the milk left in his bowl.

Mrs. Waldens sighed as Jason brought his empty bowl to the kitchen. "We're glad you have video games to keep you connected with your friends. But when you're not working, you stay on that computer for hours. Instead, why don't you finish narrowing down that list of colleges?"

"Because school stuff is not for the weekend, dear mother." Jason smirked and kissed her on the cheek, sneaking the cereal box for seconds behind her back.

"Oh!" Mrs. Waldens scoffed and swatted him playfully with a towel. "So *you're* the one eating all the cereal!"

"Who, me?" Jason backed off, feigning shock.

"You'll eat us out of house and home with how many bowls you have!" Mrs. Waldens shook her head. "Make some eggs or something if you're still hungry. Feed those muscles some proper nutrition."

Jason laughed. "But doesn't the box say magically nutritious?"

"It's magically delicious, and you know it, goofball."

CHAPTER 10

Visions

Melanie didn't see Scalaed for the rest of the day, and before she knew it, Jason pulled up in his own vehicle. She waved, then finished tidying the camper before stepping into the late afternoon sunlight.

Jason stepped out and gave his sister a hug. "How's it going, Sis? Are we flying today?"

"I hope so, but I don't know." Melanie squinted at the sky. "Let's talk inside."

The two entered the camper, and Melanie gestured for Jason to sit down at the table. Melanie opened the little fridge and pulled out a plate of BLTs. She offered a sandwich to Jason, then said, "Scalaed has been acting a little strange lately."

Jason stopped eating mid-bite. "…Like, strange how exactly?"

Melanie grabbed a sandwich and studied it, lost in thought. "I don't know. He was zoning out. Maybe he's a little lonely. Maybe he misses something."

Jason took a huge bite out of his sandwich. "Want me to hook him up with a crocodile?"

Melanie stood outside and called for Scalaed. Then she waited. The pine trees carried her voice deep into the forest.

"He can hear you from all the way over here?" Jason asked. He hefted the heavy double-seater saddle in his grip. Melanie had found it at Coincidence Antiques and modified it with safety straps and extra clips.

"If he went back to the cave below the plateau," Melanie answered, her brow furrowing in suspicion. "Otherwise I'll just use the heartlink."

"Does he usually take this long?" Jason asked after nothing happened.

"No." Melanie retrieved her bike from the carport. "Give me a few minutes to find him." She pedaled off down a barely existent trail, zooming past pine trees and tiny yellow flowers as she shouted for Scalaed.

Worry crept in. Scalaed should have found her by now. She pedaled to the edge of the forest, then stopped at the top of the canyon.

"Where on earth can he be?" she asked the open air. Melanie placed both hands on her hips and gazed at the vast landscape before her. No dragon.

"Scalaed!" Melanie called for what seemed like the umpteenth time. "Where are you?" Her voice echoed as it bounced and faded.

Suddenly, her heart skipped a beat. Maybe Scalaed had been captured. Clasping a hand over her heart to check the heartlink, she slipped her gaze down the cliff and saw a black shape, still as a shadow.

"Scalaed?" she called.

He didn't respond.

"Scalaed, oh my gosh, there you are!" Melanie laughed in relief. "Get up here!"

Scalaed didn't move a muscle. His back was to her as he stared at the sky.

"Scalaed, I know you can hear me," Melanie shouted adamantly.

The dragon was still frozen.

"Don't make me come down there," Melanie warned, as she started climbing down the cliff. "Scalaed!" Melanie snapped as she marched up to the motionless dragon. Now that she was closer she could hear him giving off a low rumble, his spikes and wings vibrating. In a much quieter tone, she asked, "Scalaed? Are you okay?"

The dragon stopped humming and turned around.

"I've been calling you forever!" Melanie explained as she stroked his nose. "What were you doing?"

Scalaed looked back at the horizon, then back to Melanie. He rubbed against her shirt and snorted.

Melanie sighed. "Can I get a lift? Left my bike up there."

Jason walked out of the camper and crossed his arms. "If I had known you'd be gone for that long, I would have come with you. I have horrendous cell coverage out here, and I couldn't reach you. So…I ate all the other sandwiches…and all your potato chips." He shrugged in a not-so-sorry way. "And some of your chocolate milk."

"I know, I'm sorry. It just took me a while to find him."

"Almost an hour."

Melanie glared at her watch. "We can still catch the sunset. Believe me, you don't want to miss it from where we'll be watching." She grabbed the saddle next to Jason and hoisted it on Scalaed's shoulders. "Ready to go, boy?"

"As long as he doesn't lose it and buck me off," Jason said.

"I'll make sure you get a lovely mahogany casket." Melanie smiled sweetly, then mounted as Scalaed snickered under her.

Jason huffed as he climbed in front. "Thank you for easing my conscience." He patted Scalaed's foreleg. "Wussup, Kool-Aid?"

"You'll be fine," Melanie reassured him as they clipped snap hooks to their belt loops. "Though you might want to hold on."

Jason stared blankly at his sister over his shoulder. "Yeah. Thanks for the tip, Captain Obvious."

Melanie patted Scalaed's hide. "Take us out, bud."

Scalaed crouched on his front legs, then leaped to the sky.

Jason clutched the saddle as powerful wind tried to peel him off. The scenery took his breath away, especially as it slowly turned from gold to pink in the sunset's light.

Scalaed dropped to the bottom of a canyon where white, foaming rapids raced. He glided down to the river and let his underbelly skim the surface of the water, spraying mist around them. Then, jerking his head up, he flew down the canyon, stretching his magnificent sixty-foot wingspan to its full capacity.

They were no longer racing, but floating slowly and peacefully over copper-stained cliffs with majestic pine trees daringly growing on their steep faces. Who knew a canyon of sand and rock could be so captivating?

Scalaed blasted straight up from the canyon. He looked back at his two passengers whooping excitedly, then shook his head and roared happily. The mighty dragon increased his speed as he leveled out while Melanie and Jason took in the cliffs' grandeur. Tilting west, Scalaed headed towards the dying light of sunset.

Suddenly, Scalaed stiffened and felt his body buzzing again. The sunset seemed to roll away to a bright spring green. The vision was distorted, but Scalaed could just make out the rough shapes of a unicorn…and a woman. She looked at him and said, from what seemed like miles away, "Your time there is over. You have grown and you are ready. Come…"

The woman's voice faded until she was only mouthing unintelligible words, but her command echoed in Scalaed's mind as the vision swirled together like a rippling pond. Colors mingled as the sight blurred and smeared, then faded away. The rusted rocks of Arizona zoomed and cleared into view.

Scalaed performed the tricks that Melanie had taught him, but he felt more distracted than ever.

The last stretch of the flight was a slow, peaceful glide. Oblivious, Melanie sighed contently at the world around her. Dark clouds flashed with silver and white as they slid past the moon. It's true that Melanie had ridden Scalaed hundreds of times throughout the years, but each ride was better than the last.

Melanie yawned. "We've been out here for hours." She squinted her eyes at her watch, but it was hard to read in the dark. "Why don't we head back?" she suggested.

"I'm already asleep," Jason joked tiredly.

Scalaed ignored them and continued on. After a few more minutes of silence, Melanie's eyes began to feel very heavy. "Scalaed," she said, "take us home, please, I'm…" Melanie's voice trailed off as the drowsiness enveloped her. Her eyes blinked more and more slowly, then they shut tight.

Scalaed glanced back to check on his riders. When had they fallen asleep? That vision must have distracted him. What did it even mean? Hearing a low whooshing sound, Scalaed looked ahead and saw a ring ripple into existence. Glowing white ribbons and sparks whipped around the ring as it grew larger and larger. Before he could react, Scalaed soared through it as streaks of light surrounded him.

Melanie's eyes fluttered. Something warm sat to her

left. When she opened her eyes and adjusted to the light, she realized she was lying down next to Scalaed. His hot side heaved in and out as he slept. When Melanie nestled down again and closed her eyes, her hand brushed against something leafy. Her eyes shot open, and she sat up in an instant to find herself in a completely unknown forest.

CHAPTER
11

The Flüm Thrae

Melanie stood up and looked around, dumbfounded. She stood in a glade carpeted with lush clover and pink, velvety flowers in the middle of a vast, wild wood of enormous trees. Their wide leaves ruffled in shimmery shades of green and yellow. There was no way this was Arizona.

Scalaed yawned, lifted his head, and looked quizzically at Melanie's baffled expression.

"Scalaed!" Melanie shouted. "Where are we?" Jason snored from the other side of the dragon, but Melanie didn't pay him much attention; Scalaed appeared drowsy, almost disoriented. She extended her arm and stroked Scalaed's neck. "You okay?"

The dragon grumbled and dropped his head to the ground.

Melanie sighed at his lack of help and began walking away. "Fine. I'm going to find out where we are." *Home can't be that far...right?* She kept that thought cycling through her mind as she marched off, despite the haunting possibility she was nowhere near home.

After looking in vain for any kind of trail, Melanie paused. The warm, morning breeze gently brushed her face, tossing her dark brown curls. The rich scent of wildflowers filled the air;

not a whiff of pine could be found anywhere. Birdsong carried in the wind, and the majestic trees—not coniferous—swayed to and fro, their branches rustling peacefully and blending with the faint sound of rushing water.

What is this place? Melanie wondered.

She continued to walk, hoping the water source was somehow the Colorado River. Noticing a clearing up ahead, she quickened her pace. The ground dropped, and the trees gave way to meet an angry, thunderous rushing river. Apprehension stirred in her gut as she stepped out from the safety of the forest's shadow.

Melanie knelt down, inspecting the river with a critical eye. The opposite bank stood below more trees. No canyon cliffs in sight. She placed two fingers into the furious water, letting the force tug her hand. It was the clearest water she had ever seen. Melanie quickly withdrew her hand when she heard a loud snapping twig somewhere behind her. Spinning around, Melanie looked back and met the icy blue eyes of a gray wolf. It stood at the edge of the treeline, its silver coat glistening in the sunshine. Melanie blinked. *Is that a tattoo on its forehead?*

It approached, staring her down. Thoughts raced through Melanie's mind as the wolf approached. Did Arizona have wolves? She glanced to her right at a tree standing at the edge of the river.

"Scalaed!" Melanie called weakly, afraid of startling the wolf. She backed up to the tree slowly; the wolf kept its confident pace. "Scalaed, help!" Melanie yelled louder as she swung herself upon the lowest branch and climbed higher into the tree. Out of danger, she shouted once more, "Scalaed!"

The wolf stopped and hunched its back, snarling nastily at the forest. Both waited for Scalaed's entrance.

"You stupid dragon! Help me!" Melanie ordered angrily.

The wolf straightened and looked back at Melanie, frozen.

"Yeah, that's right," Melanie taunted. "My dragon is gonna barbecue you."

The wolf seemed to lose its confidence, looked back and forth between Melanie and the forest, then scurried warily into the woods.

Melanie was greatly relieved...for the moment. Then a loud creak erupted below her. Her heart leaped into her throat, and her eyes widened; before she could react, the branch shook, bent down towards the river, and snapped.

Melanie splashed into the water. The river felt like fangs piercing her skin, injecting icy poison into her veins and stealing whatever warmth remained in her blood. The wild currents slapped her. The biting cold surrounded her. The water engulfed her. Foam splattered her face every time she surfaced, threatening to choke her every desperate gasp. Melanie noticed with alarm the currents racing faster and faster, and as she cleared a small cascade, she saw the water vanish over a much, much larger cataract ahead.

Panicking, Melanie fought furiously against pummeling fists of unforgiving water. As she approached the upcoming drop, she heard a loud noise through water-clogged ears. Not the sound of falling water, but a horn or a howl. Choking, she managed to cry for help. Melanie gasped for air, but water rushed into her mouth and lungs. As she convulsed in the depths, the world slipped away into dizzying blackness.

Jason rolled over in his sleep, then freaked out after nearly swallowing a mouthful of grass. Disoriented at first, he sputtered and spit. His hand froze mid-wipe when he realized he was *not* in his bedroom. Shooting to his feet, he marched in front of Scalaed and held out his arms.

"Excuse me, what is this?"

Scalaed blinking groggily, one lid at a time.

"Whoa, you okay, dude?" Jason asked the dragon. "You look like crap."

Scalaed felt like crap. His muscles throbbed, and his core burned painfully. His vision was slowly clearing, as was his hearing. His shoulders, still strapped under the saddle, ached.

"What happened?" Jason asked.

Scalaed had the same question. Struggling to stand, he found his ailments fading, much to his relief. Both he and Jason scanned their surroundings.

"These are *not* ponderosas," Jason said, putting his hands on his hips.

Scalaed agreed. These trees were even taller, with huge glossy leaves.

"Where *are* we?" Jason asked.

Scalaed's senses returned with a slamming weight, and he straightened at the strange smell that assaulted his nose.

Jason took notice, but before he could ask about it, a bola spun from the depths of the woods and tangled Scalaed's legs. Then another, and another. Within seconds, the dragon had been immobilized by half a dozen weighted ropes.

The forest exploded in shouts as hooded figures descended upon the grove. Scalaed inhaled to blast them, but a rope lassoed over his muzzle and clamped it shut, nearly causing him to choke on his own flames.

Jason tried to run, but someone tackled him to the ground. Shouting in protest, he strained against his arms being bent behind him. His head pulsed with sudden harshness, black spots encroached his vision, and his cheek melted into the grass.

CHAPTER
12
Eavesdropping

Melanie's head pounded, and her bloodshot eyes opened slightly with a quiver. She shut them again wearily. No sooner had she recovered her senses than she succumbed to a coughing fit, violently vomiting water. Air filled her lungs again.

Why can't I see? She opened her eyes once more and widened them, but could only see blackness. Next came the smells: stuffiness, sweat, horse. Melanie was on her stomach, slumped over an animal, and her whole body jostled with the creature's bouncing gait.

Melanie squirmed, panic seeping in. She needed to stand up, but to her horror, her wrists were bound, and she was wrapped in thick fabric. Melanie calmed her frantic breathing. She felt beads of sweat trickle down her face as a blaring horn, its sound vaguely familiar, pierced the air.

Melanie stopped bouncing. A muffled chorus of noises surrounded her. She listened fearfully as voices, eerily close, communicated in whispers:

"What do you intend to do with the prisoners, Helnah?" asked a low voice. "They're a little old for your uses."

"Interrogation, of course. Those lights streaking across

the sky were a sign," replied a calm voice, older and feminine. "It led us to them and this dragon, Elken. Finally, a Pyrium within our grasp! Perhaps they are the ones described in the Spire's Scroll."

Melanie's mind swarmed with questions as puzzle pieces of memory reconnected in her brain. She listened intently as the voices continued.

"We are that much closer to protecting the world." The woman called Helnah sighed, then continued, "For now, be vigilant, for I have seen a trarewolf lurking just beyond our company."

"Trarewolves? This far from their country?" asked the man named Elken.

"The sign was visible for many miles. I suspected we wouldn't be the only ones to follow it. But the savage will have no chance against us if it attacks."

"How many have you seen?"

"A lone trarewolf has been tracking us since the river, but there could be others."

Melanie had to remind herself to breathe. *What is going on?* Confusion swarmed her mind, making her dizzy. She remained silent as she felt a hand on the back of her neck.

"So," Helnah said, "I suspect there's something very special about these two wanderers."

Someone tore the fabric from Melanie's eyes, blinding her.

"And I," Helnah said, "would like to know what it is."

CHAPTER 13

A Face in the Tree

Helnah yanked Melanie's bound arms and pulled her from the creature's back. They were large, brown, equine-like animals with a pattern of green stripes on their coats. A small curved horn protruded from the center of its forehead. Black fur framed electric green eyes like thick eyeliner.

Melanie twisted on the clover to face her captors. Beneath a dark blue cloak, Helnah had piercing black eyes, and midnight brown hair covered the right half of her face. Her lips were painted a shade of dark plum like those of a vampire. Helnah squeezed Melanie's shoulder and lifted her off the ground with alarming strength.

Roughly shoving Melanie into a standing position, Helnah ordered, "On your feet."

Melanie twisted her arm, releasing it from the woman's harsh grasp. "Hey!" she sputtered. "What is going on? Who are you?"

They were deep in the woods. Riders in great numbers surrounded her, mounted on the strange beasts. All wore dark blue cloaks with hoods veiling their faces. They wore long, dark green tunics and leather boots. Quivers of arrows and beautifully carved bows swung lazily on the riders' backs as they regarded their unfortunate prisoner.

"You fail to recognize our banner," Helnah marveled in disbelief, her voice cold as stone. "Most interesting."

"Are you guys, like, cosplayers or something?" Melanie asked, trying her best to hide her nervous state. "Because your horses look amazing." Melanie gestured at the strange beasts.

"Those are tarothyls," said the man Melanie assumed was Elken, seemingly perplexed by her ignorance.

"You guys do good accents by the way; you from England?" Melanie added. "If you guys wanted me as part of your act, you should've just—"

Elken dragged Melanie towards the end of the line of tarothyls.

"Aren't you going to tell me who the heck you are?" Melanie asked. "You're not an evil cult, are you?"

"How is it you speak so much, yet make no sense?" Elken accused. "Care to explain yourself, you ignorant peasant?"

Offended and confused, Melanie's mouth dropped open. "Well," she sassed, "you get less frightening the more you talk."

Elken seemed to take that as a challenge. "Frightening? I'll show you horrors you've never seen even in your darkest nightmares."

"Wow, real cliché, dude," Melanie critiqued, her confidence replacing her fear. "You need to work on your script, because—" She stopped abruptly, and her brown eyes widened in horror. "Wait! Where is my brother?"

"Separated. We have no desire for you both conspiring an escape."

Melanie scoured the hunting party for Jason as she was led to the rear of the company, and instead saw Scalaed. Bound from nose to legs, he was being dragged behind six tarothyls. The rough treatment peeled his scales and bruised his knees and shoulders, which swelled from the pressure of the rope. The scratched saddle had slipped off-center and dug under his foreleg. His eyes were filled with anguish and confusion. The heartlink, no longer drowned out by Melanie's own fear, strained with pain.

"What did you do to my dragon?" Melanie cried, pulling away from her captor. Not bothering to look back, she ran over to him. She rested her bound arms on Scalaed's head. Her hands softly caressed his bound muzzle. "Oh, Scalaed, what have these freaks done to you?"

"How else are we to get him to the fortress?" Elken asked.

"You!" Melanie spat with venom. "You're no cosplayer, you're a demented psychopath! Untie my dragon this instant!"

"This...is your dragon?" Elken asked, trying to veil his disbelief.

"Yes!"

"Now he belongs to Helnah," Elken explained coldly, regaining his composure.

Scalaed could do nothing more than heave his sides and give Melanie a pained sigh. Melanie's head began to pound, as if her brain had no more room to hold her frantic thoughts and questions.

"Excuse me!" Melanie cried to everyone. "Who are you people? I'm going to call the police for kidnapping and animal abuse! And—"

The riders looked at Melanie; clearly, they had no idea what she was talking about. Melanie lay her head on Scalaed's cheek, tears painting her face and fear filling every inch of her being. This was no act. Melanie trembled as she stroked Scalaed, trying to comfort him until she was dragged away again, kicking and screaming curses.

"Due to your insubordination, you will not be given the privilege of riding a tarothyl," Elken said. "Instead, you will be tied behind one for the next hour. You will either keep the pace or be dragged in the dirt."

Melanie's wrists ached as the rope dug into them and rubbed them raw. Her headache now threatened to split her very skull. Even though her sandals had survived the river episode, debris caught in the straps cut and blistered her feet. Miles of walking bathed her in sweat. Her hair hung in wet strings, dripped onto her purple tie front, underneath which her white tee clung to her chest. Melanie untied the knot in a pointless attempt to feel less muggy.

The company gained speed, so the tarothyls broke into a trot. Melanie finally collapsed to the ground blanketed with leaves. The tarothyl did not seem to notice and continued to pull her along by her wrists until a hunter dismounted and helped her up. The ground beneath Melanie began to tilt and sway. Losing her balance, Melanie fell back into the hunter and slipped from consciousness.

When Melanie came to, she was in the arms of the hunter who helped her, riding on his tarothyl. She felt a wet cloth on her forehead.

"You'll be of no use to Helnah dehydrated," said the hunter in an all-too-familiar voice.

"Oh," Melanie groaned, recognizing Elken. "You."

"My name is Elken," he introduced himself as he slipped off his hood, uncovering his long, tousled hair. Dark like the soil beneath their feet, the rugged look suited him as a hunter, and it matched the short goatee on his chin.

"Yeah, I know," Melanie said hoarsely.

"Then address me as such."

"Other words come to mind."

"I think you should restrain your tongue."

"No, I want answers! Who are you, where am I, and why are we tied up?"

"You and your brother are prisoners of Thornbrill. You were rescued from the Flüm Thrae by Helnah, High Huntress of Thornbrill. You and your dragon will serve in her army. Now, silence."

Every word intensified Melanie's clenching of her hands. *How is any of this real?*

They pressed on through the evening. Occasionally, Melanie could swear she saw a pair of eyes staring at her from the black shrubs and shadows of the forest. She hoped Scalaed could confirm, but the heartlink was numb. Her dragon was too tired to respond.

When night had fallen, Helnah signaled the entire troop to stop and begin setting up camp.

A loud cry pierced the air and sent a chill up Melanie's spine. She knew that scream all too well—it was Jason. She looked around frantically for her brother and finally saw him. He was wrestling a hunter and had him pinned to the ground. It was quite an accomplishment, given that he was bound at his wrists. Feeling new energy flow through her veins, Melanie gathered her strength and jumped from Elken's tarothyl, ignoring his warning. Focusing on her brother, Melanie wove herself through the maze of resting tarothyls and dismounting riders.

The hunter was trying to take Jason down. Finally, the brute kicked Jason and punched him in the stomach. Jason doubled over and gasped for air. Opening his eyes, he saw Melanie approaching. Jason kicked the hunter between the legs and raced towards her.

"Melanie!" he shouted.

Melanie lassoed Jason's body with her bound arms and squeezed him tightly. "Thank goodness you're okay!"

"I've been better." Jason hugged back. "What about you?"

Two hunters crashed their reunion, pried them apart, and dragged them towards a fire the Thornbrillians had started. Jason thrashed around, trying to free himself. He wanted to believe this whole thing was some awful act or prank, but he had the sickening feeling it was not. That wouldn't explain the tarothyls.

The two men shoved the prisoners onto the ground and immediately tied their ankles with fresh rope.

Minutes dragged into hours as the siblings lay tied up and alone. The only interaction they had with their captors was when they were given a small portion of food and water. Whatever it was, neither Jason nor Melanie could recognize, but it did satisfy their hunger, however tasteless it was. The air that had made Melanie sweat was now bitter and cold.

Looking over at the hunters, Melanie frowned. They were laughing and talking while they sat on logs around a hot, blazing fire. She and Jason had been cast behind them where the fire's warmth could not reach. Melanie closed her eyes and prepared for a miserable, lonely night.

"What is happening?" Melanie asked Jason.

"We're...prisoners," he replied. "And these people are serious. How do you think a normal person would react to a dragon? Completely flip out and call some government agency, right? Not these guys. They took Scalaed down like it was just another day in the office."

"He didn't even faze them. It's like they're used to seeing dragons around," Melanie added. "I don't think we're on Earth anymore."

"That's insane." Jason shook his head. "But somehow it makes sense. You'd think we'd see someone pull out their phone to send a text or play a mobile game or something by now. Who the heck doesn't have a phone? Mine doesn't even work."

Melanie frowned. "I lost mine in the river." She angrily thumped the ground at the loss. *Another thing gone wrong.*

The night creatures of the forest began to wake, congesting the evening with chirps and chatter. While Jason fell asleep, Melanie stared into the forest. The heartlink told her Scalaed was asleep. Alive, but restless. With a sigh, she turned, looking at a tree with a large knot on its trunk. Through the expiring, orange light from the fire, Melanie thought the tree looked roughly like a wolf's head. The large knot was its snout, two branches its ears, two dark spots in the wood its eyes, and roots the front legs and paws. The longer Melanie stared at it, the more detailed it became. Now she could see a heavy branch wagging in the wind like a tail. The image seemed so real.

The eyes blinked.

Melanie blinked back.

What would have been the mouth opened to show a bared row of deadly white teeth. Melanie could hear the wild dog's breathing. Her teeth stopped chattering, and she fixed her terror-filled eyes on the tree.

This was not a tree. This was a real, live wolf mere feet from her face, ready to tear her apart in seconds.

CHAPTER
14

Hündr

Melanie stared motionlessly into the blackness. The wolf glared back with unblinking, ice-blue eyes.

The shadow of a passing archer drifted over it, and Melanie saw the wolf's face change. Fur receded into the skin, and the wolf morphed into a human—a young man—his wolf ears twitching and tail still wagging behind him. He wore gray pelts and a leather belt from which hung a curved dagger. Melanie didn't know whether to be relieved or horrified.

Remaining on all fours, he silently motioned to an enormous tree overhead. Quick and quiet as a squirrel, he climbed the tree and out onto a limb, then held out his hand to Melanie. Her eyes darted from his face to his hand, hesitating. He flexed his hand open even more, an order for her to take it. Quelling the voices of doubt and suspicion in her mind, Melanie grabbed it, and he pulled her into the thick branches.

Safe in the tree, she studied his face. His eyes were that same ice-blue as the wolf from the river. His chiseled jaw bore a serious expression of determination and vigilance. Under the dusky hair on his forehead was the same tattoo.

Melanie opened her mouth to say something, but he put a finger to his lips, silencing her. So she pointed down at Jason, begging with her eyes for the wolf-man to save him. The stranger assessed the layout below, then motioned for Melanie to stay put. Like a shadow, he descended to the ground and crept up to Jason.

"What the—" Jason yelled at the strange intruder, who instantly and instinctively slipped back into the tree.

"The prisoners!" shouted Helnah. She stepped aside as a hunter ran to Jason. He looked around for Melanie, but she was safe and hidden in the tree by now.

"The girl has escaped!" the hunter shouted.

Helnah marched up to him, her deep red lips pinched tightly in a furious frown, and her black eyes flamed with anger. She slapped the hunter across the face, causing several hunters to cower back. "That's on you. Find her!"

The hunter yanked his huge bow from his back and nocked an arrow to the string. Other archers followed his example as they spread about the camp. Elken scanned the forest, his face illuminated by the fire.

Helnah grabbed a grunting and kicking Jason and disappeared into the camp.

Up in the tree, Melanie and the wolf looked down with ever watchful eyes. Melanie screamed in her head as her brother was taken. She motioned frantically to the wolf-man, who simply put his finger to his lips and shook his head. Melanie didn't understand. *I need to help Jason!* He would no doubt be punished for attempting escape, and potential scenarios barraged her with fear.

The wolf-man pulled out his curved knife and cut the

ropes binding Melanie's wrists and ankles. He thrust the bonds into a hole in the tree so no one could find them.

Melanie looked back at the camp for one last glance at Jason, but instead met Elken's unshakable gaze. Still holding eye contact with Melanie, he mouthed, "Run."

Noticing Elken's message, the wolf-man grabbed Melanie's hand, and both descended into the forbidden-looking blackness.

"We can't leave them!" Melanie said in a quiet whisper. The wolf-man ignored her. "Why are we abandoning my brother? My dragon? We have to save them!"

The wolf-man again paid no heed, and on and on they ran through the woods. Melanie looked back many times, but no one was following them. The night engulfed them as they retreated farther into the woods. Melanie was exhausted from her escape. Her legs ached, and her lungs burned. Her clothes were torn and filthy. Her guide panted as he led them through the winding maze of trees. By the time Melanie was sure her legs would collapse beneath her, they slowed their pace.

Melanie began to replay the escape in her head. Desperate for answers, she asked, "How did you do that shapeshifting back there? What kind of a place is this?"

The wolf-man was too distracted to answer as he cautiously tread through the forest.

"Will no one in this stupid forest give me answers?" Melanie demanded.

The wolf-man stopped and looked at her incredulously. "Does silence mean anything to you?" Arms crossed, he continued, "It's a wonder those barbarians haven't found us."

Offended, Melanie snapped, "Oh, I'm sorry, but I planned on waking up snug in my bed this morning, not getting kidnapped by evil, gothic Robin Hood! So you will excuse my attitude, because I've had a *very* bad day!" Rubbing her face, she mumbled, "This can't be happening." When she looked back at her mysterious guide, who seemed amused, she asked again, "What *are* you?"

"My name is Briefur, son of Brefiüll." His expression bore either shock or confusion, Melanie couldn't tell which. "You don't know what I am?"

"A werewolf?" Melanie guessed while stepping back and examining him.

"It's pronounced 'trarewolf,' actually."

"So that trick back there, turning into a wolf…that was real?"

Briefur was now undoubtedly offended. "You clearly aren't from around here. It's my nature as a Hündr." He tapped his forehead tattoo. "Have you never heard of the trarewolf tribe before?"

"Those words mean nothing to me. Where am I? Someone said Thornbrill?"

"Thornbrill is the fortress. We are in the country of Tharretill." Glancing at her clothes, Briefur raised an eyebrow. "Now, who are *you*, and where do you come from?"

"I'm Melanie. I'm from Arizona."

Briefur knitted his eyebrows. "Where is that?"

"The…United States?"

Briefur's blank stare caused Melanie to reflect on her remark about not being on Earth.

Briefur shrugged indifferently and changed the subject. "We best find shelter in the trees lest those barbarians catch up to us." He scurried up a tree. "Unless you are taking first watch, Melanie of Arizona, I would climb up here."

Knowing no place else to go, Melanie hoisted herself into the tree's branches.

"You must rest," Briefur told her, "for we have far to travel tomorrow. I will keep watch to make sure no one has been tracking us."

"Not a chance," Melanie retorted. "I'm not sleeping so you could kill or eat me."

"I just rescued you!" Briefur argued. When Melanie gave no response, Briefur held out his hand reassuringly. "I give you my word: I shall not kill or eat you."

As Melanie shook his hand, she mumbled doubtfully, "I bet it's a full moon."

Briefur shook his head, befuddled and amused. "You confound me." He climbed higher. "I will keep watch as you are in more need of rest than I."

"Fine."

Briefur lay prostrate on the branch above. With his curved dagger in hand, he scanned the area with unblinking eyes.

Melanie found it terrifying to sleep ten feet up in a tree while armed barbarians hunted her somewhere below. Laying on her back, she stared at the canopy of stars. The heartlink thumped, unchanged, which told her Scalaed was fine. If only she knew Jason's fate, too. She twisted around and winced as the tree bark scraped her back. *Ugh*, she thought. *Just one more thing that won't let me sleep.*

Looking at the sky, she saw the full moon shine behind the trees. Something tugged at the back of her mind, telling her something was wrong. Melanie furrowed her brow as she looked through the branches towards a soft, golden glow. She sat upright, climbed a few branches higher, and saw the forest stretch out for miles. Melanie's mouth dropped open. A *second* moon hovered just above the horizon. The realization dawned on her like an unwelcome Monday morning. She had known it was coming; she had suspected it, but tried to push it away. Deep down, she realized she had known all along.

This is not Earth.

Melanie had been plucked from her life and dropped into who-knows-where. What would happen when her family couldn't reach her? The police would be notified. She couldn't bear the idea of causing such panic and distress. Anxiety amassed in her throat. She tried to swallow. She tried to breathe. Her heart beat on the verge of a panic attack.

Then...fatigue. Sudden and thick, it began to swallow her up like a drug. Melanie sank back down into the tree and gave in. Still staring at the celestial proof in the sky, she let her eyelids shut out the world to sleep.

Melanie bolted upright and gazed around her surroundings. She sighed in relief that she hadn't fallen off.

The forest glowed pink and gold as morning returned. Looking down at the branch below her, Melanie whispered, "Briefur...Briefur?"

No response came. Melanie's eyes darted around the scenery. She carefully crawled to the edge of the branch and looked down. Briefur was creeping closer and closer to a shadowy bush. Two golden eyes gleamed at him from the shadows. The next second, a flash of orange leaped from the darkness and pounced on Briefur.

CHAPTER
15

Fugitives

Melanie climbed down the tree and was preparing to help Briefur when he shoved his attacker off him and dusted himself off angrily. "Get off me! Why are you here?"

His attacker was a slender, blonde girl with large fox ears and tail. She, too, had a small tattoo on her forehead. "You disappeared from the village! Never had I thought that I would locate you in our enemy's territory. Why are *you* here, cousin?"

Briefur answered quietly, "While following those lights, I received a message from a Thornbrillian spy. They found a rare dragon and two alien prisoners, and he needed assistance with their protection. He suspects they wield great power. I managed to aid one of the captives."

"Yes"—the fox girl's golden eyes glimmered—"and Helnah has dispatched hunters on your scent. I came to help you."

"Why assault me, for stars' sake?"

"I missed you?" The girl shrugged.

Melanie had been watching the exchange. Seeing another Hündr only hammered her brain the more with the fact she was in another realm. Panic clawed up her throat, but she swallowed it back. She had to be clear-headed. Or at least try.

Briefur turned to Melanie. "This is my little cousin Fallon, a froxil."

"Of course," Melanie said, accepting it in stride. "A froxil."

"How far are the hunters?" Briefur asked.

Fallon stiffened. "Too close." Her nose twitched as she looked behind them. "I can smell them."

Briefur darkened. "Me, too."

He yanked his dagger from his scabbard and held it firmly. Fallon did the same.

Feeling helpless, Melanie picked up a large branch from the ground. She cringed at the sound of a twig snapping.

Fallon noticed twinkling in the bushes: the tips of many arrowheads. "Run!" Fallon fell on all fours and changed into fox form—albeit much larger than a normal fox—and darted into the thicket. Briefur grabbed Melanie and followed. Hunters shouted after them, and arrows whizzed by, many missing them by a hair. Melanie dodged shrubs as her feet barely touched the ground. She tried to keep going, but her lungs burned and cried out for more air.

As shouts of their pursuers faded, Fallon switched forms again. "We must head for the Anguill Swamps. They will not follow us there!"

"Why not?" Melanie asked.

"The Thornbrillians would never dare to enter it; they say a dark force dwells there, and they fear it more than death."

"Oh, but *we'll* waltz right in? How is this safer for us?" Melanie asked incredulously.

"Their culture is steeped in superstition," Fallon explained.

"From what I overheard in the camps during my espionage, it's all rubbish."

"Very well, Fallon," Briefur consented. "Lead the way."

They journeyed through the woods at a brisk pace, the two Hündr ever vigilant and utilizing every sense. Their ears twitched, listening for the hunters. Their eyes latched onto anything that moved, and their noses searched for an enemy presence. Their feet carried them soundlessly on patches of moss.

Disliking the silence, Melanie asked Briefur, "Were you the wolf at the river?"

Briefur smiled and nodded. "Yes. I assumed you would recognize a Hündr, so I did not expect you to flee like you did."

Melanie shrugged. "Wolves aren't friendly where I come from."

Fallon stopped abruptly. Ahead, dense vines and trees twisted together to create an impassable barrier.

"We'll climb that tharlyps tree. It looks to be the only way into the swamp," said Fallon. She pointed to a huge tree with a wide, gnarly trunk, the top of which vanished into a canopy of green fog. The tharlyps tree stood on the bank of a vast swamp that spanned for miles, its banks lost in the mist. The swamp smelled damp and metallic, like air before the rain comes. The swamp's still surface lay infested with thick green pulp.

Fallon jumped and grasped the trunk of the tharlyps. She walked around the tree using grooves in the bark as footholds. "Follow my lead," she said as she wound higher around the tree.

Melanie grabbed the tree and climbed with Briefur at her heels. When they reached a huge branch that hung over the swamp, Fallon pricked her ears and listened. "No sign of those barbarians, as expected."

Briefur sat quietly, his eyes staring down the swamp.

Melanie noticed his solemness. "What's wrong?"

Briefur lowered his head. "I don't like this place."

"Yeah, me neither. It's gross." Melanie shuddered. "You sure there's no dark force here? Seems like a prime location for zombies."

Fallon blinked at the unfamiliar word. "I know nothing of these zombies you speak of, but we are safe from our enemy here." She hopped out of the tree, Melanie following suit.

Briefur tilted his head, then crawled the length of the branch.

"Briefur, what is it?" Melanie called up to him.

Briefur dropped in front of her and spoke very quietly, his finger pressed to his lips, "We shouldn't have come."

"What's wrong?" Melanie asked as she felt herself tensing up.

Briefur's eyes darkened. "There's something in the water."

"How can you tell?" Melanie whispered.

"There's a scent." Briefur eyed the swamp warily. "A drifting presence in the wind. We must move away from here."

"And go where?" Melanie asked. "I don't know how much time my brother has."

"I understand your loss," Briefur said, "which is why we will lead you to someone who can help. He is very knowledgeable and lives in the outskirts of Hvitria."

"Then let's get started." Melanie began climbing back up the tree, purging the fear that had stiffened her body. "I'm really hating the vibes of this place."

"She confounds me," Fallon said when Melanie was out of sight.

"My thoughts exactly," Briefur agreed with a smirk, and followed his cousin up the tree.

Atop a branch, Melanie placed a hand over heart. Scalaed must have been awake, for his heartbeat sounded alert and steady. The hunting party must be on the move again. Melanie could only hope Jason was still alive.

"Your brother is not the only one who has been captured by Helnah," Fallon revealed as she reached Melanie's side. "Children all over Tindoria are disappearing."

"Wait, Tindoria?" Melanie asked. "I thought you said we're in—"

Blungk!

The three froze and looked back. A squirrel had dropped a nut from the heights of a tree before scrambling out of sight.

Melanie stared at the swamp in anticipated horror. The once placid, scummy surface erupted in furious waves. Melanie did not see it at first, but after the waves and green froth cleared, the monster emerged.

One hundred feet of glistening eel broke the surface with long fins that waved from the top of its head down to its tail. Its tongue flicked like a whip. Black smudges and scars mottled its slimy skin. Unblinking, poison-green eyes glared from the edge of its snout, which opened to reveal a mouth dripping with acid and saliva. Five rows of fangs, uneven and caked with decay of former meals, filled its maw. A breathy roar blared from the monster's mouth.

"Anguison!" Briefur yelled.

Melanie screamed and struggled to leave the tree. She heard Fallon cry out in horror. Looking back, Melanie saw the anguison's terrible tongue pluck Briefur from the branch. Briefur yelled and pulled out his dagger. Enraged, he hacked at the meaty lasso confining his body.

"Melanie, go!" he shouted, continuing to slice at the monster.

Melanie wanted to refuse, but no matter her desire, she could not move. She watched in fear as the anguison shook Briefur off, and the trarewolf sank below the scum. The monster dove in after him.

Fallon rushed to the edge of the swamp and started screaming her cousin's name through tears.

Briefur resurfaced, spitting out pulpy water, and screamed, "Go!" A huge tail smacked him, sending him under again. Melanie scrambled to Fallon's side, both screaming for Briefur to make it back.

Briefur resurfaced and tried to swim to shore, but was sucked back under. Fallon and Melanie watched him struggle, knowing he could never make it.

CHAPTER
16
Reveal

The swamp grew eerily quiet. Melanie's eyes stung from not blinking.

"No," Fallon whimpered, her fair face now flushed and trembling.

Not far down the shoreline, a figure floated toward land. Fallon strained her eyes to focus. Melanie saw it too, but Fallon sped past her.

"Briefur!" she cried.

His dark hair was streaked with green slime and black anguison blood. His own blood flowed from a nasty gash in his shoulder. His eyes were barely open as Fallon and Melanie splashed in to pull him to shore.

Briefur's icy blue eyes rolled back in his head. His chest rose and fell with shallow movements. Suddenly he rolled over onto his stomach, choking on the water expelling from his lungs.

Fallon sobbed. "You're alive!"

Briefur groaned as he strained to sit up. He pressed his hand against his wounded shoulder, but it continued to bleed. "I will survive. I've suffered worse."

Melanie knew Briefur was lying. He needed immediate

medical attention.

Fallon stared in awe at Briefur. "Did you kill it?"

"I cleaved it open," Briefur seethed through clenched teeth, "straight to its heart, so I had better. It would be a dishonor to lose a fight against something with no arms."

His head swirled, and his vision doubled. Briefur's shoulder throbbed and began to burn as the venom settled into the wound and stung his veins. He knew he would die from the poison. Wincing, he tried to stand, but his legs gave way and he buckled.

Melanie caught him just in time. "Don't get up so fast, okay?"

"I'm alright," Briefur said.

"Why does everybody say that?" Melanie huffed. "You are *not* okay. We are going to find you some medical treatment. Fallon, help me."

Fallon and Melanie carefully helped Briefur to his feet.

"Where is the nearest town?" asked Melanie.

"Not a town, the Fortress of Thornbrill," answered Fallon.

"That's where the bad guys are?" Melanie frowned. "That won't work."

"The city of Yolderain is across the southern border in the country of Rhydrah," said Fallon.

"Girl, I'm new here, I don't know what any of those words mean."

Fallon's nose twitched in irritation. "It doesn't matter. Yolderain is too far away, and Briefur would not survive the trip."

"Fantastic," Melanie said sarcastically. "Well…" She bit her lip. "For now, let's just get out of this marsh."

They made their way to a less marshy part of the woods. When Fallon sensed something to her left, she stopped, nearly pulling Briefur's bad arm out of its socket. Briefur cried out in pain, then tossed Fallon a nasty look. However, his expression changed when he noticed Fallon's reason for stopping.

A Thornbrillian archer stood in the shadows, an arrow nocked on his idle bow. Fallon unsheathed her dagger and pointed it at the archer.

"You've got to be kidding me," Melanie said flatly. "You again?"

Elken gave her a wry smirk. "We meet again."

Melanie shook her head, fury filling her chest.

"Stand down." Elken held out his hand and returned his arrow to his quiver. Fallon didn't lower her dagger. Elken unslung a bag from one arm and approached them. Melanie stepped in front, not letting him pass.

Elken sighed. "Will you let me tend to him?" He gestured to Briefur, whose eyes were slowly closing. "He is my accomplice."

"Wait, what?" Melanie backed up, and Elken walked past.

Reaching into his bag, Elken brought out a roll of bandages and a glass bottle filled with a strange blue oil. He said, without looking up, "From now on, you can count on me as your ally." Elken rubbed a little of the blue ointment into Briefur's wound.

"*You* are the spy from Thornbrill," Fallon interjected.

"Elken, yes, and I am pleased to make your acquaintance." Elken studied Briefur's wound. "I cannot heal him," he explained, "but this will last long enough for him to reach Thornbrill, where we can get proper supplies." He placed a hand on Briefur's shoulder. "Hang in there, mate."

Elken turned his head to the woods and gave a short, shrill whistle. Two tarothyls trotted out from the vines and branches. Their camouflage was so incredible, Melanie jumped when they moved. One strode over to Elken, and he petted its curly brown mane.

"This is my steed, Lythoras. She will carry us to Thornbrill."

Melanie yelped as Lythoras's horn swung too close to her face. "Thornbrill? That's where the enemy is."

"Elthar is the healer there, as well as a sort of sorcerer. He will have the remedy. As for you, you will ride with me." Elken smirked as he mounted Lythoras.

"I don't trust you." Melanie folded her arms.

The archer smirked again, a dimple pressing into his left cheek. "You have nowhere else to go."

Melanie shifted her weight and stared at his outstretched hand. *Yesterday he was my enemy, and now he's a friend? Not buying it.*

"Do not cost Briefur precious time." Elken moved his hand closer. Melanie said nothing, but reluctantly accepted his hand to help her mount.

Fallon, wanting to be close to Briefur, mounted the other tarothyl and held her cousin close. Elken urged the steeds to a quick and steady pace.

"We've got these horse creatures now, why can't we go to Yodeling-vain or some other city?" Melanie asked. If this Elken guy wanted her trust, taking her back to the enemy wasn't the way to earn it.

"Yolderain is still too far a ride for Briefur's critical condition, even with tarothyls."

"Come on, there's got to be somewhere else."

"There are only six countries in Tindoria—"

"Is that what this whole world is called?" Melanie interrupted. "You're throwing around a lot of names."

"I apologize," Elken said. "Yes. The entire continent is Tindoria. There are six countries. We are in the country of Tharretill. Yolderain is the city in Rhydrah."

He spoke not with irritation but patience. *Maybe he's not that bad.* Melanie asked, "So if you're really not the enemy, then who are you?"

"I was not always a Thornbrillian," Elken said. "I was born in Yolderain. I had just come of age and was visiting my parents when Thornbrill attacked the city, nearly five years ago. My father forced me into the cellar. When I came out, everything had been scorched to the ground. Father was dead when I found him, but my mother died in my arms."

Melanie let out a small gasp. "That's awful. I'm so sorry."

"Very few survived." Elken shook his head. "I wanted to avenge my parents' deaths. So, I left Yolderain and joined Helnah to destroy her empire from within. Thus they trained me as an archer. Through the years I earned Helnah's favor, but despite my privileges, I could never find that perfect moment to destroy her. I have done nothing of worth…except rescuing you." His voice softened.

"Is Jason okay?" Melanie asked. "Why does she want us?"

Elken took a deep breath, his chest pressing against Melanie's back. "It's not just you she wants. She has been searching for Pyrium Dragons like yours for years. For half a decade Helnah has been capturing dragons, collecting them, amassing an army. I haven't been able to divine the reasons for her desperate need, and I know even less why she would want you or your brother. You are too old for..." Elken's voice faded, and he shook his head. "Helnah has never taken this much interest in prisoners before, so I am at a loss. Just know she certainly has no plans to harm your brother."

"What made you want to help me?" Melanie asked, almost in a plea.

Elken frowned. "It's obvious you don't hail from Tindoria. This makes you special—both Helnah and I agreed on this— but I refused to let you fall into her possession. Yet I could not aid you without betraying my cover. Once Helnah told me a trarewolf was nearby, I seized the chance to secretly message Briefur, who was to rescue you until I could steal away to help you further."

"Surely your cover is blown now. Won't Helnah miss you?"

"She believes I've taken a company to hunt you down, but I slipped away while they murmured among themselves about entering the Anguill Swamp."

Melanie only nodded. Elken had opened up to her without

hesitation, even sharing his painful past with her. And he had clearly helped stabilize Briefur. *Could it be enough to trust him?* She wanted to think so.

"Well, I've shared my part, and I know you must have quite the story," Elken said.

"There's not much to tell." Melanie shrugged, her hands clenching the saddle in front of her. "I was out with my brother and dragon and woke up on another planet."

"Oh, surely there's more to it than that," Elken said.

"I don't even know where to begin."

"I would love for you to share," Fallon piped up, "but we need to hasten our pace." Briefur had paled and slumped forward against the tarothyl's neck. Fallon gripped his waist, struggling to keep him mounted.

Elken noticed and stopped their steeds, saying, "Fallon, let me help. Trade places with me."

Melanie watched him help the froxil dismount and take her place without letting Briefur fall. Fallon settled in front of Melanie, and Elken spurred his tarothyl to a gallop.

As they journeyed to the fortress, Melanie thought of what could be happening inside its walls. Then her heartlink throbbed rapidly and full of terror.

"Scalaed!" Melanie's whisper caught in her throat.

A nearby blue jay listened, cocked its head, and followed.

CHAPTER
17
Her Slaves

Jason shrunk in the looming shadows of the black mountain range, giants of rocky shards that erupted from the earth. A narrow road switch-backed up the sheer cliff face, at the top of which stood an old fortress. Two towers bridged by parapets flanked the three-story structure. Four large, slitted windows glowed on the east side. Built from blackish-blue bricks, it taunted Jason with the fact it would soon devour him. The mountains breathed a chill over him, making him wish he had his shirt. As punishment for trying to escape, he had been dealt a whipping that shredded it to ribbons, and it had been thrown away. Unfortunately, it was his favorite Jurassic Park shirt with sentimental value, so he had a personal vendetta with Helnah.

A commotion drew his attention to the rear flank of the hunting company, and the tarothyls tethered to Scalaed broke formation, dragging the dragon away in a different direction.

Scalaed kept his eyes on Jason—the only way he could communicate his terror.

"Hey! Where are you taking him?" Jason demanded.

"We cannot keep a dragon in our home." Helnah looked over her shoulder, hair falling over her face. "Rest assured he will be safe."

Jason was shoved forward, and all he could do was hold Scalaed's wild gaze as the distance between them stretched. Soon the dragon vanished behind the mountain's rocky foot, and Jason found himself walking through two giant red doors which slammed shut behind him with a despairing thud.

Scalaed moaned through the ropes as he was dragged away. His only comfort was knowing Melanie had escaped. According to the heartlink, she was safe.

The Thornbrillians and their tarothyls dragged him through a towering doorway in the mountainside. It exhaled heat, which did little to calm Scalaed's nerves. Darkness wrapped around them as they entered. Scalaed smelled ash as they reached the end of the cavern, which had two entryways. On one side, an archway wound towards a hot orange glow. To its left was a doorway hewn from stone that would have blended into the cavern wall had a Thornbrillian not opened it. Nothing lay beyond it but cold blackness and a smell that froze the blood in Scalaed's veins.

The Thornbrillians brought him to stand in front of that door. Scalaed squirmed to free himself, breathing out angry smoke through his nostrils. The men led the team of tarothyls around Scalaed, pivoting them towards the mountain's entrance. Scalaed studied their systematic movements. They had done this before.

What happened next was executed with the swiftest precision. A Thornbrillian yanked a chain between the lead tarothyls, and their harnesses disconnected. At the same time, other hunters whisked the animals outside. By the time Scalaed realized his bonds had been released, a man pulled a lever outside that sealed the mountain and threw Scalaed into darkness.

Scraping off his muzzle with his freed claws, Scalaed roared in broken defeat. That was when something cold wafted by his legs. Igniting his mouth, he shed light on the ghostly vapors that leaked from the dark doorway.

Something uncurled from its depths, a massive black shape that coiled around Scalaed and reeled him inside. Roaring, he blasted it with fire, but to no avail. Deeper into the cold darkness he went until he was pulled into an open cavern. A pale spotlight fell through the cavern's ceiling, streaming down in white light and illuminating the horrifying shape that lounged in the center.

A massive dragon over three times Scalaed's size lay in the cavern. Its smoky black hide gave it a deathly appearance. Its eyes, pupil-less and steamy white, hammered into Scalaed's soul. And he was wrapped in its tail.

In a deep, raspy voice, the dragon spoke. "After all these years."

Scalaed wanted to growl, roar, blast, anything, but he was frozen.

His captor studied him, unblinking, and hummed a shivering tone. "You look no more remarkable than the others."

Letting Scalaed drop to the floor, the foe-dragon swiped shut the entrance and sneered.

"Come now, show your power. Your ability."

Scalaed had no idea what that meant. So he blasted a pillar of flame at the dragon's face.

The dragon was not impressed. "Not that, you fool."

Scalaed did not take kindly to the insult and launched himself at the monster only to once again be caught in the dragon's tail. It was cold like a corpse. Holding him in a tight grip, the creature brought Scalaed close to its haunting face. White vapors curled from the tail like liquid nitrogen as the dragon shook its head. "Suit yourself. I do not need you to be willing."

The mountain shook as the monstrous captor shifted around, revealing a cage of stone tendrils. The dragon flung Scalaed inside like he weighed nothing, and the saddle jabbed into his back. His captor latched its terrible claws shut around the cage.

"Do not fight. It will only make this more painful."

Scalaed felt the voice rumble through the cage. A mental weight suddenly rammed into his mind, causing him to roar. The hungry force pressed itself into his brain, clawing through muscle and skull.

Scalaed thrashed in the cage, trying to escape the thick chill tunneling its way to his heartlink. His one comfort slowly beat softer and softer, and the feeling of Melanie's presence drifted away.

"Let me in!" The mountain shook again at the dragon's frustrated shout.

Scalaed roared long and loud in defiance, using his last bit of strength to repel the force. The weight vanished, and Scalaed felt steely mental walls erect themselves around his mind and core, protecting him from any further invasion. But they also muted the heartlink.

"Impossible!" The dragon loomed, its decaying breath suffocating Scalaed, who managed a weak smirk at its failure. "You *will* yield to me, beast. Until then, you will rot in this cage."

Jason sat on the cold, hard floor. His arms, wrapped around a black iron pillar, had grown numb. Glaring down at him from the top of the pillar with empty eye sockets and fangs was a blackened dragon skull.

He had been tied up in this room to wait for Helnah, who had separated shortly after they entered the fortress. The stone room had slit windows on one wall, while the other was the raw face of the mountain. At one end of the room stood a pair of grand, arched double doors leading to the front gates, and on the other end, a single, narrow doorway where Helnah had disappeared down. Pickaxes, crates, buckets, and crumbled wheelbarrows littered the rest of the room. A forge collected pounds of dust in the corner. Nothing looked like it had been used in decades.

The smaller door opened, and Helnah strode in wordlessly. Jason met her unblinking gaze as she paced around Jason with an unbreakable calm that made him shiver.

"What is your name?" Helnah asked.

"Elvis."

"Tell me, Elvis," Helnah asked. "Where is your family?"

Jason kept his answers as vague as possible. "At home."

"Where is home?"

"At my house."

Helnah's mouth twisted into a smirk as she descended to his level. "I will extort the information I want one way or another."

As she rose with a joyless smile, Jason bit his lip. Unable to look at her anymore, he stared down at his shoes.

"What are those?" Helnah asked, noticing the footwear.

"You've never seen sneakers?" Jason asked incredulously. "Wow, what planet are you from?"

The question seemed to strike a chord with Helnah. She inhaled softly. "Ah, so you *are* from a different realm?"

"Yes, and it's a whole lot better than this place."

"Have you any experience in fighting?"

Jason scoffed. "I am a master at thumb-wars."

Helnah was unfazed. "So, you have no knowledge of weapons of any kind? No experience in great battles?"

"Oh, I have experience. You know how many video games

I play?"

Helnah looked at the ground, trying to decode his replies. When she looked back at Jason, she had a dark glimmer in her eyes. "Your defiance could be converted to courage, boy. You could be a great warrior."

Jason rolled his eyes. "Even when I know absolutely nothing about what's going on or how to fight?"

"For what else have you been sent?" When Jason narrowed his eyes at her, she continued, "If you refuse to cooperate, I have other ways to make use of you..." She glanced at the skull mounted above, then bent down and grabbed his face, squeezing his cheeks as she inspected him like he was livestock at an auction. "Good age." Jason cringed when her cold hand squeezed tighter and tilted his face to the other side. "Many useful years ahead." Her gaze scanned the rest of him. "Wasting such fresh manhood would be a shame." Helnah trailed her fingers down his neck to his chest, pressing his muscles. "Lovely physique for a warrior," she noted with a small smile. "...What makes you *so special?*"

Jason scrunched his nose and snarled, "Lay. Off."

"Be grateful we found you," Helnah continued, dusting her hands off like he was a contaminate. "The savages could have found you first."

"Well, I don't know anything about these 'savages,' but I'm sure they're better than you."

Helnah laughed a cold, hollow laugh that echoed throughout the room. Jason looked with disgust as she stood again, and he swore she grew taller.

Helnah continued, "Ours is the rising power of the world. We will see glory and praise from other kingdoms. You must join my forces, for I believe the fate of the world rests with you."

She glided behind the pillar, and Jason heard a knife being drawn. It cut through the air with a loud whoosh, and he instinctively shut his eyes. His arms fell to the floor with a thud; his bonds had been cut. Lifting his arms in front of him, he felt the blood rush to fill them again. He was unharmed, for now.

Jason stood up, and Helnah sheathed her knife. She clicked her tongue in distaste.

"You'll need more suitable clothes…" She pointed to his shorts and sneakers. "Come along. Thendrell will prepare you for assessment."

She pushed him out the door she had come through, where a winding stairwell led to floors above and below. *This must be one of the towers,* Jason recalled. Helnah gripped his shoulder and prodded him down to the darkness. At the bottom of the stairs, Jason turned into a hall that must have stretched the entire length of the fortress. Prison cells and torches lined both walls. The dungeons. As they passed, Jason glanced into the barred windows in curiosity.

Children and teenagers sat behind the bars. The oldest, a girl around Jason's age with rose-gold hair, slunk back in terror until she seemed to sink into the stone itself. Jason noticed that her hand was a strange shade of blue, and her nails were black and long. Before he could look more closely,

Helnah pressed him forward. They passed many other cells, all filled with emaciated youth who cowered when he and Helnah passed by. Jason was appalled. *What could they have possibly done to deserve this?*

His question must have been written on his face, because Helnah answered, "For the sake of a secure Tindoria, sacrifices must be made. Don't make me throw you in with them."

Jason found himself gaping at one little boy of about eight rocking himself in the corner. His little voice was quiet but Jason could hear him trying to comfort himself saying, "Everything will be fine."

"What did you do to them?" Jason asked, his anger towards Helnah heating to a boil.

Ignoring him, Helnah shoved Jason through the other staircase at the end of the hall. Jason climbed the stairs back to the main floor.

Helnah led him through the back of the throne room. A blood red carpet stretched toward an elaborate chair carved with tiny dragons outlined in gold, bronze, and silver. They wove around the chair's back, slithered down to the armrests, and rested at the foot of the chair. To the right of the throne was a long table set for twelve people. A golden dish filled with fruit served as the centerpiece.

The man sitting at the table was tall with a dark blue cloak draped around his shoulders. His short, trimmed beard and hair were the same shade as Helnah's—dark brown, almost black. But unlike Helnah, his eyes were a brilliant blue.

"Ah, the new recruit," he said, standing to greet them.

"Thendrell," Helnah said, "this is Elvis."

Jason had to bite his tongue to prevent himself from smiling.

"Before he begins his assessment, he needs a new wardrobe." Helnah picked at Jason's shorts disgustedly as if they would come alive.

Thendrell smirked. "I think I may have something." With a bow, he exited the grand double doors to the main corridor.

Helnah walked up to the throne and dropped into it. She seemed worn out.

"So," Jason said, summoning his courage, "you're the queen of this place?"

Helnah laughed aloud. "No, my dear boy, I prefer the militant title of High Huntress, for I've captured nearly every dragon in the realm. From mountain lairs to forest caves, I've amassed a force of hundreds to wipe out anyone and anything that opposes us."

"What about the children you've kidnapped?" Jason asked, disgusted.

Helnah's lips twitched. She stood slowly and approached Jason. He swore the room grew colder with her every step. The candles flickered and a few died out.

Helnah, silent and unblinking, stopped mere inches from him. A frosty uneasiness squirmed through Jason's limbs.

Helnah leaned down to his level and whispered with a crooked smirk, "They're hardly children anymore."

The grand doors opened, and the cold disappeared. Thendrell strode in, carrying a neatly folded bundle of clothes.

Helnah waved her hand dismissively. "Take Elvis to his new quarters and dress him in his new attire."

Jason was whisked away, back up the staircase to the second floor of the fortress. He had counted three floors in total, and then the dungeon. This floor was all halls and rooms. Passing one, he saw they were indeed the hunters' quarters. Most had double bunks, but there were other more private ones.

Jason thought he saw Thendrell nod suspiciously at the guard standing post at the room he was ushered into. The room was furnished with a bed in one corner, a large barred window, a table and chair, and a tiny crackling brazier. In another corner was a chamber pot next to a bowl with a brick Jason assumed was soap. The door closed behind them, leaving Jason alone with Thendrell.

"Take off your shoes," Thendrell ordered.

Thinking it was a cleanliness thing, Jason slipped them off. Thendrell promptly threw them into the fire.

"Dude!" Jason exclaimed. "Those were sixty-five dollars!"

"Everything that you once were must be erased," Thendrell explained coolly. "You are Helnah's now."

"This is ridicu—"

"Now take off your clothes," Thendrell interrupted.

"No way, you pervert!"

Thendrell's mouth curled subtly. "I presumed as much." He opened the door, took a dirty bucket from the waiting guard, and splashed its contents onto Jason.

"Aaauggh!" Jason yelled, his pants soaked with the liquid. "What was that for? What is this stuff?"

The foul odor that reeked from his pants was followed by Thendrell's reply. "Tarothyl urine."

Jason gagged in horror.

"And it appears your attire is ruined," Thendrell noted.

The door opened again, and the guard dropped off a bucket of water and washcloths, trying not to laugh as he shut the door.

"Clean yourself and change into these clothes," Thendrell said. "You'll be fed once you cooperate."

Food! Jason couldn't remember when he'd last eaten.

Thendrell stepped out of the room, though Jason suspected he hadn't gone far. Grimacing, Jason peeled off his pants and visibly yellower socks. Not urine-proof, his ruined phone joined the clothes as he dropped them into the brazier with a soggy *squish,* which was followed by hissing and steaming. Jason grabbed the wet washcloths and bucket and began scrubbing himself down, praying he wouldn't contract some disease. After cleaning himself as best he could, Jason changed into his assigned clothes: a long beige tunic that dropped above his knees, a brown leather belt, gray pants, and sandals. He scowled at the awkward attire. *This is what I have to wear?* Jason adjusted the tunic. The odd clothes made him feel like a stranger, and their plainness taunted Jason with his new reality of being a prisoner. Helnah's slave. He hated every thread of the thing.

The door opened. Jason's guard looked him up and down, then wheeled a cart into the doorway. There were multiple plates of identical servings of some sort of meat and mash.

Jason guessed it was the prisoners' food cart. The guard handed him a plate and spoon and turned to leave. Thinking quickly, Jason snagged a knife off the cart and slipped it up his sleeve. He sat down at his table to eat and waited for Thendrell.

The chopped meat was a little dry and tasted like cheap steak. At least it was salted. The mash, colored an unappetizing gray, had more smell than flavor. It was less palatable, but Jason's hunger allowed him to finish it.

When Thendrell did appear, Jason stood to present himself. "Happy now?"

"Indubitably," Thendrell replied and walked toward him.

Jason lunged at him with the knife, but Thendrell jumped back. The Thornbrillian's expression of shock changed to anger, and he unsheathed his sword.

"Come on, man," Jason taunted, flicking out the spoon as well, "you can't hurt me. I'm Helnah's new favorite."

Thendrell huffed and dropped the sword in frustration. "Will nothing be simple with you?"

Dropping the spoon, Jason scrambled for the sword, but Thendrell grabbed him. He squeezed his arms around a thrashing Jason, who threw his head back into Thendrell's. As the Thornbrillian stumbled back to clutch his nose, Jason broke free. Knife still in his other hand, Jason yelled and attacked his opponent in a fit of rage. Thendrell leaned to the side, seized Jason's arm, and pried the knife from his grip before shoving Jason to the ground. Taking possession of the knife, Thendrell plunged it toward Jason, who grasped the opposing force in his hands, shaking as they almost touched his chest. The rough floor bit into his back as Thendrell pressed him harder.

As faint as a breath, Jason heard a soft voice say, "Be strong."

Before Jason could question where the voice came from, the fatigue instantly melted from his muscles. Fresh stamina fueled his body and reflexes, and with this new surge of strength, Jason hooked his feet under Thendrell's chest and launched him across the room, sending him crashing into the wall. With a kick-up, Jason landed on his feet and reclaimed the knife and spoon. Then he rushed his opponent. Thendrell rolled out of the way towards his sword, grabbed it, and jumped to his feet. Jason's arms flicked out like whips, the cutlery clanging against Thendrell's defenses. Jason recognized the insanity of the duel, but he persisted despite his pounding heart. With short steps and calculated jabs, Jason's attacks quickened. Thendrell's eyes widened as his arms tired from parrying, and he felt the first prick of Jason's knife ping his chainmail. Jason inched the fight closer to the corner of the room, his arms a swift blur—a whirlwind of metal stabbing from every direction. Thendrell panted, his opponent's attacks making more contact until in one fluid motion, Jason slid his weapons to opposite ends of the sword, and rotating his arms, spun the blade from Thendrell's grip. The sword twirled right into Jason's waiting hand, and the duel ended with him aiming the sword's tip at Thendrell's neck.

"You lose," Jason said.

Thendrell sat stunned as Jason tossed the sword across the room. Pointing at Thendrell's bloody nose, Jason added,

"And that's for dumping a toilet on me. Along with"—he gestured to the rest of his injuries—"everything else." Jason left the room where his guard met him around the corner.

"He's fine." Jason rolled his eyes before the guard had a chance to ask what happened.

The guard returned Jason to the throne room but did not enter. He instead opened the door and gestured for Jason to pass. Apprehensive, Jason slowly exited the stairwell, which shut behind him with an echoing boom.

Helnah was looking out of a window at the valley below. Creeping closer, Jason saw Helnah's one visible eye that was not covered by her hair staring wildly out the window. The stone room suddenly became colder. Jason wrapped his arms around himself, and his breath emerged as a frosty cloud. The fire in the fireplace sputtered and coughed, then was extinguished. The room now seemed forbidding and eerie, reminding Jason of a tomb.

The cold aura vanished as quickly as it had appeared, and the huge fireplace blazed with fire once more. Helnah turned her head, and Jason saw that her face was drained of color like she had seen a ghost. Jason wondered if she had. Helnah looked exhausted, but when she saw Jason, she raised an eyebrow at his battered state.

"Had a skirmish, did you?"

Jason didn't know how to respond without making things worse.

"Hmm." Helnah looked thoughtful. "I shall get Thendrell's report on how well you fought."

Her unexpected reaction relieved Jason, and he walked closer. He put his hands on his hips, then asked, "So, what now?"

"Now, you come with me."

CHAPTER
18
A Chat in Jail

Helnah took Jason up the east tower stairs. After entering the door at the top, Jason stopped. A huge stone patio stretched out over the mountainside. The far wall rose four feet, with glossy black pillars climbing the rest of the way to the ceiling. Racks of weapons were stationed at Jason's right.

Helnah closed the door, crossed her arms, and leaned against the doorway as Jason took a few steps into the room. He gazed out over the edge of the railing at the towering rocky mountains encircling the fortress.

Jason turned around and faced Helnah. "What is this place?"

Helnah strode over and gazed blankly at the world beyond. "This is where we will assess your abilities."

"Abilities?" Jason echoed.

Helnah walked over to one of the many racks bearing an array of weapons. Jason recognized most from the various video games he played: swords and daggers, bows and arrows, maces and clubs. But others he had never seen before: something with a bunch of ropes like a scourge, small pointed discs, and a short double bladed spear.

Helnah gestured to the collection. Without looking at

Jason, she said, "We will find what skillset you have after you have been tested with each of these weapons."

Jason pulled three arrows from the quiver. Two of them immediately clattered to the floor. With a glance at Helnah, who watched his every move without emotion, he shook his head and tried again to nock the arrow. Finally succeeding somewhat, Jason pulled back the bowstring.

"Tsk tsk tsk," Helnah said. "Nock the arrow on this side of the bow."

"It slides off," Jason grumbled under his breath. Helnah heard it anyway.

"Doing it your way will cost you a precious half-second. It means the difference between life and death."

"Thanks," Jason said, but he hardly meant it. He only had to play this role long enough to devise a plan of escape.

Helnah kept him on the expansive patio until night fell and stars filled the sky. He had tried many different weapons, but the sword seemed easiest to handle.

Helnah blinked, waiting for something more. "Is there… anything else of promise you can show me? Thendrell said you fought quite strongly today."

Jason did not tell her of the voice that had come to his aid.

Helnah took a step closer. "Tomorrow I have another task for you. Tonight, you are excused." Helnah left the patio without another word, and Jason's guard once again appeared and directed him to his quarters.

His room was much darker now that the sun had set, and pale moonlight shimmered through the tiny window. Jason trudged over to the windowsill and rested his chin on his folded arms.

He had been in this mysterious land for only two days, but he was haunted by the thought of staying much longer. *Where is Melanie? Is she safe? Will she come for me?* He gazed up at the night sky, even more questions escaping his lips, "Where am I? Why am I here?"

Jason gasped. A silver moon glowed with radiance perfectly in the center of the starry domed sky, but just touching the horizon on the south was a second moon. Jason rubbed his temples. "It can't be!"

Hail, most fortunate human!

Jason stumbled, looking frantically for the source of the voice.

A blue jay had landed on the sill. *For I have come bringing good tidings.*

Jason's eyes widened. The bird's beak didn't move, but he could hear the voice in his head.

Yes, it is I who speaks. The blue jay fanned out his wings in a fluttering bow.

Jason's voice pitched higher, "What?"

Dear me, have you never been graced with my palpitating

presence? The bird swatted his heart, offended to his core. *You must be cursed. Allow me to introduce myself. My name is Azeur, an Avis Messenger—a rare, precious being blessed with telepathy. I deliver messages faster than any other creature in existence and am therefore held in highest esteem by the Hündr who use our services. We truly are the best.*

"Okay," Jason said slowly, instantly disliking the bird's vanity and condescension. "So, you have a message for me?"

Of course, my poor, deprived recipient, Azeur replied. *Fate led me to a froxil who begged with her heart and soul, trembling in my majesty. Her tears flowed like the Flüm Allarway, and I, being the compassionate creature that I am, gave her great comfort in telling her I would deliver her urgent message with such haste that—*

"Please"—Jason cut him off, not believing the story to be that true or dramatic—"just tell me the message."

Oh, most certainly. Your sister Melanie is on her way with companions to rescue you and the dragon. Now, as she appears to be an alien, I can only assume that goes the same for you. It would be in your best interest to find someone to educate you about this realm. Now, as lying, scheming Thornbrillians would most definitely be the poorest tutors, try to find yourself a source of honesty. Perhaps the dungeons will have a poor wretch to answer your questions. I would enlighten you myself, but I have other messages to deliver, you understand. Yes, I fly to lords, kings, and empresses! Even... Azeur's voice dropped to barely a whisper, his eyes wide with wonder...*gods!*

There was a brief moment of awkward eye contact before

Azeur stretched his wings and flew away.

Jason stood there in bafflement. A minute later, he took a deep breath. "Dungeons it is, then."

Jason peeked around the corner. Guards kept watch in every hall and doorway, but he had to reach the dungeon and find that rose-gold-haired girl. She might know more than the younger prisoners. Jason knew it was no mistake his quarters were in the middle of the floor, far from the staircases.

Thinking of a distraction, he grabbed a torch from the wall and threw it down the hall. It clattered to the floor and rolled down the hallway, trailing flaming pitch behind it.

"Fire!" he shouted.

Jason backed behind his door as the two nearest guards ran towards the flames to extinguish them. Jason ran right behind them and dashed to the tower door. Flinging it open, he leaped down the stairs, into the dungeon, then leaned against the door behind him to catch his breath. Wiping his forehead, he crept down the dungeon corridor and peeked inside each cell. Where were the guards?

Jason picked up his pace and found the cell he was looking for. The rose-blonde-haired girl lay on her cot, curled up and shivering.

Jason did not want to wake her, but he had to. Tapping

the barred door, he whispered, "Psst!"

The girl's turquoise eyes shot open, and she tumbled off her cot on her back, breathing heavily. She appeared to be a light sleeper.

"Sorry! I didn't mean to scare you," Jason whispered.

"Who are you?" The girl's voice lilted in a brogue much different than that of the Thornbrillians.

"My name's Jason, and I'm not going to hurt you. I came to ask you a couple questions."

The girl seemed to calm down a bit. "I'm Laena," she said softly. She tiptoed to the barred window, giving Jason a good look at her face. Freckles dusted her dainty nose. Her hair glistened coral and was streaked with copper in the torchlight. But her lips; they were a sinister blue like the bottom of an ocean trench.

Taken aback by her appearance, Jason managed to ask, "Where are the guards?"

Laena scoffed. "Does it look like we have the strength to escape?"

"What did you do to get thrown in here?"

She took a shaky breath before answering. "When they attacked Endlewood, I was separated from my father and captured. 'Tis the same story for all of us here. War was used as a mask to steal us away, and all for what? Service under the lie of a brighter future." Laena looked at the floor and rubbed her arm.

Jason now realized with shock that half of it was blue, and her knuckles were covered with thick flakes.

"What did they *do* to you?" Jason asked.

Laena looked up into Jason's hazel eyes with her teary ones and said quietly, "Helnah, she tortured us, cursed us—told us our sacrifice would save…" She bit her lip to prevent herself from crying, but tears still flowed down her cheeks, memories searing her mind. Her burning district, the fleeing vendors. The purple dragon pouncing on her and carrying her off. Her father's screams fading behind her as she dangled from the beast's grip. Helnah strapping her down on a table. A crude black vial. Poison. Seizures. Migraines. Burning blood. Laena willed the memories away and held her thin shoulders as she shook, crying silently.

Jason's heart ached for Laena, and he wanted to reach through and comfort her. "Cursed or not, I will try to get you out of here. All of you!"

Laena shook her head. "There's no point, Jason. By the time you rescue me, I will not be the same."

"What are you talking about? What did Helnah *do* to you?"

Laena covered her eyes and whimpered in pain as Jason inched closer. "Laena?"

When Laena looked up, Jason quickly stepped back. Laena's beautiful eyes had changed. Her pupils were dilated slits like a reptile's, and they bore a hungry glare.

"I am a dragon," Laena said, "and there is nothing you can do about it."

CHAPTER
19

Trapped Under a Bed

Melanie breathed heavily as the heartlink throbbed and pounded. Fear and dread radiated from her heart. *What is happening, Scalaed?* She clutched her chest, and Elken took notice.

"Melanie, are you alright?" His gentle voice was laced with authentic concern. He rode beside her on the other tarothyl, supporting Briefur. The trarewolf was groaning, slumped forward in a daze.

The heartlink's pulsing heat faded, and the strange distance worried Melanie more. "I don't know," she finally replied.

Elken wished Melanie would trust him, but he did not press her for more. His dark eyes were glued on the path ahead, occasionally scanning the area around them.

The blackness of the night engulfed them, and the world felt different. Before, the crickets had been chirping, and the occasional cry of an owl had echoed through the woods. Now only the steady walking of the tarothyls and Melanie's rapidly beating heart could be heard. The forest was cold. It felt abandoned, forbidding, and devoid of all life.

Melanie's eyes began to close. The urge to sleep was too

overpowering. She fought it as best she could so as not to become vulnerable, but the sweet temptation to sleep and forget the day's worries won. Melanie felt her head reeling back, the forest slipping in and out of view.

With a snap, she jerked her head up. She was on the ground behind a small ridge at the edge of the forest. *Did I fall off?*

On the grass next to her, Fallon cradled her dying cousin. Briefur's face was ghastly pale and drenched in sweat. His eyes were shut, his hand weakly held onto his wounded shoulder, and his breathing came in labored gasps.

Elken was with them. "Fallon, wait here and care for Briefur until we return," he said. Fallon nodded.

Melanie stiffened as Elken approached her, but he looked beyond her. She followed his gaze as he pointed to a towering cliff side, where a winding gray road led to an ominous fortress at the top.

"The Fortress of Thornbrill," Elken said with obvious disgust. "Any aid for Briefur lies behind those walls." He offered Melanie his hand, but she helped herself to her feet.

"We need to hurry," Elken said. He walked back to his tarothyl, grabbed a rope, and faced Melanie. He smiled at her, but his voice hardened. "I am a man of my word, Melanie, and I told Helnah that I would find you." Taking the rope, he began to bind her arms.

Melanie sat in front of Elken astride Lythoras, his knife pressed into her back almost to the point of drawing blood. Ropes wrapped her arms from biceps to waist. *A bit excessive,* she thought. She looked at Elken, whose expression was unreadable.

The Fortress of Thornbrill glared down at Melanie from the mountain. She tried to steady her breathing as every step pushed her closer to the enemy. A horn sounded somewhere to her left, and she saw startled birds fly from a lookout tower peeking just above the trees. Elken pulled out a small whistle tucked under his cloak and blew loudly in response.

"Now they know who we are," he explained.

After a suspenseful ride up the mountain path, Elken dismounted at the red gates and pulled Melanie off the tarothyl. Melanie held her breath as Elken greeted the squad of guards. The eyes of four rugged men roved over Melanie, making her feel queasy. With congratulatory words for Elken, the men opened the gates to let them in. Elken marched her to the throne room, where Helnah sat alone on her throne. She appeared weary, her skin unnaturally pale and her expression distraught. Half of her face was still covered by her dark hair, and Melanie wished she could swat it out of the way.

Helnah had been staring at her hands squeezed together in her lap. She looked up at their arrival and stood gracefully. "I assumed you were dead when the party returned without you from the swamps. Yet you are safe. And successful, no less." Helnah scanned Melanie and continued, "There is a vacant room for her confinement. See to it she arrives there." Helnah sat back down hard and rubbed her forehead.

Melanie began to think the woman was very sick. Elken bowed stiffly and shoved Melanie out the door. After the great doors shut behind them, he pulled Melanie close and whispered, "Well played."

"Thanks, but that knife was a little too close for comfort."

"It adds to the effect." Elken smirked playfully. Melanie ignored the fact she found his dimpled smile attractive.

"Now that Helnah believes you are under my watch," Elken continued, "we can safely tour the fortress. Now, our healer Elthar has delivered purple vials to Helnah frequently."

"She does look like crap," Melanie noted. Elken made a face at the word, and Melanie almost smiled. "She looks bad," she reworded.

"Ah. But after taking that vial, she improves greatly. If there is anything to save Briefur, that would be it."

"But anything could be in that," Melanie said. "How do you know it would help Briefur?"

"No matter her ailment, he always brings the same vial. It's in her quarters two floors above."

"Oh, boy," mumbled Melanie. "How do we even get there unseen?"

"There's nothing to question about us. Just a loyal Thornbrillian leading his prisoner to her room. If we can access her quarters within the next few minutes, we may be able to get what we need before Helnah retires for the night."

"Eesh, no pressure." Melanie sighed.

"Going back into the throne room would raise suspicion,

so we must use the west stairwell," Elken said as they crossed the main corridor into an empty room of dust and pillars. Melanie wanted to ask what the room had once been, but Elken quickened his pace. She kept silent and began climbing the stairs—an awkward task with her arms bound.

"Listen, Melanie." Elken stopped at the top and looked down at her. "These stairs continue straight into Elthar's laboratory, which we *must* avoid. He is a secretive man of ill-temper, and I do *not* want to barge in uninvited with a prisoner. However, Helnah's room is on the same floor."

"Okay, so how do we get there?"

"We will cross at this floor to the east stairwell, which makes entry to Helnah's room much less conspicuous."

"I understand."

"Stay close. This is the floor with all our rooms, so there will be many men."

Elken positioned Melanie in front, one hand gently pressed against the small of her back, and opened the door with his other. Melanie scolded the flutter of her heart at his touch.

As he had predicted, they encountered many Thornbrillians, most of whom sneered at Melanie or nodded approvingly at Elken in passing.

"We are almost there," Elken whispered as the two turned into a hallway. He suddenly stopped and quickly untied Melanie.

"What are you doing, this is our cover!" Melanie hissed, the sound of chattering men growing louder.

Elken stuffed the rope into his pack. "Go down this hallway, turn right, go up the stairwell, and pass through the training court. Helnah's door is the green one in the hall. Search the drawers for the vial. I'll be right behind you."

Frantic, Melanie wanted him to repeat the directions, but there was no time. She nodded, then raced down and around the next bend.

"Elken!" boomed two voices.

Melanie froze and peeked back around the corner.

Elken had been intercepted by two Thornbrillians who stood with their backs to Melanie. One wore a gold circlet on his head, and the other had a chain around his neck with an ivory dragon tooth.

"Ah, Helketh and Keth," Elken greeted through a forced smile.

The man with the necklace cracked a grin. "Thendrell told us that you had returned."

"Oh," said Elken. "So, you have come to welcome me home? My heart is touched." He noted his subtle sarcasm was lost on the two men.

Helketh, the one with the circlet, crossed his arms and said, "Actually, my friend, we have come to ask for your help in the dungeon."

Elken's expression hardened as Keth continued. "Yes, the prisoners must be moved to the Arfire Maze."

"Already?" Elken looked beyond the two men at Melanie, his eyes clearly reading: *Run!*

Melanie nodded and disappeared around the corner.

"Come on, my friend." Helketh clapped Elken's shoulder. "We've done this often enough; it should no longer come as a surprise."

"But at this hour?" Elken asked.

"We always have a small window to operate," Keth said.

"I don't want another incident like last time we were too late," Helketh continued. "It took us over a month to rebuild that dungeon!"

"Come, the more men we have the quicker this will all be over," Keth said.

"A fortress of one hundred and twelve men, and you can't find *anyone* else to help?" Elken raised an eyebrow.

"Well, we also want to hear how you survived the Anguill Swamps and found that little wench." Keth wrapped his arm around Elken and led him away.

Jason had been locked in his room for hours with absolutely nothing to do. The punishment could have been worse. Thendrell had caught him in the dungeons. With a disappointed sigh, the Thornbrillian had put down what looked like a checklist and charcoal stylus and dragged Jason back to his room, saying nothing more than how he was lucky he had no time to reprimand him properly.

Jason paced around his small room, trying to formulate

an escape plan for those poor prisoners who were mutating into dragons.

The shock at Laena's revelation turned his stomach over and over. According to Laena, Helnah had strapped her to a table and injected poison into her chest. When he asked how such a poison was possible, Laena had merely shrugged, her gaze distant. She'd been the first victim of the batch, and the vial had been given to Helnah by a black figure in the corner. Laena had squeezed her eyes shut at the time, so she saw little else.

Jason stopped pacing. Screaming in frustration and anger, he threw his chair at the wall, followed by the candle holder. Fuming, he glared at his door before slamming himself into it. The wooden bolt snapped and popped off, but he dislocated his arm. Gasping and clutching his left shoulder, he pushed the door open and poked his head out.

There were no guards in sight. Jason hoped they were assuming he'd be asleep all night. Slipping out of his room, he crept down the hall. He would be no use to anyone as long as he was stuck in the fortress. It was time to escape. Melanie was coming for him, and if he could find her, together they could get help from another city to save the young prisoners.

Melanie successfully followed Elken's directions and

found Helnah's room. She carefully opened the green door, then slipped inside and closed the door behind her.

Helnah's spacious quarters were furnished with a large four-poster bed at one end of the wall next to a huge window. A desk covered with ornately carved runes sat in a corner, and banners hung like tapestries along the walls.

An ornate purple vial stood on the desk, practically begging Melanie to take it. She picked it up and studied it. Although she could not read the strange runes written on the label, her head felt clearer when she smelled it. It must be the healing potion Elken had mentioned.

Her heartlink began to pulse. It was weak, somewhat veiled, but it called for her to follow it.

Melanie straightened. *Of course!* The heartlink had led her to Scalaed many times in the past. And if she could find Scalaed, she would find Jason.

I'm coming, guys.

She slipped the vial into her pocket and ran to the door. Her hand froze on the brass knob when she heard the sound of hurried footsteps. Melanie's heart raced faster as she desperately tried to find a hiding place. Dreading the thought, Melanie dove under Helnah's bed just as the door opened.

Helnah hurried in, and she did not look happy.

CHAPTER 20

Thrown to the Flames

Seizing his chance at an escape, Jason continued sneaking down the hall. Once free of the fortress, he would hunt down reinforcements of some kind to save the prisoners. *Perhaps the nearest town can help. Why wouldn't they?*

He passed the dimly lit stairwell that led to the dungeon just as an awful scream pierced the air.

"Laena!" Jason gasped. He turned on his heels and descended into the dungeon, which had been thrown into chaos.

Nearly a hundred hunters were opening the cell doors and gathering the prisoners. Jason had no idea there were so many. He calculated around eighty. Thendrell yanked a prisoner—the little eight-year-old boy—from his cell. The poor child, or what was left of him, was clawing at the air and shrieking through pouring tears. He writhed in pain, gasping for air. White horns emerged from his scalp, and red scales covered every exposed inch of skin, including a deadly, spiked tail. His arms elongated into dark red wings that slowly stretched through his clothes.

Jason had never seen anything so horrific in his life.

The boy screamed and thrashed as two guards dragged him to the opposite staircase at their end of the hall. One pulled a torch whose hidden mechanism folded the stairs into the wall, revealing a secret passage that shone with an ominous red glow.

The hunters continued dragging children out of their cells and shoving them into the passage. Jason saw Laena screaming hysterically in the clutches of her captors. He found his legs and ran down into the crowd. A girl with braids blasted fire, then wrapped her hands around her pain-seared throat as her face turned from green to blue. The hunter pried her hands away, and she collapsed unconscious. A Thornbrillian with a gold circlet threw the poor girl like a trash bag into the tunnel.

A man with a tooth chain slammed into Jason and looked at him quizzically. "What are you doing down here, boy?"

"If you want to get another kid, you're gonna have to go through me!" Jason said, electrified with righteous anger.

"And I thought you were on our side," the hunter sneered. "You can join them!" He grabbed Jason's dislocated arm, sending a wave of fresh pain through his muscles. Jason was shoved past another man whom he recognized as the hunter who had let them escape back at camp.

Elken looked at Jason with recognition, then horror. He tried to make his way towards Jason, but it was too late. His captor shoved Jason into the blackness of the tunnel, which concealed a deeply sloped floor.

Jason stumbled and rolled down, down, down until he lay sprawled on his stomach. He groaned in pain, squeezing his injured shoulder. When he looked up, the stairs were folding back into place twenty feet away. The closing door snuffed out the light of the dungeon with a loud thud, telling Jason clearly there was no way back.

Melanie stopped breathing.

"What now?" Helnah asked, her voice weak. "Leave and let me be!"

Melanie didn't dare to move. *Is she talking to me?* Melanie knew there wasn't anyone else in the room. Melanie's breath came in soft clouds, and she wrapped her arms around herself as the bedroom dropped in temperature. She clenched her jaw to stop her teeth from chattering, and goosebumps crawled on her skin. Melanie held her breath as Helnah threw herself on the bed and screamed, a terrible noise that somehow felt colder to Melanie than the frosty air. *She must not have seen me,* Melanie thought with great relief.

Helnah dragged herself off the bed, crying in anguish, and clawed her way to her desk with one hand pressed against her forehead. Melanie watched her throw and swipe things from her desk and drawers.

"Where is it?" Helnah shrieked. She dropped to her knees. "It's gone!"

Who is she talking to? Melanie watched uncomfortably.

"Go away!" Helnah sobbed bitterly and banged her fists on the floor. A second later, the room was warm again.

Helnah looked up, tears streaming down her anguished face and hands pressing against her head. "Just let me die," she begged, sinking further down on her knees. Her shoulders shook, then stilled, and Helnah slumped into a quiet motionless heap. At that moment, the door flew open and a Thornbrillian with dark hair and bright blue eyes rushed in.

"Helnah!" Thendrell gasped, "where's the potion?"

Helnah gave no response.

Thendrell scooped her up and laid her on her bed. He jumped back to the drawer, searching for a potion Melanie knew he would not find.

"Elthar!" he called, and dashed out of the room. "Elthar, quick, Helnah is draining!"

Melanie lay still, her hand on her pocket. After she was sure Thendrell had cleared the hallway, she crept out from her hiding place and peeked over the edge of the bed. Helnah lay still as a corpse, her black hair tossed over face.

Melanie stood and ran, not looking back.

"Do you have any idea what you've done, you fool?" Elken yelled at Keth, who stood as stiff as an iron rod, his face distraught. "You've condemned Helnah's apprentice to the flames of the Maze! How a clot-head like you remains in rank is astounding. Just have Helnah behead you now and rid us of your incompetence."

Keth took a sudden interest in his boots. "He was a traitor. I punished him as I thought appropriate."

Elken rubbed his forehead and stared at Keth, exasperated. "It's not your job to think!" Elken turned his back and pinched the bridge of his nose. "No one will ever find him now. He'll be either incinerated or eaten." Elken could feel his face heating up in his anger.

Keth stood there, subtly scuffing his boots in shame. "We could go after him," he offered.

"Oh, yes." Elken stared at him incredulously. "You've somehow stayed alive this long; you're bound to be successful."

"We'd have to rescue you as well, you dolt," Helketh said from behind them. He uncrossed his arms and pushed off from the wall. "I'd go in myself, but Helnah has us on nice little salaries, so I prefer to live for the next raid." Helketh looked at Elken and wryly smirked. "You're the noble boy, Elken— always smuggling your extra food to those slaves. *You* go fetch the wretch. Spare us all from Helnah's wrath."

Crawling to the top of a ridge, Jason gaped at the size of the place.

Carved out of the black volcanic rock spanned a cavern that would dwarf a football stadium. Stone arches and bridges soared from edge to edge, from gateway to gateway, and stone dragon heads poured lava from their mouths. Levels of doorways surrounded by golden runes led to darkness. Ledges hung from daring heights. Huge, twisted pillars rose past the cloud of red smog to the hidden ceiling. Lava flowed in rivers and falls to form lakes.

Below, the dragon youth screamed and shrieked as they ran blindly into various tunnels. The boy with the red scales threw himself into a nearby lava lake. Jason's heart dropped to his stomach.

A large lava bubble bloomed, and a red dragon with white horns loomed from the depths. He would have looked terrifying if it weren't for his innocent eyes brimming with steaming tears. The dragon stepped out of the lava and collapsed from exhaustion, no doubt dreaming of his stolen life.

Not knowing what else to do, Jason wandered through the tunnels of the Maze, avoiding the scorching heat of the open caverns when he could. The constant stream of flowing lava, a sound like crinkling glass, drilled into Jason's head, and he was sure the noxious smell would take a few years off his life.

Around the next corner, he found himself face to face with a dragon. He yelled and tumbled backward. The dragon studied him woefully, and Jason recognized its glowing turquoise eyes. They had once been so bright and beautiful—lights in the depths of a prison.

The dragon was Laena.

CHAPTER 21

Through the Walls

Melanie sat curled in the dark stairwell behind the door that led to all the bedrooms. *Where is Elken?* She had been rolling the vial around in her hands as anxiety seeped into her bones. He had said he would be right behind her.

Has he abandoned me? Melanie felt herself shrinking. *I…I wanted to trust him!*

The negative thoughts followed. *But look at what happened when you did. You trusted him to return, and he broke his promise.*

Melanie shook her head, defying the voice of distrust for the first time. *No. Maybe something happened to him? What if he was caught?*

Hearing voices and laughter, she pressed an ear against the door. Was it Elken?

"Oh, I'm glad that's over!" one hunter said. The voice was too gruff to be Elken's.

"Agreed!" the other replied. His accent was too heavy. "Look at what that boy's talons did to my wrist."

"They're the Maze's problem now," said the first hunter.

Melanie held her breath as the hunters walked past. What did that guard mean by "the boy's talons"? She slunk even further into the shadows, turning to her heartlink for comfort.

"Scalaed? Can you hear me?" she whispered in a voice so soft the dust in the air didn't move. "I'm here, buddy. I *will* come for you and Jason. Be strong."

The heartlink beat even more faintly now. But there was a twinge of hope in the rhythm.

Elken stormed out of the dungeons and marched up the stairs, searching for Melanie. He wanted to punch something. He should have expected going behind Helnah's back would be difficult, but that buffoon Keth had made things more difficult. He had no plan now. The only thing he could do was find Melanie. The poor woman was lost and alone in a foreign world, with Elken himself as her only ally. She was his mission, his noble purpose. Protecting her from Helnah's possession would be the first thing he accomplished against the tyrant. He prayed she just hadn't been captured during their separation.

He ascended the stairs, quickening his pace, and sighed in relief upon seeing the curled form at the door.

"Melanie!"

Melanie popped her head up, her heart jumping at the sight of him. Was she merely startled, or was she actually happy to see him? "You came back."

Elken knelt and searched her face. "Are you alright?"

In the dark security of the stairwell, Melanie studied his face. She dwelled on his eyes, whose color hid in the shadows. A small smile played on her lips as she lifted the vial. "I got it." She pressed the vial into Elken's hands. "You give this to Briefur, and I'll go after my brother. I've got this sixth s— Elken, what's wrong?"

Elken wore a pained frown. "We have a problem."

When he finished telling her how Jason had been thrown to the Arfire Maze, Melanie sank against the wall, barely able to think.

"Tell me he'll be okay," she demanded, voice shaking.

Elken winced. "I wish I knew."

"Then we have to get Scalaed. He can take us to Jason." Melanie launched to her feet and started down the stairs.

"Melanie, wait!"

"Trust me." Melanie held his gaze, shocked by her own sternness. Then she descended the stairs, two or three at a time, until she reached the bottom and entered the dungeons.

She stopped to notice all the cells were open. Empty. The heartlink compelled her toward the stairwell at the other end. It beat harder as her hand floated toward the torch mechanism. Then a hand locked around her arm.

"Oh, you don't want to open that door, girl," a guard said. Desperation had blinded Melanie, and in the darkness of the dungeon she hadn't seen him hidden behind the wall. The hunter dropped a bottle of ale, then grabbed her other arm. She spun, trying to free herself from his strong grip, but he only squeezed more tightly.

"Let me go!" she yelled. "I have to get him back!"

"We're not making that same mistake twice," the guard hissed, his warm breath reeking of alcohol. "We already lost one of Helnah's apprentices." He swung Melanie around and dragged her away. "Your brother has been cast to his fiery death. Probably been eaten by now, limbs bitten off one by one…just imagine the pain."

Defeated, Melanie stopped writhing and sobbed. The heartlink faded, like a crying voice growing more distant.

"Helnah will know what to do with you," the guard continued.

Despair coiled around Melanie's heart, squeezing her lungs. Like a heavy blanket, it weighed on her, pressing her into the ground. The passing stones in the floor seemed to draw closer. *If only they would swallow me up.*

Her arms slipped through the guard's grip. Then, impossibly Melanie's legs sank through the floor. Suddenly weightless, she passed through the stone.

"Where did you go?" the guard yelled as he spun around, eyes glued to the floor.

Melanie somersaulted through walls and floors, tumbling faster and faster until the fortress spat her into white moonlight. She landed on her back.

Melanie didn't dare move. *What…just happened?* Cautiously, she fluttered her fingers to feel grass beneath, and as her eyes adjusted, the silver moon came into focus.

"I'm outside," Melanie said. "I'm *outside?*" Launching upright, she looked around, utterly stunned. "I escaped?"

A distant commotion drew her attention to the forest a hundred feet away. Howls and yells rolled from the green depths. She knew wolves when she heard them.

Confound it all, Melanie! Elken thought as he left the stairwell. Invisible as a Thornbrillian was in his own fortress, he exited the stronghold with no interference. Free, he dashed down the hillside, the vial's purple contents sloshing against the sealed cork. He had to reach Briefur, give him the potion, and return to Melanie before she got herself killed.

If he was being honest with himself, he found her courage and determination attractive. But neither those qualities nor her soft, amber eyes had anything to do with Briefur. It had been almost an hour since he'd left the two Hündr, and he hoped they were alright.

When Elken reached the bottom of the hillside, the other tarothyl was gone. So were Briefur and Fallon. His bow immediately in his hand, Elken cautiously approached the scene. He stepped slowly through the brush as he scanned his whereabouts. Before he could check the ground for tracks, he was tackled to the ground by a mob of angry trarewolves that pounced on him from the trees.

Elken cried out as he was bound from his shoulders down to his ankles. "Where is Briefur?"

Another trarewolf, no doubt the leader, stepped forward, and he was a whole head taller than Elken. He wore a fur cape clasped to one side of his shoulder by a silver clip with a crest Elken did not recognize. His feet bore tall leather boots, and a thick leather belt secured his gray pelt garment, from which hung two scabbards for his curved swords. He stood perfectly still, with the exception of his wolf ears twitching, then unsheathed one of his swords and pointed it at Elken's neck.

At that moment, a trarewolf girl with silvery blue eyes and dark hair swept up in a twist pushed her way through and said in a furious whisper, "Let me kill him, Father! I will avenge my brother!" Her long black lashes shook, betraying her anger.

The leader glanced at his daughter for a moment. "Silence, Bareth." Then he said to a defenseless Elken, "You will beg for death when I'm through with you."

He nodded to another trarewolf, who promptly smothered Elken's face with a drug-laced cloth. His limbs began to feel like they were melting.

"This renders you immobile but vividly conscious," the leader snarled. "You will feel *everything*."

"No! Stop!" cried a voice that silenced the entire glade. All eyes turned to face the speaker. Melanie, breathless with her hands on her knees, emerged from the treeline. "He's not a Thornbrillian."

"And who are you who sees so poorly?" The leader narrowed his eyes at her intrusion. He pointed accusingly at Elken. "He wears their colors! How can you deny his allegiance?"

"Just hear me out, please!" begged Melanie. "Elken saved Briefur, who saved me at the Anguill Swamps. That's how Briefur was wounded. Elken has a vial of healing potion that can save him. If Elken hadn't shown up, Briefur would be dead."

The trarewolves murmured among themselves. At a signal from the leader, the cloth was taken off Elken's face, and he leaned over, gasping for clean air. The ground rocked beneath his limbs buzzing back to life, and his stomach felt heavy.

"I rarely believe strangers," the leader said.

"My Lord Brefiüll!" Fallon panted as she finally reached the crowd. "I was there. She speaks the truth."

Brefiüll paused and, after some consternation, said, "Then I offer you my sincerest apologies."

Melanie snatched the vial from Elken's floppy fingers and handed it to Brefiüll. "Give it to him, now."

The chief trarewolf nodded. He entrusted the deed to Bareth, who was disappointed at Elken's survival, but obeyed her father. She made her way to the back of the company where Briefur lay on a makeshift woven stretcher. Gently sitting him up, Bareth poured painstakingly small sips into his mouth until the vial was empty.

"Good as new," Briefur croaked with a weak smile.

Bareth rolled her eyes, but she was relieved. "Not so fast. You will stay on this stretcher for the journey home."

"Ordered around by my younger sister. What nightmare is this?"

Bareth flicked his ear then left him in the care of their other companions.

Meanwhile, Melanie had grabbed Elken's hand and pulled him up. "You okay?"

Elken groaned, "I feel like I've eaten stones."

"Ah. Sounds fun."

When Fallon approached the two, Elken added, "You might have come a bit sooner?"

"I was tending to Briefur," the froxil said. "His condition worsened, and it really frightened me, but your success will surely save him! You are to return with us to our country so we may thank you."

We're leaving the country? "No, we can't!" Melanie said. "Elken, I was caught." Her voice cracked. "I was so close to Scalaed, I could feel him, but I was dragged away before I could free him."

"How did you escape?" Elken marveled.

"I...I don't know." Melanie hesitated. "You won't believe me." She stared at her crumbling sandals and watched numbly as a tear dropped to the grass.

Elken's calm voice directed her misty gaze to him. "Melanie, you can tell me."

The breath caught in her chest as she willed it to turn into words. She had to be honest. To trust him. "...I was being dragged to Helnah when the ground collapsed beneath me. I floated through the floors and walls like they were empty air until I passed through to the outside." As the event replayed in her mind, so did her failure. "Jason," she sobbed. "He's going to die now, isn't he?"

Elken gently reached out and brought Melanie into his arms, holding her tightly. She didn't resist this time. Elken didn't know what to make of her miraculous escape, but right now, this broken woman needed him. He said, "I swear to you, I will face the flames of the Maze to return him to you, Melanie."

She just shook her head and sniffled. "The guard told me that he was already dead."

Elken said, "Well, he's wrong. If Jason is anything like you, he is smart and strong-willed, and will give his all to outlast the Maze."

Bareth approached. "My brother is stable. It is very late, so we leave this forsaken land in the morning."

"What else can we do?" Melanie's voice was quiet.

Jason screamed in pain as his shoulder shunted back into place. His vision blurred for a moment, then cleared. He gingerly lifted his arm out of the crack in the wall and flexed it again.

"Well, it's good," he told Laena.

The dragon just snorted.

Jason could not understand how he knew how to fix his arm. Maybe it was natural instinct or luck.

Laena looked at the cavern's ceiling in a daze.

"Hey, are you okay?" Jason asked softly.

Laena looked at him sideways, her eyes squinting.

"Right, dumb question." Jason scratched his neck awkwardly. "Are you in any pain?"

Laena's expression softened, and she shook her head gently.

Jason bit his lip in the awkward silence. "There's a lot of space in here if you want to, uh, try out your new wings…"

Laena stared at Jason as if he'd just grown out of the ground.

"I'm not helping. I'll just shut up."

Laena slowly lifted her wings and looked at them for a long time, hardly believing they were hers. Looking up, Laena started to flap her wings. In just a matter of seconds, her movements changed from timid shaking to powerful beating. Her hind legs lifted off the ground, and she looked at Jason.

He gave a happy, encouraging thumbs up. Seeing the confusion in Laena's eyes, Jason remembered that he was on an alien planet where, apparently, a thumbs up didn't exist.

So he shouted, "You're doing great! Add some more power. You're stronger than you think!"

Laena's wings beat with powerful strength, and she ascended faster. She dove forward and soared around the cavern.

Jason watched as Laena's stability and speed improved with every passing second. The way she moved suggested her dragon instinct was taking over. Hopefully, when she landed,

Laena's humanity would not have completely disappeared.

CHAPTER 22

The Arfire Maze

Pain.

It sank its teeth into Scalaed's consciousness, injecting anguish in waves. Within its grasp, he felt everything—his identity, his purpose, his heartlink with Melanie—slipping away. In its place was only agony.

The foe-dragon's voice returned with a snarl. "Do you even know what you are?"

Scalaed twitched, panting wearily against the mental onslaught. When at last the scorching, invasive tether receded, he glared at his captor. He refused to entertain a conversation. "Are you even aware of where you came from?"

Scalaed blinked. Of course he was curious, but he did not like that this monster held the answers.

"Surely you felt out of place in your old world," the foe-dragon crooned, lowering its steaming maw closer. "Because you were stolen from this one."

Scalaed huffed.

"I imagine it must have been very hard. Were there no other dragons to keep company?"

Scalaed lowered his head a little.

His captor chuckled, sending a cold shiver through

Scalaed. "I thought so." With a great sigh, the dragon straightened. "We could have made a powerful team."

Scalaed snorted. He would never team up with such a beast.

"No one would have feared you, you know." The dragon looked down at him sideways. "We would have been the defenders of this realm. You never would have had to suppress your true ability. With my guidance, you never would have had to hide. Any sky would have been yours to soar as you pleased." It tilted its head to face Scalaed, lips curled faintly in disgust. "Not...cowering alone in fear...in a cave...in the desert like some common snake."

Scalaed jerked his head up, suddenly aware of the tickling in his mind that poked into his memories. He shoved away the intrusion, severing his mind from everything, which muted the heartlink altogether.

"That all can change, of course," the dragon said, "if you allow me to help you unlock your true power. Don't you want to know what you're capable of?"

Scalaed tensed his jaw. He hated that he wanted to know more than anything. He wanted the answer to his lifelong question: who was he?

"Ponder it, little dragon," the foe-dragon said. "I'll return tomorrow."

With a thunderous shuffle, Scalaed's captor settled back over his cage and stilled, frozen like a statue. The chill in the cavern dissipated, and Scalaed sat in the darkness, turning his thoughts over and over.

Jason smirked when Laena landed with a huff. "Looks like you've got the hang of it," he said.

Laena's gaze was blank. Leaning uncomfortably close, she sniffed Jason.

"Laena?" he asked hopefully.

The dragon gave one last look, huffed again, and swooped out of view. Jason's heart sank. Laena was gone, lost to her own body. It was only then he realized how lonely the Maze felt. He was on his own.

Melanie! Jason's legs buckled as the thought crashed down on him. *She better be okay.* He raised his eyes from his knees. *Will she find me?* Struck with a new resolve, Jason returned to his feet. *Yes, she will, because I'm busting out of here. I already made it out of the fortress. I can get out of here, too.*

Jason took a deep breath and began walking. Hours slipped by as he crossed the vast halls and caverns of the Arfire Maze. He saw rivers of lava and fountains of fire, columns of black stone and bridges of obsidian. Jason stared in awe at the magnificence of it all. The place was beautiful in a dangerous way, and he feared every turn would lead him to a hungry dragon.

At one point, he walked through an archway only to reel back as a yellow dragon crept by, its eyes unblinking and wild. Jason had no idea what the dragons would eat here, but he had no intention of adding himself to the menu.

The dragons were not the only ones growing hungry. Jason had no idea when he'd last eaten, or even what time it was, but his stomach started to punish him with threats to eat itself if he didn't find food soon.

The heat made it worse. He sweated through his clothes, becoming dangerously dehydrated. His tongue stuck to the roof of his mouth, and his perspiration evaporated, encrusting his skin in salt. He needed to find a way out *now*.

Crossing yet another bridge, Jason found another hallway. When he stepped into it, rainbow lights streamed like veins along the walls to the end of the hallway. He touched one. A little thread of green light traced his hand and continued its course down the wall. More lights streaked the walls until the whole hall was lit up.

At the end of the hallway, he found yet another soaring cavern of corridors and passageways. "Are you kidding me?" Jason cried in frustration. "Get me out of here!" Screaming, he kicked a rock. "I miss you, Melanie. You've always been the problem-solver."

How would you *get out?*

Jason leaned against the warm stone, panting heavily in the rippling air. He melted backwards into a crevice, his eyes growing heavy. What time was it? Maybe all he needed was a nap. Yes, sleep would refresh him. Fresh sweat trickled down his forehead, stinging his eyes, and he closed them. Immediately the arms of sleep cradled him, heavy, black, peaceful…permanent.

"Wake up!"

The voice jolted Jason awake like an electric shock. He jumped to his feet and wobbled. "Melanie?"

No one was around. Sweat dripped from his soaked clothes, and his mouth tasted ashy. *How long was I asleep?* Jason shook the fog from his heatstroke-addled brain. *Sleep is bad. Sleep is death.* Panting, he pressed on.

The lava river flowing next to him reminded him of the Colorado River, of home. Melanie. Scalaed.

Jason stopped in his tracks. He remembered the hunters taking Scalaed to the mountain. To the Maze. *There is a way out! To think I almost went to sleep instead.*

"Thanks, Melanie," Jason said. He jogged down a corridor that descended into the mountain. If there was a door at the foot of the mountain where they had taken Scalaed, then he needed to go lower. At every junction, he chose the descending path.

Fighting a migraine and parched throat, Jason pushed onward, through baking caverns and winding hallways until he entered a wide chamber. Carved dragon heads of black rock vomited lava into holes in the ground, but Jason didn't even notice them.

At the other end of the chamber stood two huge slabs of iron. *Doors?* Hoping against hope that he had finally found the way out, Jason pressed a hand against them. They were cold. His heart skipped a beat, and he began pounding on the metal. The sound echoed and vibrated through the whole room.

"Come on!" Jason yelled. "Open up!" He scanned the

room, then muttered, "There must be some way to open this thing." He felt around the door's edge, but found nothing. When he backed up for a different perspective, he saw a chain woven around a series of gears climbing up one side of the doors. He scanned the chain, and seeing it vanish into the rock below, reasoned the mechanism to open it must be outside the mountain. That wasn't going to stop him. Jason pulled the chain with all his might, using his body weight to weigh it down, and the iron doors groaned. Slowly, slowly they opened. The glorious sunlight blinded Jason, and he cackled in disbelief as he began sprinting toward blazing freedom.

His tired legs quickly gave out. Jason tripped and tumbled down the grassy mountainside for several hundred feet before slamming into a wooden wall. His head spun, and he saw stars. Through his blurry vision, Jason saw he had crashed into a stable. He wearily picked himself up, and as the dizziness subsided, he saw a water trough. Ignoring all precaution, Jason scrambled to it and dunked his head in, gulping in what felt like gallons of life-giving coolness. When he finally came up for air, the animals were staring at him, stunned.

One side of the stalls housed tarothyls; the other, horses. The different tack beside each animal distinguished the fact that horses were for labor and tarothyls were for hunting.

"Don't judge me," Jason said breathlessly as he rose to his feet. He jabbed a finger at the nearest horse. "You'd do the same thing if you'd been trapped in a freakin' pizza oven."

One mare tossed her mane, catching Jason's eye. She stared at his approach with large, brown eyes. Her coat shimmered midnight black, and her mane and tail rippled with silvery white hair. Jason immediately fell in love. The mare reminded him of the one he used to ride at Uncle Conrad's. Thornbrillian runes were carved on the mare's stable door. While he couldn't read them, Jason thought they looked like the word "ivy".

Reaching in slowly, Jason stroked the mare's white blaze. "Right then, Ivy," he said in a soothing voice. "I think I'll take you with me." After a cautious glance in every direction, he opened the door to Ivy's stall. The horse looked at Jason, then took one step out.

"That's it," Jason encouraged her. "Let's go find my sister."

Ivy trotted fully from the stall and circled Jason once before stopping at his side. He held onto her blue bridle and mounted. Memories of Uncle Conrad's horse ranch went through his mind. Conrad had taught him to ride bareback. *It's all in the legs,* he'd said. *Yelling at the horse won't do anything. Kick softly to get her moving.*

Jason gave Ivy a soft kick. She obeyed immediately, walking forward.

Good, Conrad's voice said in his memory. *Now get her into a trot.*

Jason signaled Ivy to trot with another nudge of his foot, and she obeyed.

You call that posting? That stinks! Watch her front leg and rise with it. Up, down, up, down, up, down. Good!

A rush of adrenaline shot through Jason as he and Ivy fell in sync, and he grinned.

Get her to a canter! Gotta keep your butt on the horse's back, son! It's not comfortable for a horse when your butt is bouncing all over the place. Move with the horse, sync with her movements.

Jason obeyed. Ivy was a force of midnight muscle beneath him, rider and horse blending to one mind. He let out a loud victorious holler.

Good job! Go for a gallop. Excellent!

Fire!

The memory shattered. That last voice hadn't been his uncle's. Whipping his head around, Jason saw five archers atop a watchtower.

"Fire!" one yelled again. "Shoot the boy, you shoddy failures!"

Jason cursed. *How could I have missed that stupid tower?*

The forest was not far away. If he could just make it, he would be out of range. Heart pounding, Jason spurred Ivy to gallop faster. They crossed the treeline as arrows struck the trees around them. Suddenly, Ivy snorted and bucked Jason off her back. He somersaulted onto the forest floor.

When the world stopped swirling, Jason groggily checked himself for injuries. He stopped when he saw Ivy, who lay on her side, kicking and snapping at a huge arrow that had pierced her foreleg.

Jason ran to help her. He pulled out the shaft, causing Ivy to bray loudly. Jason held the tip in his hands. It glistened with a pale substance. Poison. Like a fungus, a black scar spread in a diamond above her foreleg. Jason tried to calm Ivy down, but he had to step away to avoid getting kicked in the head or chest by her hooves. He watched helplessly as Ivy thrashed about on the forest floor, just like the kids he'd witnessed in the dungeons. Having nothing to put her out of her misery, Jason turned his head to avoid seeing her suffering.

Without warning, Ivy quieted.

Jason looked back. Ivy had risen to a crouch like a sphinx. Glistening green scales now coated her flanks, and she stared at Jason with luminescent fuchsia eyes. She spread two massive wings, smattered in shades of green, gold, and blue, then brought them to her sides. A long, black, flame-like fin had replaced her silver mane. Two black horns protruded from her skull, and a spade-shaped spike tipped her tail. Ivy's nostrils flared, emitting trails of smoke twirling like ghostly snakes.

She bared her carnivorous teeth, and Jason prepared to run. But Ivy slowly stood, then began walking towards Jason.

Three thoughts hit Jason in quick succession. He would never find Melanie on foot. He needed a ride. And this dragon-horse was his only option. She might eat him…then again, she might not. Laena hadn't.

"Heel!" Jason commanded.

Ivy froze and stared at Jason in confusion. He held out his hand and crept closer. "I'm not gonna hurt you."

The dragon remained still.

"We can be friends," Jason said. "Guess I can call you Poison Ivy now, huh?"

Ivy cocked her head and blinked several times.

Jason stepped even closer to Ivy. "Or just Pi?"

Ivy seemed to recognize the name and took a step forward.

"Yeah, that's right," Jason said. "That's your name. Don't

you remember me?"

Something shifted in Ivy's eyes. The hungry fire evaporated, and she lowered her head and nuzzled it against his chest.

Relieved, Jason stroked Ivy's nose. "There, there," he whispered. "You're alright now. I got you." He petted her forehead. "You're going to be okay. Come on, let's go find my sister."

Then he thought, *And how exactly are we going to do that?*

Another voice broke into Jason's thoughts—unfortunately, one that he recognized. *Oh, praise the Celestial Emperor, you are saved!*

Azeur descended from a tree overhead. *All thanks to me, somehow, I'm sure!*

"Where is my sister?" Jason asked, keeping a taut hold on Ivy's bridle. The dragon-horse growled hungrily at the bird.

Ah! To know such valuable information, I require... remuneration.

"I'm not paying a bird."

An Avis Messenger! Azeur corrected. *Our talents must be compensated.*

"What talent? I only asked a question."

The bird froze, caught in his greedy scheme.

Jason snarled. "Tell me where Melanie is, or I'll have Poison Ivy here gobble you whole. I'm sure she's starving."

Ivy growled and licked her lips with a forked tongue.

No! Mercy! Azeur begged, bowing prostrate. *The world would not be able to function without me! Please! I will tell you. She has left for Hvitria. Journey southwest to the Diamond Mountains. The snowy ones. You shall find her in the White Village at the center of the storm.*

"Thank you. Was that so hard?"

My dignity…ravaged!

"Scram before I change my mind." Jason stomped a foot toward the blue jay, who shrieked a sob and fled. Wasting no time, Jason mounted Poison Ivy and spurred her onward. But instead of galloping like the horse she'd been, the dragon rocketed into the sky. Jason squeezed the bridle, surprised at how naturally Poison Ivy had taken to her change. Perhaps for an animal, the transition was more seamless.

The forest dropped away as they ascended higher, and Jason was thankful he had experience in both horse and dragon riding. He would reach Melanie in no time.

CHAPTER 23

The White Chief

After three days, Melanie's destination finally felt close. She regarded with dread the heavy gray clouds shrouding the peaks as she pressed on behind the trarewolf party. Worry oppressed her mind. The journey to the Hündr home had given her time to reflect on everything that had happened, and she agonized over what she left behind in Arizona. She wished she could call her parents to let them know she was okay. Five days had passed since Melanie's arrival in Tindoria; she couldn't imagine the torment they must have been feeling. She wished she could tell them she loved them.

Elken kept their conversations brief and light, mainly about the scenery and the weather. Understanding fully well the loss of a loved one, he respected Melanie's space. She had opened up to him once; perhaps she was finally beginning to trust him. He watched her as she walked, adrift in her emotions. Her brown hair, lovely and curly, whipped in the wind. She didn't acknowledge his presence or even blink. Her eyes bored into the ground, seeing nothing but flashes of a former lifetime. Elken hoped she would speak to him again. He wanted to help.

The wind grew colder as they ascended into the Diamond

Mountains. Cloaked in a forest of purplish, arrow-like trees, they were the tallest mountain range in the realm, and their peaks were battered with a never-ending snowstorm. The trarewolves and Fallon took on their animal forms. Even Briefur was able to change form, lying on his stretcher-turned-sled. The wolves' thick fur, ranging from silvers and grays to deep charcoal, rustled in the crisp wind. Fallon's carrot-orange coat stood out like a burning ember in a bed of dead coals.

Melanie feared frostbite above everything else. She didn't have a fluffy fur coat like the Hündr. Her toes tingled in her sandals, and her bare arms and legs shivered with goosebumps. As the first of the snowflakes brushed past her face, she squeezed her arms to keep warm. Each inhale burned her nose.

When he noticed her state, Elken unclasped his cloak and gently wrapped it around her. Melanie accepted his gesture but said nothing. Only a puff of cold escaped her mouth.

"You shouldn't walk in this terrain in that footwear," Elken advised. "May I carry you?"

Melanie finally met his eyes. *What color* are *they?* She didn't have a name for the hue, but one word came to her: kind.

She nodded, and Elken scooped her up effortlessly. He felt her relax. "I know this might not mean much," he said, "but I know your pain."

"I'm losing my mind, Elken," Melanie said. Using his name for the first time didn't feel as scary as she'd thought it would.

Elken loved the way it sounded in her voice. "But unlike me, Melanie, you have hope. Jason is alive, that I firmly believe.

I will return with you to free him, but you are spent both physically and emotionally. Tend to yourself when we reach the Hündr's village. Eat and rest. Will you help me by doing that?"

Melanie nodded.

"Thank you."

"No," Melanie said softly, "thank you."

"Oh, you don't weigh much," Elken smiled.

"Not that." Melanie resisted a smirk of her own. "Thank you for staying with me. I never had anyone besides Jason to help me before, so…it means a lot."

"You are most welcome."

Elken thought he saw life bloom in Melanie's face. Life given from hope. And she smiled.

The trees dropped away in the high altitude, exposing the travelers to the full might of the storm as it met them. The ground disappeared completely in the snow. Thick, white flakes blasted their faces as they trudged through the blizzard.

"What's the name of your country again?" Melanie called over the deafening wind.

"Hvitria," Brefiüll answered. "We will provide aid and provisions. Also, the White Chief has summoned you."

The trarewolves and Fallon bounded over a ridge and disappeared. Fallon's head popped out from behind it. "Almost there!" she called.

The snow reached its thickest, and neither Melanie nor Elken could even see each other's faces.

"Only the sense of a Hündr can find this place!" Fallon

cried above the storm. "All others fall victim to the storm." She came back to grip Elken's hand and guide him as they pushed deeper into the blizzard.

When Melanie felt as if the storm would sweep them away, they broke through what seemed like an invisible barrier. Melanie looked behind them to see the raging winds and swirling snow blocked by a transparent wall. Ahead the Hündr descended a road carved into the side of the mountain. The wolves in front ran through a tunnel at the end.

Beyond the tunnel, Melanie was shocked to find daylight and warmth. Elken put her down, and Melanie held his shoulders for support as he did so. He had been very strong to carry her through such terrain. Chasing away those thoughts, she followed the company into a secluded mountain valley.

The Hündr village was nestled at the bottom. The approaching trarewolves returned to their human forms, a few waving to their neighbors as they entered the village. The inhabitants, like Briefur and Fallon, were half human and half canid—mixes of wolves, foxes, coyotes, and jackals. A little girl with large coyote ears stared at Melanie from her porch. Melanie smiled and waved. The girl's tail flicked as she sped off into the arms of her mother inside.

The buildings were huts of tall reeds and thatched roofs. Most of the dwellings sat high in the trees, encircling the village center on the ground—mostly shops, gathering places, and gardens. Rope bridges swung between some of the tree houses, connecting their circular porches together. A hefty fence of sharp-tipped stakes around the perimeter of the village served as a barrier to any trespassers who would brave the eternal storm. At the far end of the village stood a beautiful gate woven from vines, roots, and leaves.

Elken had never seen the land of the Hündr. He saw the houses and their beams carved with gracefully curving vines and leaves. The gardens burst in ripe colors. The villagers talked and laughed with their neighbors. Smells of chimney smoke, food, and crafted leather blew on the breeze. *And to think Helnah calls them "savages,"* Elken thought with disdain. As he walked with the others deeper into the village, the Hündr stared at Elken. Some snarled. Others glared with murderous intent. Despite this, Elken held his chin high. He knew who and what he was, and no one could convince him otherwise.

Bareth approached Melanie and Elken. "Remain here. My father is gathering the chiefs of the tribes to a meeting."

"Where's Briefur?" Melanie asked.

"He is resting," she replied, "and improving greatly."

"Then maybe you can tell the villagers to stand down? They might kill Elken with their looks alone."

Bareth cast a glance at the scornful glares of passersby.

"He saved your brother," Melanie reminded.

"He still dresses like the enemy." Bareth returned her icy eyes to Melanie and Elken. "They know what Thornbrill has done to other kingdoms. Our children have been spared thanks to the storm, but the children elsewhere have not."

Melanie felt a weight sink in her stomach. "What does she mean, Elken?"

Elken opened his mouth to speak, but blaring horns

echoed throughout the village, cutting off his response.

"The White Chief is returning from his hunting party," Bareth said. "He is expecting you."

"How does he know we're here?" Melanie asked as they followed.

"Father relayed a message through an Avis Messenger. Insolent creatures, but highly valued."

"Don't let them hear you say that," Fallon scoffed as she joined them. "They may just increase their compensation. Pray you never meet one."

Fallon led them through a crowd of tails and furs towards the gates. They opened, and a pack of silver wolves and white foxes entered the village in orderly fashion. They walked regally past the crowd toward the longhouse in the village center. Then Melanie saw the chief.

A snow-white wolf the size of a lion walked behind his hunting party toward the longhouse. Around his neck rested a necklace of woven silver strands. Before entering the longhouse, he met Melanie's eyes. She felt like an intruder under his penetrating stare. Another white wolf, slightly smaller and more slender, followed the chief into the longhouse.

Brefiüll and three other tribal chiefs motioned for Melanie and Elken to follow into the longhouse. Inside, a blazing fire in the center burned in a variety of colors. At the far end rested two thrones of twisted branches and autumn leaves woven together into a work of art. Sitting in each were the White Chief and his wife, who had assumed their human forms.

The chief was younger than Melanie expected. He was a regal man in his prime, and his clean-shaven face was tanned and creased from many long years of rule and experience. He held a staff of gnarled oak and silver. His white hair matched his lupine ears, and half of it was pulled back to frame his face. Around his head and above his tattoo was a woven silver circlet. He wore a robe of white and silver fur, black moccasin boots, and a long cloak of white, from behind which his tail flicked. His steel eyes penetrated Melanie, exposing what a deadly foe he could become if challenged.

Like the chief, his wife's hair was white. It twisted upward, then dropped in shimmery locks to touch her bare shoulders. Her dress was wrapped around her slender frame and was ruched to her side with a large silver pendant. Her warm, brown eyes sparkled as she glanced at Melanie, the ghost of a smirk playing on her pink lips.

Melanie looked over at Elken. Despite being surrounded by many who would desire his execution, he walked on without hesitation, his expression calm. When Brefiüll nodded to the wooden bleachers where other members of the village were seated, Melanie and Elken joined them.

The White Chief, his eyes never blinking, rose from his throne and thumped his staff against the stone-tiled floor. He walked into an open square of light from a hole in the roof. "Before we discuss any matter of aid, we must address the presence of this man. Please stand, Elken, son of Elkarim."

Elken stood without delay.

The White Chief continued, "One of my premiers, Lord

Brefiüll, informs me you had enlisted Briefur's help before he was left wounded in the Anguill Swamps while aiding this foreigner." His stare landed on Melanie, who shrunk back. "Despite your appearance being that of our enemy, you acquired a cure for his son, and it has saved his life. What clarity can you add to this account?"

Silence reigned for three seconds. They seemed like an eternity to Melanie.

"I am not a Thornbrillian," Elken began. "When I learned of Briefur's presence, I sent him a message to help me free Melanie and her brother from Helnah's possession. I believe they have been sent to Tindoria for the purpose foretold in the Spire's Scroll."

Whispers flitted through the crowd, and Melanie caught expressions of astonishment.

Elken continued, "Briefur was to aid their escape until I could steal away to protect them from that point on. He is my ally and has kept his word, which cost him an encounter with an anguison. Our plans since have failed us, as Melanie's brother remains imprisoned, but I've sworn to do everything in my power to return him to her. My allegiance was never with Helnah or Thornbrill. I was born and raised in Yolderain, but when the dragon fire rained down and killed my family, I vowed to wipe out Thornbrill. Only now have I made any progress against them. Protecting Melanie is vital to Helnah's downfall."

All was silent as the chief pondered Elken's words. The air lay heavy with suspense as everyone waited for his response.

At last, he rose and approached Elken. "You have the trust of Chief Helmir. But should you betray your words, you will be struck down where you stand."

Briefur fully recovered, to the relief of the village. After a happy reunion, Fallon insisted that Melanie and Elken stay at her home for the night. She led them first to the river to refresh themselves and rinse out their clothes. Elken insisted Melanie go before him; he would bathe after she returned. Melanie thanked him for his decency.

The fresh scents of the lush valley enveloped Melanie like a much-needed hug. As she floated in the river with eyes closed, soaking up the sun, she drifted downstream at a lazy speed. The flowing water melted away some of the stress and drowned out all sound as it covered her ears. Suspended in this state of rejuvenation, Melanie didn't want to leave, but now that her legs had been given a respite, she swam back to shore. She returned to the base of Fallon's tree house, where Elken had been introduced to Fallon's younger twin brothers and her parents.

"River's all yours," Melanie told Elken, her voice lighter than it had been.

"The whole river? How generous." Elken smiled, and Melanie finally returned the expression, unable to resist his dimpled cheeks.

Later that evening, the village ate at the Great Hall. Even though Melanie had eaten rations during their journey here, she was famished. She tried to pace herself so as not to appear rude. Succulent meats and vegetables swirled in a vibrant, flavorful stew, and the overwhelming scent nearly brought tears to Melanie's eyes. She must have had three helpings by the time dinner ended.

As the Hündr began to disperse, Fallon led Melanie and Elken back to her home: a cozy house nestled in one of the huge trees. Climbing the rope ladder, Melanie finally reached a little porch. The home was divided into three open-faced rooms with no doors. It was a place to sleep and refresh oneself. The largest of the rooms had cushions on the floor for guests, while the others were simply furnished with plush feather mattresses wrapped in rabbit fur on beautifully crafted frames. Melanie and Elken lay soft fur mats on the floor of what Melanie considered the living room.

As night fell, lanterns, one by one, twinkled to life in the village. Like hundreds of orange stars, they flooded the sleepy tree-homes with warm light.

Unable to sleep, Melanie stared at the ceiling. Placing her hands behind her head, she sighed as the week's events replayed through her mind.

"Can't sleep?" Elken asked.

Melanie shook her head. "I've been in another world for five days. My family has no idea what happened to me."

"I wish I could help bear your distress," Elken said.

"Why?" Melanie turned, searching his face for answers. "Why are you doing all this?"

"You came to Tindoria on ribbons of light. Surely you are destined for greatness. Destined to be the one who ends Helnah's reign of terror."

Melanie nodded, realization creeping in. "All this time I've been telling myself Scalaed was meant for something more. I never expected this! I dedicated years of my life to protecting him, keeping him a secret from the world."

"Sounds like a lonely existence."

Melanie stared back at the ceiling. "Yes."

"Your sacrifices will not be in vain, Melanie. We will rescue Scalaed and Jason when we set out tomorrow."

"I just hope they're still alive. What if..." Melanie's voice caught. "What if Scalaed sided with Helnah?" It would have kept him alive, but at what cost? Jason clearly picked his side, which had landed him in a volcanic hellscape.

"Helnah would have launched her plan—whatever it is—if he had. Your dragon's spirit won't be quenched easily. Do you not trust your family after all this time?"

Melanie opened her mouth. "No, I do. I think. I mean... we've never been through something like this. Wouldn't this make anyone doubt?"

"Or make their faith stronger," Elken suggested.

Melanie was silent as she pondered his words.

Hoping a change in subject would ease her worry, Elken asked, "What is your world like?"

"Oh, wow." Melanie sighed. "Where to start? My world is called Earth. Um…it has a population of eight billion people, and—"

Elken opened his mouth, dumbfounded. "Your world must be enormous!"

"I guess. Seven continents and four oceans. How big is Tindoria?"

"Our cartographers say one can walk the length of the continent in five to seven days."

"Length?" Melanie propped herself on her shoulder, eyebrows furrowed.

"Yes," Elken said, mirroring Melanie's position. "Imagine the world is like…a pie."

"A pie?" Melanie smiled uncertainly.

"Bear with me," Elken chuckled. "Imagine that pie has six slices." After a quick glance around the room, Elken snatched a clay plate from a nearby table and crawled back, holding up his reference. "Each slice is a country. Tharretill"—he pointed to the upper right area of the plate and worked clockwise—"which is where Helnah lives…Rhydrah, the country where I was born…Hvitria, where we are now…Lethios…Endrial, which has the capital city of the realm, Endlewood…and Allendia, the country of immortals."

Melanie gasped. "Wait, so you can actually reach the edge

of the world?"

"There's a halo of water around Tindoria, yes," Elken added with mystery. "No one dares explore it, for those who do never come back. To be bound to a ship's mast and sent sailing over the edge is the cruelest execution reserved for only the most corrupt of kings. Not only is one faced with inevitable death, but also the crippling fear of the unknown. How they really die remains a haunting mystery."

Melanie gawked. "Wow." When Elken raised an eyebrow, she laughed. "Sorry. I mean, that's a *horrible* execution, but the fact that your world is flat fascinates me."

"Is Earth not flat?"

"No, it's round. Like a sphere."

Elken leaned back, his face a mask of stupefaction, unable to process what a spherical world would be like.

Melanie stifled a laugh, trying not to wake Fallon's family in the next room over. The tiny release of joy refreshed her soul. "You know…it's so nice having someone else to talk to."

"Oh?" Elken leaned closer. "How do you mean?"

"Back home, I didn't—couldn't—make any close friends because it was too risky. And the one friend I did have…I had to end the friendship to keep Scalaed a secret. It's freeing to be on the same page with someone who already knows about dragons."

Elken smiled, which made Melanie feel warm. "I must agree, it's nice to have a friend," he said.

Melanie hadn't noticed how relaxed her hands had been the whole conversation, but she did feel the butterflies in her stomach. Unable to look away from Elken and his irresistible smirk, Melanie felt the flutters rise into her chest.

The silence was broken by a horn that echoed throughout the village, raising shouts of alarm from the villagers below. Melanie twisted around to see Fallon standing as still as a statue, staring wide-eyed out the open door.

"What is it?" Melanie asked.

"We've never had to sound that alarm," Fallon gasped, not even hearing Melanie's question. Snatching a dagger from its wall mount, the froxil leaped out the door, slid down the ladder, and raced through the crowds.

"Briefur!" she called, seeing her cousin looking around, "is this what I fear it is?"

Briefur nodded, his expression grim.

Hündr swarmed behind the gates and took on their animal forms, while the White Chief snarled at the sky. A single froxil stationed in a small lookout nest atop the wall jumped down and whispered something to Chief Helmir. The chief howled loudly, silencing his army, leaving only the sound of crackling torches.

Elken and Melanie ran up behind the ranks.

"Is something coming?" Elken asked.

Fallon turned. "Dragon. How did it find us?"

A black shape—most definitely a dragon—circled above them. The village remained silent as the creature made a final descent, then landed just beyond the wall.

The White Chief turned to face his troops. His eyes gleamed red in the torchlight.

A voice beyond the wall shouted, "Don't shoot!"

Melanie's heart stopped.

"We come in peace! Open the gates, please, or we'll jump over! You think a wall is gonna stop Pi from getting in?"

The dragon leaped over the gate and landed in front of the ranks. It was green, but Melanie thought it looked more like a pegasus with scales. Then, to her shock, her brother slid off its back with hands raised above his head.

"My name is Jason," he said. "I'm looking for my sister Melanie. I went through hell and back to get here, so I'd *really* appreciate it if you don't kill me now."

CHAPTER 24

Helmir's Ally

"Jason!" Melanie's breath escaped her as she pushed through the crowd. Through tears and laughter, she squeezed her brother tightly, never wanting to let go.

"I've missed you too, Mel." Jason hugged her back. "I'm safe now. We're okay."

Melanie grabbed his face, verifying he was her actual brother. "How did you escape?" Melanie wiped the tears from her eyes. "And what on earth are you wearing?"

"Long story, I'll explain later."

The White Chief interrupted, "Is this your beast?" He glared at Poison Ivy.

"Um," Jason began, but was speechless having never seen a Hündr. "Yes…"

"Keep it outside my village."

"Sure. Sorry." Jason motioned for Poison Ivy to return to the other side. She did so, snorting smoke as she bounded back over the wall. Satisfied, the chief signaled his troops to disband and return to their homes.

"Quite the welcome party," Jason told Melanie as he looked around at the army. "I would have gotten here a lot sooner, but with bathroom breaks, no GPS, and my horse having to learn hunting to eat, it took—"

Melanie squeezed him again in another hug. "You're here now."

Jason patted her back and added in a lower voice, "Do you know where I could get some food? I learned I'm not a great woodsman."

"Of course, you must be starving!" Fallon approached them. "Please come this way."

"Hey, mind reader over here," Jason joked as he followed Fallon.

Fallon smiled sweetly. "Hardly anything goes unheard when you have the ears of a fox."

"Yeah, I mean…no offense, but what *are* you?" Jason asked.

With great enthusiasm, Fallon launched into a lengthy explanation of her culture as she led Jason to the Great Hall.

The next morning, Jason slipped on a clean shirt and a pair of trousers Fallon's mother gave him to replace his ash-soiled prisoner clothes. He was now a new man, rested and refreshed. Not only that, he had a plan. He knew the way out of the Arfire Maze, which meant the dragons could now be freed from Helnah's control. All he needed now was reinforcements.

Jason made his way to the town square to discuss the

journey ahead. Melanie and Elken had been up before him, chatting, and Jason could have sworn Melanie's ears looked redder.

"Good morning, sleepy head." Melanie patted Jason's shoulder as he joined them. "I never got to hear about your escape. All you did was eat and fall asleep."

"Oh, that?" Jason chuckled nervously, then recounted his side of the whole adventure: waking up in Tindoria, pretending to be Helnah's apprentice, getting thrown into the Arfire Maze, finding Ivy before she was poisoned and transformed, and meeting the pompous blue jay who sent him to Hvitria.

"Did you see Scalaed?" Melanie asked hopefully.

Jason scrunched his eyebrows in confusion. "No, I didn't. The place is ginormous."

"Is there somewhere else he could be?" Melanie asked Elken.

"No. The Arfire Maze is the only place," Elken explained.

"Scalaed would be a great asset against Helnah," Melanie said. Her heartlink, despite its cold feebleness, beat in agreement. "And I know how to find him."

"Without her dragon army, she's just a loopy lady and a bunch of dudes," Jason added.

"Do not underestimate her." Elken crossed his arms. "She was formidable before her forces grew."

Briefur and Fallon volunteered to assist them on their mission. Fallon walked past Jason and gave him a huge smile, which he found amusing, while Briefur stood beside Elken.

Chief Helmir addressed the group. "Our ally Baraden

lives in the outskirts of the valley, to the southeast. Considering Elken's claims of your potential ties to the Spire's Scroll, you will find his insight invaluable. May fortune find you on your quest."

"Thank you." Melanie nodded respectfully.

Jason mounted Poison Ivy, and the group left the White Village. Melanie looked back and saw Chief Helmir, his wife, and Bareth raise their arms in a somber farewell.

Briefur and Fallon led the group down a grass-trodden path further into the valley. Green hills stretched higher up the mountainsides, fading away to bare rock caked with snow. Only the faintest wisps of storm clouds licked behind the peaks. The green valley was safe in the eye of the storm. The path led them into a forest of dense trees.

"I hope this Baraden guy can help us fix all this," Jason said after the village disappeared far behind them. *Maybe he knows a way to reverse Helnah's poison.* Suddenly impatient, he asked, "How much farther is his place?"

"We are nearly there," Briefur replied.

The forest cleared after ten more minutes of walking, revealing a humble cottage and a small stable.

Jason chuckled. "You'd think Snow White and her seven dwarves lived here."

A dog guarded the porch. Its entire coat shimmered gray, and its pointed ears lay flattened behind its head.

Melanie did not appreciate the way it glared at her. Its eyes penetrated with the message: "Kill, kill, kill!" It had been lying on the front porch of the cottage, but it stood up and approached the intruders when they drew near. The dog's black lips curled back, and it barked as if trying to wake the dead.

Briefur walked in front and held out his hand to the dog. The hound growled, its eyes glued to Briefur's hand like it was a juicy steak. It took one step closer, sniffed Briefur's hand, and instantly calmed.

As the dog trotted back to the porch, Jason dismounted Poison Ivy. He led the rest of his companions onto the porch and to the door. The dog let them pass.

Before Jason could knock, a distinguished figure opened the door. His dark blond hair was long but neat, combed back with faint sprays of gray over his ears. He wore a short beard and a blue tunic. His long mantle of sky blue matched his eyes.

"Welcome, my friends," he said warmly, his voice rich and accented. "It is good to see you, Briefur and Fallon."

The Hündr bowed in respect. "Baraden," Briefur said, "this is Melanie and her brother Jason, and Elken son of Elkarim."

"A pleasure to meet you." Baraden smiled.

"Your dog is beautiful," Melanie said, "though I was worried it would kill us."

"Oh, you have nothing to fear of Byrn; he would never attack a Hündr. We vowed to protect Hvitria after I was banished from Lakéthion."

"Banished?" Jason asked. "What happened?"

Baraden stepped aside. "Please, come in."

The five of them walked into a little kitchen, and Melanie saw trophies of war all over the wall: spears, banners, swords, arrows, and scythes. The place looked more like the Huntsman's house than Snow White's.

Baraden gestured for them to sit. The Hündr's craftsmanship was evident in his beautifully polished, wooden furniture.

"We were told you could help us," Melanie explained.

"Why were you banished?" Jason interjected, which earned him an embarrassed shove from his sister.

"Let me start by introducing myself," Baraden began. "As you know, my name is Baraden. I was a scribe in the city of Lakéthion."

"That's the main city in Lethios," Elken whispered to Melanie.

"Many years ago, I lived in a tower that overlooked the Sea of Starlight," Baraden continued, "and I rose every morning to watch the sun rise and burn it gold. My duties were to make copies of historical manuscripts, and discern the meaning of prophetic documents, namely, the Spire's Scroll.

"I grew older, and the newer, younger scribes began complaining I was spreading a mistranslation of the Spire's Scroll. I said the hero foretold would not hail from any city known. Despite the Scroll's clear support of my translation, the other scribes grew angry. I suspect they had schemes to raise a hero under their own control, and the idea of a warrior from alien lands would be discordant. They labeled me unfit for service, then banished me."

Melanie frowned in disapproval. "That's so unfair."

Baraden shrugged. "I kept no grudge. I viewed it as

the beginning of a new chapter. So I journeyed across the Diamond Mountains, where I lost my way in the snowstorm. I would have died from the elements had the White Chief and his company not stumbled upon me. He showed compassion, and I vowed to help protect his village ever since. And in my solitude, I devoted myself to divining the true meaning of the Scroll."

"Do you know whom the Scroll speaks of?" asked Briefur.

"Alas, no one knows," Baraden answered. "There are but mere whispers."

Baraden rested his hand on the hilt of his sword hanging in its scabbard. Elken could not see much of the weapon, but the hilt glistened and shimmered like no metal he had ever seen.

Baraden caught his gaze. "Your eyes do not deceive you. This is no steel sword."

He stood and unsheathed the weapon, which rang like crystal. A huge diamond made of glass protruded from the pommel, and two more decorated either end of the silvery cross guard above a navy blue leather grip.

"Long ago, a star fell from the sky into the Sapphire Mountains," Baraden said. "The king of Endlewood found the star, blazing brightly as if still hanging from the night sky. When he reached for it, the star dimmed, becoming an orb of glass. The king brought the star to Yolderain, where three swords were forged from the glass. Two went to his sons, and the other was a gift to an immortal in Allendia. Alas, the sons were slain in battle, and their Indomitable Glass swords became lost to legend. Centuries passed until they were no more than a myth. Shortly after my banishment, however, I heard a rumor in a highway tavern that hoards of ancient treasure lay in the sands of the Deplorable Waste. With no obligations elsewhere, I braved the forsaken landscape—all dust and death and the essence of evil. Using my knowledge of the land's ancient geography, I finally found the legendary sword in a desert cave amidst the spoils of history."

Jason scratched his neck. "Forgive my blatant ignorance, but wouldn't a glass sword just, you know, break?"

"It is Indomitable Glass, forged from the heart of a fallen star."

"So how strong is it?"

Baraden sliced a nearby stack of firewood, which parted as if it were butter.

Jason watched wide-eyed as the sword split the air in a glowing white arc. "Geez! That thing is like a lightsaber!"

Baraden smiled as he smoothly sheathed his weapon. "I apologize for my lengthy tales. Service as a scribe tends to make one into a bit of a storyteller. Tell me, why do you seek my assistance?"

"Jason and I are from a different world," Melanie began. "We came with my dragon Scalaed, but he's been captured by Helnah."

Baraden seemed to look beyond Melanie, thoughtfully stroking his beard. "So the Separate Realm does exist," he mumbled. Jason and Melanie exchanged looks, but the old scribe shook his head. "Continue, please."

"Scalaed is now imprisoned somewhere in the Arfire Maze," Elken said. "It's a volcanic system of tunnels and lava where Helnah keeps the children she's abducted. She poisons them, turning them into dragons."

"I can get to Scalaed," Melanie added, "but I'm sure Helnah has strict security to prevent her dragons from just walking out. Any ideas on what we might face?"

"Or if there's a cure for the children?" Jason added.

Baraden stroked his beard, casting a glance at Elken. "The Ruby Mountains were once thought to be a new resource for the medical communities, so a baron of Yolderain moved to Tharretill and founded a mining establishment that is now the Fortress of Thornbrill. However, everyone vanished one day under mysteriously dark circumstances, and the fortress lay abandoned until Helnah lay claim."

Elken knew what Baraden would say next, but he had been hoping it was a myth.

Baraden continued, "I fear the baron's greed led them to mine too deep. My theory: something dwelling in the Arfire Maze was disturbed from its slumber and annihilated them all."

"I didn't see anything." Jason suddenly felt cold as he realized how close he had been to meeting this mystery threat.

Elken took a deep breath. "It's there." He continued in a lower voice, "We have stories in Thornbrill. No one has seen it. Many a foolish Thornbrillian searched for it, and most never returned. Those who did spoke of strange markings on the wall not made by any dragon. Some say they heard a distant noise like laughter, dissonant and chilling. Whatever this beast may be, it is cunning and remains well hidden. Helnah has lost many men to their own stupidity."

"What about the kids?" Jason asked.

Elken shook his head sadly. "No cure exists."

"I'm afraid that may be true," Baraden sighed. "In all my manuscripts, I have never seen a poison of that power before. I can only say such a harrowing substance was created under dark means. Perhaps even the dark magic of old."

Baraden might as well have stomped on Jason's heart. *No cure?* A wave of gloom washed over him.

A loud roar outside interrupted them, followed by a bark.

"Oh, excuse me for just one second." Wincing, Jason ran from the house. "Pi!"

"I will provide whatever I can," Baraden said. He stood and walked to a large scenic painting that nearly spanned the whole wall. He pulled the top edge of the frame, and the painting folded open on hidden hinges. A spread of spears, swords, bows, daggers, and knives were clipped to the display.

"If you plan to confront Thornbrill," Baraden said, "you should be well-armed."

"Not funny!" Jason yelled at Poison Ivy. "That's a dog! Not lunch!"

Byrn had aggravated Ivy, snapping at her legs, and now she wanted to blast him. Jason stepped between the two animals, waving to get his dragon's attention. "Hey, hey! Look at me, girl, he's not gonna hurt you; just calm down."

Byrn made a hasty retreat into the house.

"Everything okay, Jason?" asked Melanie as everyone exited Baraden's cottage.

Jason grinned nervously. "We should get moving before Ivy decides she's hungry for dog."

Fallon snickered. When Jason faced her, she handed him two long knives. A matching set, their angular blades stretched from dark green grips with brass ornaments. "Might I recommend weapons other than your sharp wit?"

She slipped the weapons into his hands. They felt at home in his grip, and he twirled them with an unexpected flourish. "Thanks, Fallon. These are awesome."

Beaming a smile, she patted her own set sheathed at her belt.

Baraden approached them, leading a dappled gray stallion and a buckskin mare from his stable.

"Oh, he's beautiful!" Jason said.

"This is Silvedus," Baraden said, stroking the stallion's nose affectionately, "and Starlark, his mate. May they bear you on safe travels."

While Briefur and Jason saddled the horses, Baraden pulled Elken aside and presented the glass sword to him. "Its name is *Clavnir*, which means 'Passionate Defender.' It will do more good with you than it does hiding in the outskirts with me."

Stunned, Elken bowed and took the weapon with reverence. "Thank you," he managed to say.

The horses were bridled and ready, with Elken riding Silvedus and Melanie riding Starlark. Shifting to canid forms, the Hündr trotted alongside.

"This group should get an awesome name," Jason said from Poison Ivy's back. "Too bad all the good ones are taken. The Fellowship, the Avengers, the Magnificent Seven, the Impossible Missions Force."

Melanie laughed. "Oh, you'll find something."

"Yeah." Jason smiled. "Eventually."

CHAPTER 25

The Abrielstones

The sky was dark violet, and the first of the stars shone high above the trees, reflecting in Melanie's eyes as she lay awake under a tree. They rested on blankets that Baraden had given them. The horses snorted in their sleep. Despite countless nudges from Melanie, Jason continued to snore on the blanket next to her.

Melanie adjusted her position, unable to sleep through her restless mind. Nighttime left her alone with her thoughts and fears. She had tried to reach Scalaed, but his heartlink remained dull. It had been fading in the five days since her escape, and she hadn't seen him in six.

Frustrated, she tossed to her other side and winced when she realized she had accidentally bumped Elken with her elbow.

He sniffed loudly in his sleep, then dozed back off.

Melanie watched Elken sleep for a while. *Where would I be without him?* His constant sturdiness had grounded her, kept her moving when all she wanted was to sink into despair. Now his determination began to reflect in her. Destiny had intertwined their missions and given Melanie a real friend. Those warm eyes with their mysterious hue that reflected his genuine heart. That smile that left just one dimple in his left cheek.

A gentle trill sounded next to her. Facing the noise, she gasped.

A creature perched in a tree above them, glowing like moonlight. Arrayed in opalescent feathers, the creature was no bigger than a house cat. Large, feline eyes blinked brightly with pupils dilated to black pools of innocent curiosity. Pointed, feathery ears atop its head twitched, and the petite beak set in its round face opened again to purr. Wings rested by its side, motionless, unlike its four fidgety claws and puff-tipped tail.

"A griffon!" Elken whispered as he woke the others.

Briefur and Fallon watched as the griffon took off and floated a few feet away. It cried again and stayed hovering in the night air. Melanie stood, as did the others.

Then, a soft voice whispered, "Melanie…"

She looked around, but everyone appeared just as bewildered as she felt.

"Melanie…"

Melanie slowly approached the griffon. It flapped its wings and flew a little further as Melanie came closer.

"It wants us to follow it," she said.

"Do you hear that?" Jason asked. "Who's calling my name?"

"Mine, too," Fallon said.

Leaving their blankets and supplies, they entered deep into the forest, following the griffon.

"Glow-boy just keeps going." Jason sighed.

After they had gone a hundred feet or so, the griffon zipped away in a streak of light and disappeared into a thicket.

The others did not follow, for to their left a round hill rose from the ground, with a gold-and-ivory staircase leading to a marble fountain blooming with clear water. Two trees unfolded at either side of it, their large green leaves shimmering in the moonlight.

"Why would the griffon lead us here?" asked Jason.

As if in response, the fountain shone with brilliant light, but it did not blind them. The trees changed to white with silver leaves, and a woman appeared at the top of the staircase, her arms outstretched like she wanted to embrace her visitors. Her golden hair tumbled freely, and she radiated light. Rows of diamonds sparkled and glittered on the hem of her soft green dress.

"Welcome to the Fountain," she said.

Elken knelt on one knee. "Empress Elethýna. To what do we owe this undeserving honor?" He had heard stories of hidden fountains that would grant an audience with the Empress, but never had he expected to find one. He motioned to the others, who knelt after his example.

"Five years ago, I found a Pyrium Dragon egg in the Golden Mountains, the nest abandoned by its mother." She gracefully descended the staircase, her long green train rippling behind her. "To save it from Helnah, I sent it to the Separate Realm. Now Scalaed's return has set into motion your perilous paths of destiny. So I have come to grant you my protection."

"Who are you?" Melanie could only whisper in the

Empress's splendor.

"I am a Celestial," Empress Elethýna replied, her ethereal voice filling the forest. "An immortal, and I have lived since Tindoria's dawn."

Empress Elethýna flourished her hands, and a long, flat silver box glittered into existence. Effortlessly balancing the box in one hand, she touched her necklace: a golden cross with a peridot gemstone embedded in the center. "This is *Mastrónias*," she said. "It is an Abrielstone. As long as I live, this stone embodies my power, and with it I can dispense protection to you through these…" She opened the silver box to reveal five silver duplicates of her necklace, though the gems were different. She faced Elken and draped a garnet-inlaid necklace over him. The red stone in the cross glowed. "Fear not. Your nobility will be rewarded," she told Elken.

Turning to the others, she continued, "You will each receive an Abrielstone. They will protect you from harm." Elethýna gave Fallon and Briefur each a silver cross embedded with a diamond. She smiled and said softly, "May you always cherish the White Village."

The Empress gave Jason an amethyst-embedded cross. "Do not fear, Jason, for you will find peace by helping others. No ailment is beyond a cure."

Melanie was last, receiving a silver cross with a ruby. "Your strength and sacrifices have led you here," Elethýna said. "This, Melanie, is what you've prepared for. We will meet again."

Elethýna stood before them and said, "Go now and rest, for

the window of opportunity is short." Walking up the staircase, she vanished. The trees returned to their normal states and the fountain stopped flowing, reverting into an archaic structure.

Jason fiddled with his new necklace as they returned to camp. When he reached the camp, he dragged his blanket over to Poison Ivy. He lay down, and draped Ivy's wing over his body.

As the Empress had instructed, everyone had fallen asleep. Everyone except Melanie. She tossed and turned, never escaping that one irritating root in her back. Soon, she'd had enough. *I'm moving.* Standing, she ripped the blanket from the ground. Something twinkled beneath the leaves and mulch. Kneeling, she carefully touched what had been hidden under her blanket.

She had not been lying on a root at all, but a sword in a scabbard. It hadn't been there before she laid out her blanket. As Melanie lifted it up, the molded red rose on the pommel glittered in the moonlight. A pair of glistening green leaves formed the crossguard, and the scabbard was carved away at the top, revealing a third leaf stretching into the blade. Suspicion crept through Melanie. She unsheathed the sword and nearly dropped it. She recognized the blade's material right away. In Melanie's hands was an Indomitable Glass sword.

CHAPTER 26

Return to the Fortress

How is this possible? Gawking at the weapon, Melanie turned the sword to study it and noticed an inscription running down the blade. At first, Melanie couldn't read the runes, but soon they blurred into letters she recognized. *Ilvir*.

Melanie shook her head in confusion. How could the glass sword have just *appeared?* While the explanation eluded her, she knew deep down that she was meant to have it. So she returned it to its burgundy leather scabbard, where "Faithful Illuminator" was written in gold leaf, then placed the sword by her head and fell asleep.

When Melanie awoke, streams of golden light rained down through the branches. She stretched and walked over to Jason, who sat with his back against a tree, chin up and eyes closed.

"Hey," she said, sitting next to him. "How long have you been up?"

Jason opened one eye, then he turned around to face her, his shoulder touching the tree.

"A while." He smirked. "Not used to waking up with the sun."

"You seem to be handling all this fairly well," Melanie

noted.

"Panicking doesn't help anyone in a crisis. Besides, what else can I do?"

"Fair point."

"How are you? Do you still have the heartlink?"

"I don't know. Scalaed is still alive, but I'm not feeling him anymore. Like..." Melanie tried to explain. "He feels farther away. Like there's a wall blocking our full connection. I can barely sense it now."

"Can you still find him?"

"I hope so," Melanie said. "But we need to move before I lose it entirely."

"It is a one hundred and thirty mile journey to Thornbrill," Elken began as they sat around the campfire. "We can cover most of the distance in a day if we ride from dawn to dusk. Our mission is to rescue the Pyrium Dragon, Scalaed, from the Arfire Maze. The only entry from the outside is through the Iron Gateway."

"Entering the Maze does us no good if we don't know where Scalaed is being held," Briefur noted.

"Scalaed and I share what I call a heartlink," Melanie explained. "I can follow it to him. This has worked in the past on my world."

"Thornbrill has a watchtower, so we'll need a distraction," Elken added.

"I could return in an act of surrender," Jason suggested. "Helnah seems head over heels for me, so maybe I could use that to my advantage."

"It might be safer if I went, Jason," Elken said.

"I agree," Fallon nodded.

"Yeah, but I kinda have a score to settle," Jason explained. "I want to do it. Don't worry, I'll have Pi. That ought to give Helnah a shock and keep her in conversation while you guys go in the Maze."

"What exactly *is* the Arfire Maze?" asked Fallon.

Everyone went quiet, and Melanie could hear the rustle of the grass beneath them. All eyes were on Elken. He looked down and sighed deeply. "The Arfire Maze is a labyrinth within the volcano's magma chamber. It is the habitat for the dragons Helnah and her hunters have captured. It is with this dragon army she attacks other cities for children, whom she adds to her ranks."

"Why does she need so many dragons?" Jason asked. "She makes dragons to get kids to make more dragons. Seems weirdly cyclical if you ask me."

Elken took a deep breath. "Helnah was once a member of King Eldrain's scientific council. She dedicated her life to finding ways to improve Endlewood's military, striving honorably to one day be given command of it. Near as I can tell, dragons had always been her passion, so one day, she suggested using them as a means of warfare.

"Helnah was then consumed with paranoia, begging the king they needed this power against the unknowns of the world. When the council deemed her unfit for service, Helnah exiled herself to finish growing an army, and she used her royal funding to hire hunters from around the realm to her cause.

"It was later I discovered she wasn't building an army, but searching for a specific dragon— a Pyrium Dragon like Scalaed. I have asked Helnah countless times what made these dragons so special. She refused to say, only that they number one out of hundreds. But her hunters thinned the dragon population, so she acquired a poison to make dragons. Celestials only know where she got such an evil substance. She abducts children, for they easily succumb to the mutation effect. But she has failed to produce a Pyrium from her experiments."

"That's horrible!" Fallon cried.

"Cities forged weapons and formed armies, and even the most peaceful of kingdoms and villages found themselves preparing for battle. All are futile efforts. Helnah's army is unstoppable. How she manages to control them in battle is a mystery to most of the Thornbrillians except for a select few. Likely the same few who know her true intentions with a Pyrium Dragon."

"But we're going to stop her," Melanie vowed as she leaned forward. Her scabbard stuck out behind her.

"Whoa, what's that?" Jason pointed.

"Oh, this?" Melanie reddened as she glanced at her sword. "Um, *Ilvir.*"

"I'm sorry, what now?"

"Yeah, I forgot to tell you." Melanie smiled sheepishly as she revealed the glass sword.

Jason gawked before finally sputtering, "How?"

"How indeed?" Elken marveled.

"It found me?" Melanie shrugged. "It was right after the Empress gave us our Abrielstones. I came back and found this under my blanket."

"Why would an Indomitable Glass sword just appear like that?"

"Maybe it's a sign, but whatever the reason, I'm grateful it happened. Now let's go."

"You mean to tell me Elvis was eaten by a horse?" Helnah's voice was like the calm before a storm.

Thendrell, Keth, and Helketh and a few others sat stone-faced along the dark mahogany table.

"Well?" Helnah drove her knife into the long table.

"Helnah," Thendrell began, raising his hands in a placating gesture, "he may have escaped into the forest."

Helnah sat down in her seat at the head of the table and took a deep breath. "He has not been seen for seven days." When her remark was met with silence, she sighed. "I want that rogue horse-dragon contained and confined in the Arfire Maze immediately. Do you understand?"

"Yes, Helnah," Helketh replied and nudged Keth to go with him. The two exited through the doors, only to reopen them two seconds later. A breathless hunter had joined them.

Helnah stood up and asked, "Dereth? What is it?"

"The rogue dragon…it has returned."

"What?"

Helketh added, "Elvis is with it."

"More like *on* it," Keth corrected.

Helnah and her men raced to the parapets, where they stood transfixed. Walking out of the forest was Jason atop Poison Ivy. Her wings fanned out in a glorious display as Jason locked eyes with Helnah.

Silvedus and Starlark carried their riders with swift silence to the foot of the mountain. Elken dismounted and tied the horses' bridles to a tree at the edge of the forest. "The heat of the Arfire Maze is too much for them. We'll see them when we return. We'll go the rest of the way on foot." Staying under the cover of the treeline, Elken led Melanie, Briefur, and Fallon past the watchtower. The hunters at the top began to shout and point at something in the distance, then they blew the tower's warning horn. Jason's distraction was working. At Elken's signal, he, Melanie, and the Hündr dashed across the open stretch of a hundred yards up the mountainside, then ducked out of sight behind a rocky wall. Before them stood the Iron Gates—two slabs of metal in the mountain face that stretched nearly thirty feet. Elken approached and pulled a lever near the entrance.

"That's strange to make this place so accessible," Briefur said.

"It's how we delivered the wild-caught dragons to the Maze," Elken replied as the Iron Gates groaned open. "Anyone entering blindly would be eaten long before they could infiltrate the fortress."

Before she entered, Melanie looked to her left and saw the towering mountain range stretch past a gaping chasm. It was so vast that the other side faded into the mountains beyond.

"What caused that?" Melanie pointed.

"Tildain's Chasm?" Elken squinted at the landmark. "A remnant from quakes of the first eruption. So named after it swallowed the cartographer who mapped this region. Now, quick, inside."

Melanie and the Hündr slipped through the gates into the mountain before Elken pushed the lever back in place. The Iron Gates closed with a grinding noise behind Elken, shutting the group into darkness, save for a single torch and the ominous orange glow of an archway at the end of the room.

Melanie patted her sword by her side, grateful to finally have a weapon.

"I pray Jason stays safe!" Fallon added. "Why did we let him go?"

Melanie answered in a grim tone, "He volunteered…"

Briefur wrapped his arm around Fallon's shoulder. She looked at her cousin with her golden eyes, worry and fear filling them. "He will be fine, Fallon," he told her, and her eyes brightened a little.

Melanie reflected on her brother. Before leaving, Jason had had a look in his eyes, something she'd never seen in him before. A seriousness, a determined glint. She had always considered him somewhat of a floater. Now she saw a man who meant business, who had initiative, and nothing would stop him. Whatever he had witnessed with those poor children had really emboldened him.

"Whenever you're ready, Melanie." Elken stepped behind her.

With a nod, Melanie honed in on the heartlink. *Scalaed?* she asked it. *Are you there?*

For the first time, there was no response.

Scalaed, where are you? "I can't reach him," Melanie said, a faint wobble in her voice. "I'm going in."

She rushed through the archway onto a ledge but stopped as she was blasted with hot winds as if she had opened a twenty-foot-high oven door.

"Melanie, wait!" Elken called as he and the Hündr ran after her.

Melanie panted anxiously as she turned to face a sloping trail that narrowed as it wound past the lava lake below. She had to find Scalaed. *He has to be okay. He has to—*

The ground gave way and Melanie tumbled off the ledge.

"Melanie!" Elken screamed.

Spinning as she fell, Melanie reached for Elken's hand. Their fingers latched onto each other, rigid like stone, and they froze. Neither dared to move as Melanie dangled above the huffing lava.

"I've got you!" Elken gasped as he squeezed her hand even tighter.

Her wild brown eyes burned with fear, looking up at her savior leaning over the remaining half of the ledge.

"I've got you," Elken said again. He tried to grab her with his other hand, but he held fast to the ground to keep himself from joining her.

Heat swarmed them, joining forces with their terror, and their grips grew slick with sweat.

"Don't let go," Melanie pleaded, afraid to breathe.

"I won't," Elken said, his eyes penetrating her with determination.

Their hands squeaked, a subtle slip.

"Elken!" Melanie gasped, tears brimming her eyes. "I can't move!"

Elken felt teeth sink into his tunic, and Briefur and Fallon snarled to hold him in place, paws planted in the ground, allowing him to free his other hand.

"Yes, you can," Elken assured her as he thrust down his other hand. "You'll be alright. Reach!"

Melanie's chest rattled with her own thundering heartbeat.

"Trust me!" Elken begged, his eyes just as wide as hers as he strained to lower his arm closer. "Please."

Melanie gulped a shaky breath and obeyed.

Their sudden movements, sweaty as they were, ripped them apart, and for a precious second their hands scrambled to join again.

They missed.

Melanie fell through the thin air.

Elken yelled in despair, a broken sound as Briefur and Fallon shouted after her.

The heat intensified as Melanie neared the lava lake below her. Just when she thought her skin would blister and split open from the heat, she hit the lava.

Elken watched in absolute horror as Melanie sank below the fiery depths, her shrieks still echoing in his ears. Screaming back, he fell to his knees.

CHAPTER
27
The Captor

Ten minutes was all he had. Ten minutes to distract the watchtower and Helnah while Melanie and the others made their way to the Arfire Maze.

Jason took a deep breath as Poison Ivy slowly walked to the fortress. Under different circumstances, Jason would have laughed at Helnah's priceless expression when she saw him.

He dismounted at the red gates as the guards opened them. Inside, Helnah was waiting for him, her face paling behind her hair.

Jason walked up to her, counting every step as they brought him closer. Eight minutes.

"How are you here unharmed and…" Helnah looked from Jason to Poison Ivy, eyes wide as she added in a quieter tone, "…with a dragon?"

The air felt thick with what Jason sensed was Helnah's fear. He loved every bit of it.

"Apparently I'm good with dragons," Jason said.

"No doubt," Helnah said, unable to look away from Poison Ivy. "Come inside."

"Oh, of course," Jason said, a sly smile following as he settled into character, "and I trust your invitation extends to my new friend." He stroked Poison Ivy's nose affectionately. "You see, she gets quite lonely and frightened when I'm not with her. And I'm sure you'd hate to see your castle burn to the ground."

Helnah's lashes fluttered. "What game are you playing?"

Jason looked deeply offended. "And here I thought I would have made you proud coming back. I thought you missed me! I didn't have to return, you know, but it's no difference to me if I change my mind. "

There was a moment of silence from Helnah. "If you are trying to deceive me, I will end you."

Jason and Poison Ivy walked down the main hall then took a right into the throne room. Helnah sat him down at the long table. "Elvis," she began, and Jason bit his cheek to prevent laughing. He'd forgotten about that little bit.

Helnah leaned forward with her pale hands folded in front of her, "Tell me, why have you *really* returned?"

"I have a skill I'm sure you'd find very useful," Jason explained, mirroring her position. "I can train dragons."

Helnah's composure changed to intrigue. "Is that so?" She reclined in her chair. "What makes your method any more efficient than mine?"

Jason was wary. "Your method?" Six minutes.

"The minds of my dragons are dull." Helnah studied something invisible between her fingers. "Malleable. Easy to bend to my will."

"Mind control?" Jason didn't like the sound of that.

"Every whim I conjure they obey instantly."

Jason folded his arms and leaned back. "So you have no use for my talent, then? Not even for the black dragon?"

"He has been most uncooperative. It appears he is immune to my ability, and it has tolled on my health as of late."

"Take me to him, and I'll get him to listen," Jason offered eagerly.

Helnah tilted her head, her eyes narrowing skeptically. "And what do you gain from all this, Elvis?"

"What do *you* gain from Scalaed?"

Helnah hesitated before replying, "I've searched for a Pyrium Dragon for many years. He possesses a magical ability." She darkened, her voice an intense whisper. "An ability I *need*."

"To…protect Endlewood?" Jason squinted, remembering her backstory.

Helnah rose to her feet, gasping in surprise. "So you *do* understand! Not just Endlewood, but all of Tindoria."

"From what?" Jason was unsure what to make of her sudden change.

Helnah's eyes darted at the shadows around them. "The end."

She really has gone nuts, Jason thought. Four minutes. He studied Helnah, whose gaze was scattered and unfocused. *Something has her legitimately spooked.*

Helnah shook her head, reentering the present. "Thendrell," she called. "Bring out the Thardenveil so we may toast to Elvis."

Poison Ivy tracked Thendrell from her post near the fireplace as he approached Jason with a tray bearing two golden goblets and an ornate pitcher. He poured a rose-colored drink in each cup, then gave them to Jason and Helnah.

Poison Ivy snarled, opening her mouth. Flames began to glow from the back of her throat.

Helnah pointed to the dragon. "Kneel."

In dazed obedience, Poison Ivy shut her mouth and did as she was told. Jason's heart dropped to his toes. He had never seen Helnah use her power before.

Acting as though it had meant nothing, Helnah raised her cup, proclaiming, "In celebration of our resurrected alliance, I propose a toast to our future victories."

Jason held his breath as he clanged his goblet against hers. Two minutes. *Is this poisoned? I just struck a deal, why would she poison me? I'm not drinking unless she does.*

Helnah smiled. "To dragon training." She lifted her goblet to her dark lips.

Jason did the same, bringing the rim to his lips but not touching the sweet-smelling drink. His eyes watched Helnah.

When she set the goblet down, Jason noticed it was empty. Clearly it was safe, as he had seen both drinks poured from the same pitcher. She really *did* want him, so he drank.

"I must say, I have many questions." Helnah rubbed the brim of her goblet.

"Like?" Jason had one minute left before he was supposed to rendezvous with the others. How was he going to get out of this with Poison Ivy under Helnah's spell?

Then it hit him. First he felt the dryness in his mouth. Then his head began to swim. Jason grasped the table and stood up, gasping for air. He clutched his chest as what felt like shards of glass scraped his lungs. His ears started ringing. His insides were on fire. Collapsing to the ground, Jason screamed.

He heard Helnah laughing in the distance. "Did you really think I believed you?"

Jason curled into a ball and wrapped his arms around his stomach as he choked. He felt like knives were cutting him open from the inside as Helnah's dark laughter echoed in his head. Walking over to Jason, Helnah kicked him over so he was facing her. She bent down and squeezed Jason's cheeks.

"You never would have been my ally. You were my prisoner! Nothing genuine would have brought you back to me." She lifted him by his neck and thrust him at the wall. Jason coughed weakly as his eyes clouded over. Helnah crossed her arms and watched her victim, amused. "I am not foolish enough to reunite you with your dragon."

Jason closed his eyes as his stomach churned to vomit. He groaned, "How did …?"

Helnah spared a glance for the half-empty pitcher on the table. "The beverage itself is fatal, but my power grants me immunity."

Foggy darkness was descending over Jason when, suddenly, his chest ignited. He grasped his shirt. His eyes shot open as he realized his Abrielstone was on fire. Instantly, the pain from the poison vanished. He sat up and looked down at his jewel, which was glowing brightly. Jason felt strength surge through his veins.

Helnah paled when she saw Jason glaring at her.

Amethyst flames of power wreathed his body, and she cowered in its blinding light. Jason stayed aflame as he slowly rose and approached her. When he reached her, his powerful aura dissipated. Inches from her face, Jason hissed, "That all you got?"

Trembling, speechless, Helnah relinquished her hold on Poison Ivy. The dragon scrambled to her feet, tossing Thendrell and a quartet of frightened guards from her path, and stood menacingly behind Jason.

"You lose," Jason said. He swung atop Poison Ivy, who snarled nastily at Helnah before walking toward the exit.

"And by the way," Jason added, "the name's Jason." He and Poison Ivy burst out the doors past unconscious guards and a completely dazed Thendrell. They plowed through the remaining hunters on their way out and crashed open the gates before leaping into the air. Guards stationed at the parapets hollered after them and loosed arrows. Poison Ivy tucked her wings in as the arrows glanced off her green armored hide and plummeted toward the foot of the mountain.

They might be a little tardy, but Jason hoped Melanie and the others had found Scalaed by now.

Shock gripped them all in silence as Elken knelt at the precipice. He'd failed Melanie. He'd asked her to trust him, and he'd dropped her. The guilt suffocated him, constricting his lungs and heart.

"Look!" Briefur's shout sliced through his thoughts.

The lava churned and boiled as a shimmering figure ascended from it. Melanie.

She grasped her shirt, thinking it was burning. She saw her Abrielstone shining with blinding light, cloaking her in ruby fire like a cloud. Melanie continued to rise from the lava until she gently alighted on the edge of the ridge. The red flames sealed themselves back into her Abrielstone.

She lifted her eyes and locked them on Elken. "How?" she squeaked.

"It is as Elethýna said," Elken gasped in disbelief. "The Abrielstone protects its bearer."

Melanie looked at her hands as if they were still glowing. "I thought I was dead."

A second pair of hands joined hers, and she looked up to find Elken even closer.

He had the sudden urge to embrace her, just to make sure she was real, but restrained himself. "I dropped you," was all he could say. "I am so sorry!"

Melanie melted into him. She heard his heart, racing as fast as hers, and felt his arms slowly surround her. She needed someone stable while she recollected herself. Someone to ground her.

Yet the heat wasn't kind to their moment. It only brought more sweat, so Melanie released Elken.

"Um, we should find Scalaed." Melanie awkwardly

gestured to the narrow path, still accessible by the now much-shorter ledge. She began her descent, leading the others into the Arfire Maze.

The heat rippled off the lava in constant waves. Bubbles grew silently, then spewed magma when they popped. While guarding themselves against the elements, Melanie and the others kept an eye out for dragons. Luckily so far, any they encountered snored in a docile slumber.

Their twisting path through the Maze led them to a tunnel. When Melanie touched a thread of pink light, it swirled around on the wall and vanished.

Elken looked at Melanie, her brown eyes sparkling in the rainbow lights, and smiled. "Melanie—"

"Wait!" Fallon held up her hand and turned her head. "Did you hear that?"

"You mean the snores of dragons?" Briefur asked.

"No." Fallon's ears shot up, her golden eyes widening.

Cautious, they exited the tunnel, which opened into another chamber filled with sleeping dragons soaking in another lava lake. But what Melanie heard next emanated from a corridor directly across the lava lake.

"That sounded like..." began Elken.

Melanie met the concerned faces of her companions, afraid to admit what she'd heard. "Like...laughter."

"There it is again!" Fallon spun around, facing the corridor. "Do you hear it?"

The sound was unmistakable—laughter, increasing in volume.

They all lay low behind jagged boulders to avoid being seen.

"Elken, we must go!" Fallon whispered, terrified.

All eyes were glued to the dark hall across the lake. Melanie struggled against her nerves to draw her glass sword. Then a squeal pierced the air, and Melanie shivered. It was not a squeal of torture or discomfort, but more like one of delight.

The hall started to glow. A stream of red fire blasted from the hall and splashed into the lava. Then another, and another; Melanie counted fifteen in total. The laughing was not as loud now and reduced to more of a mischievous snicker. A small point of red fire surfaced directly in front of a dragon sleeping on a rock. Fourteen more like it surfaced and circled the dragon. The cavern exploded in shrieks, laughs, and squeals as the fireballs ran all over the dragon, which immediately woke up and roared in pain. Within moments, the fire consumed it.

Woken by the commotion, the other dragons scrambled out of the lava. The laughing intensified as the roar of the dragon diminished. The fire finally left, leaving only a stark white skeleton.

Melanie covered her mouth in horror as the fire withdrew back into the tunnels in silence.

"What was that?" she whimpered.

"That," Elken began slowly, "was what we were worried about."

Melanie tried to exhale. What those things had done to a dragon in just a matter of seconds…"What if that's why I can't find Scalaed?" Melanie scrambled to her feet. "What if he was eaten?" Tears brimmed in her eyes. "No, no, I have to find him!" Her damp hair whipped in the hot volcanic breath as she spun, scanning the cavern for any clue on where to turn. Her frantic muttering was silenced when Elken reached out to her face and turned her to him.

"Melanie." Elken's voice stilled her. A strand of hair clung to her cheek, and Elken gently brushed it off her face and combed it behind her ear. He held her cheek in his hand, gazing into her eyes. "We will find Scalaed. You've been so strong. You won't break now. Alright?"

Melanie nodded, realizing her hands had clasped his on her cheek.

"Good."

Scalaed slowly opened one eye. His vision blurred, and he sank deeper in the floor. Day after day, the duel of minds always left him weakened. But something was different today. His dragon captor hadn't moved. Its frozen stillness was normal after a battle, but it should have awakened by now.

Scalaed pressed his nose against his stone prison and warbled quietly.

The other dragon remained silent.

Scalaed growled more loudly.

Again, it gave no reaction.

Scalaed was alone. Shaking in disbelief, Scalaed tore down his mental walls and unleashed the roars he had been suppressing.

His heartlink blazed to life, igniting the cold thread that spanned the Maze, striking Melanie's chest with intensity.

She stumbled back, then looked at the group, her face lighting up. "I feel Scalaed! This way." Melanie sprinted back into the light tunnel, breathing heavily as each heartbeat brought her closer. The volcanic fumes no longer had any effect. The heat no longer mattered. All thoughts were of Scalaed.

When the heartlink led them back to the Iron Gates, Melanie stood confused.

"We're right back where we started," Briefur scoffed.

"Scalaed is so close, though." Melanie walked along the wall, trailing a hand along the rock.

The Iron Gates opened, and Jason and Poison Ivy bounded in. "Weirdest conversation ever, but I'll explain later. Status update, Sis?"

Melanie had both hands on the wall, head craned up in examination.

"A door!" Melanie spun around. "Scalaed is right here, I know it. Help me!"

Everyone approached to feel the wall, gliding hands or sniffing the floor in front to find the means to open it. Elken reached for the torch.

"Should have guessed." Jason shook his head. "It's always a torch."

As soon as the door crunched open enough, Melanie squeezed through, ignoring her companions' protests. She fumbled in the blackness, winding through the corridor until she emerged into a huge cavern. She froze.

The largest, ugliest dragon she had ever seen glowered in her direction. It appeared to be frozen in time. Then it shuddered to life. It tilted its head at Melanie, narrowing its blank milky eyes. An unnatural smile of crooked fangs stretched across its muzzle. "So nice of you to finally join us, child of the Separate Realm." Its purr rumbled like thunder.

Beneath one of the monster's massive feet rested a stone cage. Inside, Scalaed roared and scratched at the bars. He was barely visible through his captor's talons.

Fury inflamed Melanie, and she unsheathed *Ilvir*. "Let him go." Her voice sounded small in the vast room, and not as brave as she hoped.

The dragon growled. "You do not threaten me, pestilence."

Elken burst into the room. Without hesitation, he drew *Clavnir* and planted himself between Melanie and the monstrous dragon. He cast a quick glance at Melanie, who stood determined despite the tremble in her sword.

Jason and the others entered, and the dragon's lips curled back in hatred. "Traitors!" The dragon's voice dropped to an eerily familiar sneer. "I'll have your hide for this treason, Elken. And you too, Jason!"

Elken and Jason sucked in a breath. They *did* know that voice. And the realization chilled them to the bone.

"*Helnah?*"

CHAPTER
28

Of Wrath and Poison

The cavern's temperature dropped to a chill.

Jason drew his twin knives and, with a yell, drove them into Helnah's leg. His weapons bounced off, causing a bright shimmer to ripple over the dragon.

"No!" Jason screamed. From his cage, Scalaed whined in confusion.

"It's a shield, you imbecile." Helnah cracked a grin. "No weapon can pierce me!" With a deafening roar that sent them buckling to their knees with covered ears, Helnah tightened her grip on Scalaed's cage. "Now, you will help me, or I will break your pet's mind into submission."

Like a molten poker, Helnah's mind invaded Scalaed's with a new ferocity. He began roaring and writhing in pain.

Her breath coming heavier and faster in white puffs, Melanie felt adrenaline electrify her limbs. She ran, hefting *Ilvir* to strike.

Scoffing, Helnah swiped her massive tail down toward Melanie.

With a scream, Melanie swung the glowing arc of her blade into the black flesh, cutting through it and the shield like jelly.

Helnah roared and reeled back, her wings slicing through the still cavern air. Elken and the others ducked, barely escaping the razor edges.

"Impossible!" Helnah shrieked. Bubbling black blood oozed from the severed tail, then vanished in a thick cloud of smoke. "Die! All of you!"

The mountain rumbled. Rubble fell from the ceiling as a distant noise like a storm approached.

Swarms of dragons flooded the cavern, and chaos ensued. Screams from Melanie and her companions bounced among flapping wings and gaping maws. Briefur and Fallon assumed their canid forms and darted through talons and tails, sinking their teeth in anything that crossed their path. Their claws struck with vicious fury.

"Keep that sword away from me!" Helnah screamed, hiding behind her cloud of dragons.

A green dragon rammed into Elken, knocking *Clavnir* from his grip. Turning his fall into a roll, Elken swapped weapons, rolled to the side, and sent an arrow into its wing. *Why are none breathing fire?* As Elken released more arrows with rapid succession, he realized such an amount of fire would suffocate everyone in the cavern, including Scalaed, with the fatal heat. Helnah would never risk it. Ducking a pair of greedy talons, Elken reclaimed the glass sword and locked eyes with Helnah, who melted further back into the darkness.

"We can't hurt them!" Melanie cried above the chaos. "They're only children!"

"Then how do we fight back?" Briefur asked as a blue

dragon hoisted him into the air.

"There are natural dragons among us," Elken panted as he cut through the wing of a beast he recognized from a hunt.

Melanie scrambled to the floor as dragon jaws chomped in her direction. "How can we tell them apart?"

Jason leaped behind a stalagmite for cover to rummage through memories for anything useful. What did he see in the dungeons when they were tossed into the Maze? He peeked around his rocky shield and scanned the dragons.

"The wings!" He screamed as he jumped back into the fight. He pointed at a red dragon soaring around Helnah. "A kid's arms become wings. Two wings, two legs."

"I read about this!" Melanie shouted in recognition. "They're wyverns!"

The dragons swarmed in a tornado around Helnah, separating her from the glass swords. One blue wyvern smacked Elken with her tail, sending him flying across the chamber and away from Helnah.

Poison Ivy stalked Jason, twitching her head for control of her mind.

He planted his feet and adjusted his knives. "Pi, stop!"

The horse-dragon's pupils flashed between slits and ovals, but she kept her pace.

"Poison Ivy, fight it!" Jason ordered, fear tainting his tone.

Poison Ivy curled back her lips and snarled evilly. Lunging, she pushed Jason to the ground, snapping her jaws closer and closer towards his face. Jason braced his arms against her throat, but the dragon was far stronger.

"Don't make me kill you, girl!" Jason strained.

A brown dragon pounced in front of Elken, its four legs identifying it as a wild beast.

Melanie, who had been swinging *Ilvir* like a madwoman, raced to Elken's aid.

"Hey!" Melanie tore its attention from Elken, giving him the chance to rise to his feet.

The dragon saw Melanie, then the glowing glass blade, and leaped out of the way.

Melanie's attack sliced Elken across the chest.

He stared at his bleeding wound in disbelief. Then, mouth gaping, he fell to the ground.

All sound was sucked from Melanie's world. Struck still like she had been turned to stone, she couldn't breathe as Elken collapsed. Everything slowed, and her throat burned from a scream she couldn't hear. She felt herself stumbling back.

A turquoise wyvern landed with a thud between them, blocking Melanie's view of Elken. The wyvern was joined by others who thrust their heads forward to attack.

Briefur saw Elken fall. He wriggled free from a dragon's clutches, sinking teeth into scaley claws. He bounded down on dragon backs from the heights of the cavern. Hunching over Elken, he snapped rabid jaws at their attackers.

"Kill them all!" Helnah bellowed from behind her cover of minions. A shockwave of cold rolled through the cavern.

The turquoise wyvern panted against Helnah's mind-control as she jaggedly craned her neck around to Melanie, who weakly lifted *Ilvir* in a daze.

"Melanie, no!" Jason screamed, and with a desperate grunt, kneed Poison Ivy in the throat. "That's Laena!"

Scalaed watched helplessly from the narrow slits of his prison. He could see it all—Melanie with her sword, Jason with his knives, Briefur and Fallon with their claws and teeth. Elken, dying. He had to help.

Scalaed heaved as he shifted position to look at the turquoise wyvern. She wasn't like the others. Jason knew her. An ally?

Scalaed barked for her attention, and his red eyes locked with glowing turquoise irises. He had no idea if this would work, but he had to try. He fanned out his mental walls, imagining them plating her mind and cutting off her enslavement. Laena blinked rapidly, and in suspended silence, a mutual understanding sparked between them. She twirled around and zipped through the crowd of dragons, snatching Elken in her claws. Melanie screamed, and Briefur and Fallon jumped onto Laena's back, ready to free him.

Scalaed roared in harsh opposition, and the Hündr realized they were being flown out of the volcano into blue freedom.

Jason saw it too, and he yelled for Scalaed's attention. Poison Ivy, who had recovered from a choking fit, was ready to blast Jason. Scalaed spun his shielding onto the horse-dragon, and she snapped back to reality. Swallowing her fire, she pushed Jason onto her back.

"Melanie!" Jason waved for her attention as he and Poison Ivy barreled to her. "There's too many of them!" Not waiting for her response, he grabbed her wrist and hauled her onto Poison Ivy.

"No! But Scalaed!" Melanie reached out to her dragon.

"We can't get to him, Melanie," Jason snapped. "It's either him or Elken."

Time slowed as Melanie felt imprisoned by her two choices. She held Scalaed's gaze as they flew past. He nodded in assurance, telling her through the heartlink he would be fine. Elken needed her more.

"Scalaed." Melanie's voice was lost in the cacophony, and as they spiraled out of the volcano, she screamed a sob. "I'm sorry!"

Seeing her fly toward safety gave Scalaed peace. The other dragons funneled out the vent in pursuit until the cavern was once again a pit of silence. He knew Melanie would come back for him. And he could outlast whatever Helnah threw at him.

Helnah razed him with her murderous white stare, and he gulped.

He had to last.

Jason held Melanie tightly against him as Poison Ivy zoomed up behind Laena. He shot a glance back and saw the swarming dragons ignite their throats, no longer confined to the volcanic oven.

Melanie adjusted her sword in anticipation, then looked to Elken. Laena's claws cradled him delicately as blood dripped from them. So much red. But Melanie couldn't tear her gaze away.

Briefur and Fallon had pasted themselves on her back for fear of falling off. "They're gaining on us!" Briefur shouted over the wind.

Laena craned her neck to see their pursuers, then roared something to Poison Ivy. The Ruby Mountains shrunk behind them as the two dragons barreled higher into the sky, trees waving in the sunset beneath them. Faster and faster the forests shimmered past, and the two dragons accelerated like missiles, splitting the air as they cut through the sky. Fields, rivers, and forests streaked past in flashes of green and blue, and the riders couldn't keep eyes open in the wind peeling their faces. Thankful Poison Ivy had her bridle, Jason clung to it for dear life.

Laena felt desperate claws sink into her scales for safety, but she tried to ignore them. The pursuing dragons fell far behind, but Laena and Poison Ivy pressed on. She had to get Elken to Lakéthion. He had been the only kind face to visit the prisoners in the wee hours of night to give them extra food. The least she could do was ensure he didn't die. But his pale, limp form instilled little confidence.

Melanie's eyes stung from the wind and the dried tears encrusting her lids. "Why didn't his Abrielstone protect him?" she cried.

"I don't know," Jason shouted, barely hearing his own

voice over the wind. He watched Laena. Her eyes were locked on the horizon, and her wings beat relentlessly despite the fatigue. "But I think we're being led to a place that can help."

Helnah felt her army begin to slip beyond the borders of her reach. She called them back, roaring in defeat as they funneled back into the Arfire Maze.

Scalaed prepared for her wrath as she heaved her massive, draconic form in his direction, lowering her head to within mere inches of his. His breath fogged the air between them.

"You *insufferable…*" Helnah paused. Then a crude smile twitched on her lips. "They abandoned you."

Scalaed growled. Obviously, Melanie's companion had been dying; of course she wanted to save him. She was a good person.

"No," Helnah scoffed. "Your darling human girl chose a traitorous hunter she barely knows over you."

Scalaed snorted angry coils of smoke. He knew that tone of voice from the villains in movies, and he refused to be manipulated.

"She could have freed you if she had tried a little harder, you know," Helnah purred. She lifted the stump of whatever remained of her tail. "Her sword could easily kill me and break your cage. With my mind scattered over so many vessels, it would have taken the barest effort." She leaned in closer to Scalaed, who flinched. "And she knew it, Scalaed."

The use of Scalaed's name disoriented him. He shook his head.

"Come now, you sensed her weighing her options: to save you or Elken. If she had any common sense, she could have freed you and still be able to fly her precious companion to safety. Especially if she rode with you."

Scalaed tried to deny it, but black tendrils of doubt began seeping into his heart. The saddle suddenly felt heavier.

"But I will treasure you, Scalaed," Helnah said as gently as possible. "Together, we can burn those who burn us."

Conflicted, Scalaed weakly shook his head.

Helnah rumbled in frustration. "What will it take… to…" She wheezed and collapsed onto his cage, motionless. The stillness had struck her again. Scalaed realized the sheer amount of energy she'd spent on this form must have drained her to the point of catatonia.

A snort escaped his nose as he smirked at her pathetic state. But then he thought of what she said. It couldn't be true, could it? Helnah didn't know Melanie like he did. But Melanie hardly knew Elken either.

A squirming feeling crept up on him. Scalaed didn't like how jealousy felt. It only made him crave escape more. But he was trapped under the crushing weight of Helnah's limp body.

Helnah awoke in her bed drenched in sweat. Gulping down the contents of the purple vial by her bedside, she shuffled off the mattress and caught her reflection in her mirror. Her hands shook violently, and her hair had been swept aside. A white eye surrounded by ashy scales glared back. With a shudder, she quickly covered the haunting reminder of her dragon body. *My tail!*

She needed to speak with Elthar immediately.

Helnah never thought she would ever go back to that room where she had become one with the dragon. That day she lay on a wooden table with a heavily sedated dragon next to her, chains anchoring the beast to the ground. Elthar had carefully cut away the dragon's skull, exposing its brain as he'd asked her, "Remind me how you got this…potion?" He swirled the crude vial of purplish-black liquid.

"It does not matter where or whom I got it from," Helnah snapped, scanning the room. "And I don't pay you to ask questions. I pay for your moral ambiguity."

Elthar's face twisted into a grin as he injected the poison into the dragon's brain. "Certainly my medicinal sorcery has nothing to do with it." As the brain began to glow, he continued, "You cannot fault my curiosity. I thought this was for *children*." Then, with a wave of his hand, the brain dissolved into a wild, shapeless mist that contained the dragon's entire consciousness. "Did someone grow a conscience to protect the innocent urchins?"

"That's a question, Elthar," Helnah reminded him.

With an amused *humph*, Elthar formed the mist into a cloudy blanket and draped it over Helnah, and the spirit seeped into her body. After a series of terrible convulsions, Helnah's dazed eyes shut. The dragon growled louder and raised its head, imbued with Helnah's consciousness.

"You've succeeded!" Helnah said through the dragon. The power that flooded her veins whispered of affliction and evil. It frightened Helnah, but it was necessary. Exhaling, the dragon collapsed, and Helnah sat up in her human body, a wild look in her eyes.

"Enhance this vessel with Pyrium abilities," she said to Elthar. "I must be unstoppable!"

"First, let me remind you of the risks," Elthar warned, even as he reached for the proper syringes. "You are now one with a dragon. That alone will weaken you. Being one with an *enhanced* dragon will bring *enhanced* side effects. You will require frequent dosages of a healing potion to maintain your strength, and likely your sanity. Actively controlling a force greater than you could drain you to the point of death. If either body dies, you perish."

"I care not for the cost," Helnah had retorted. "This is the only way."

This is the only way, Helnah reminded herself as the memory faded, and she opened the door.

"What brings you back here?" Elthar mused, barely

looking up from his scrolls.

Helnah quietly slipped inside the dark room, closing the door behind her. "I need help."

"How may I be of service?" Elthar strolled behind his desk. Its tiers of shelves and drawers held his collection of questionable potions, which glimmered in the candlelight.

"Your shield doesn't work."

"How so?"

"You said no known weapon could pierce the enchantment you placed upon my dragon body. Then the girl's sword severed the end of my tail. I need a new way to defend myself."

Elthar blinked. "I cannot help you."

Stepping back, Helnah jabbed a finger at the man. "You already failed to give this vessel Pyrium magic, which left me no choice but to become an abductor—"

"A choice you suddenly embraced." Elthar raised an eyebrow.

"It's that depraved dragon body!" Helnah shouted. "It's evil. Do you think I *wanted* this?"

"You don't pay me for questions." Elthar sneered. "You now know the girl has this weapon, so simply kill her before she reaches you next time."

You apathetic magician! "You understand nothing," Helnah seethed as she stormed out. "Without me, Tindoria falls, and you will be to blame!"

She slammed the door behind her, and a feverish chill swept through her body. The hallway swirled as she collapsed.

CHAPTER 29

The Doctor is In

Silver glittered on the horizon: the Sea of Starlight.

As they crossed the border into Lethios, Laena beat her wings with the last of her strength to ease their descent. Carrying three extra bodies had drained her over the past two hours. Below, the silver city of Lakéthion reflected the dying light of day in shades of pink and gold. Blue rooftops gleamed purple in the sunset.

Melanie peered over Poison Ivy's neck at the approaching city. Something moved at the top of one of the towers, and as they neared, she heard shouting. A barbed lance streamed past the dragons, causing Poison Ivy to barrel-roll out of the way. Jason and Melanie screamed as they clung on for dear life, and Briefur yelled, "Dive, now!"

The dragons obeyed, tucking their wings tight against their bodies and whistling toward the city. Another javelin zipped past, and Melanie watched the tower guards strain to pivot the large ballista in their direction.

Laena roared, hoping to dissuade the attacks, but that only enforced more retaliation. Horns bellowed around the walls as the dragons landed. A squadron of guards in steel armor charged the invaders as Melanie slipped off Poison Ivy's back.

"Stop!" she cried. "We need help!"

A guard spun Melanie behind his shield and said, "I have you now, my lady, you're safe."

"Not me!" Melanie snapped as she stepped out of his hold. "Help Elken!"

The guards, blinded by their mission to rescue Jason and the others from the ferocious dragons, thrust blades in Laena's direction.

"Laena, get out of here!" Jason cried as he strained against the guard holding him.

Tail between her legs, she laid Elken down and cowered away from the spears and swords and screams.

"Go, Laena, I will find you!"

Laena leaped from the wall.

"I promise!" Jason yelled after her.

The other guards were turning toward Poison Ivy when a voice boomed, "Stop!"

Silence befell the ranks. A guard pinned with various colored medals strode towards Jason and Melanie, flanked by Briefur and Fallon. A blue feathery plume whipped atop his helmet as he removed it.

"These dragons saved their lives," the guard said. "Leave them be and tend to this man at once."

The other guards' hesitation and confusion allowed Melanie to squirm free. She sprinted to Elken's side, cupping his face in her hands, but only for a moment before the guards came to their senses and pushed her aside. Clutching her shirt, she watched them carry Elken down the tower stairs. All that was left was a smeared puddle of blood on the floor. Melanie's mouth went dry, and she started to follow when the captain called, "Halt!"

Melanie spun around. The captain eyed her and her companions, drumming a thumb against his helmet as he assessed them and Poison Ivy.

"Will one of you kindly explain what just *happened?*"

Jason blew through his cheeks. "Well, gosh, how much time do you have?"

The captain of the guard, who introduced himself as Boliver, took note of their ragged appearance and led them to an inn in the city. For obvious reasons, Poison Ivy could not join, so Jason told her to leave the city to hunt. He would call her if needed.

The inn was called The Silver Lining, a fitting place to eat and ease their minds after what Boliver surmised must have been a frightful flight.

But Melanie had no appetite, and she let Jason do most of the talking. His responses faded to the back of her mind. She caught bits and pieces of their adventure and was vaguely aware of Boliver's eyes growing wider with each reply.

Melanie swirled her cup of water, staring blankly at her

rippling reflection. The heartlink pulsed as she searched for Scalaed's status. According to him, Helnah was still frozen, and he was fine for the time being. His heartbeat hinted he was more worried about her new friend.

As if on cue, a guard jogged up to their table. "Pardon my interruption, but I bring news of your companion."

Melanie's heart pounded against her ribs, unable to predict what the next words out his mouth would be.

"He is mortally wounded. Physicians are tending to him now." He took a deep breath as Melanie lost hers. "He will not last the night."

"Let me see him!" The words rushed out before she could stop them.

The guard looked to Boliver for direction, and the captain waved a dismissive hand.

"Fallon and I can continue your interview, Captain," Briefur stepped in and, nodding to Jason and Melanie, said, "Go."

Elken was easy to locate, though Melanie wished it hadn't been his screams that led them to him. She heard voices behind a door; worried voices. The guard excused himself, and Melanie closed her eyes to prepare for the worst. *You caused this,* Melanie's conscience told her. *He is in agony because of*

you. He is suffering because of you. Melanie shook her head to rid herself of the thoughts and gripped the door.

"Are you sure you want to do this?" Jason put his hands on hers.

Melanie answered solemnly, willing her tears to stay inside, "I have to see him and…apologize before it's too late."

Jason let go of her hands as they entered. Elken lay strapped on a stone table slick with blood. He had been stripped down to his trousers with his wrists in leather cuffs tied to the table. Doctors in soft yellow robes whispered amongst themselves as they pressed Elken's wound with bandages. Despite the layers, his chest was drenched in blood. His eyes squeezed shut, and he gripped the edge of the table so hard his knuckles were bone white. His breath came in short and shallow gasps.

In her horror, Melanie pressed her hand against her mouth, and her eyes welled up. "I am so sorry!" she said, voice shaking as she walked over to him.

Elken shouted in pain as a doctor peeled off the soaking, dripping bandage. Melanie stood anxiously as she listened to Elken's pained moans and screams. Her chin quivered. "Please forgive me," she whispered.

Elken was vaguely aware of her presence but incapable of acknowledging it. Jerking his head back, he cried out in agony as another doctor frantically tried to stitch the gaping red gash closed.

Melanie tried to hold his hand, but the doctors denied her.

"Why didn't his Abrielstone work?" she asked Jason again.

Her brother, unblinking, guided her attention with his finger. "Look."

Elken's Abrielstone glowed, a faint pulsating light in sync with his heart.

A doctor approached them, nervously wiping bloodstained hands on an already sodden towel. "His condition confuses us. While he is not worsening, he is not improving either." He looked back at his patient. "Whatever magic is in that stone is keeping him alive when he should have died long ago. We don't know how to proceed with such a devastating injury."

Jason watched the scene intently. They slowly abandoned the table. Elken had blacked out. Jason didn't understand how, but he knew that they had overlooked something. His head started to feel hot. He brushed past the doctor, who was hugging a trembling Melanie.

Unbidden, Jason's hand reached out to Elken's chest. Golden streams illuminated Jason's brain. Crossing to a row of shelves, he began shuffling through ointments and jars. His hands were guided to a tiny dusty vial in the far back. It was no larger than a shot glass, and he frantically grabbed it. Wheeling around, he emptied the vial's contents onto Elken's crudely-stitched wound and accidentally spilled the rest on himself. The sparkling powder dissolved in the blood, then bloomed in a crystalline jelly, sealing the raw edges of flesh. Jason watched the reaction, muttering the information overflowing his brain, "Not enough to connect the epidermis …" He pressed his hands onto the gash. "Amplify the crystal…" As he pressed, he thought he saw a faint glow under his hands.

Was that from the powder? Or my hands? Jason blinked rapidly as his vision peered through Elken's skin, golden light tending to the damage at Jason's command. "…reconnect the pectoralis major…reattach the thoracoacromial artery…" A final rush of energy shot through Jason's hands, and he stumbled back. Elken's chest had sealed completely. Only a fading white line across his chest remained, and a healthy pink washed over his sleeping face.

The doctors murmured among themselves in bafflement. One held the empty vial Jason grabbed and froze. The other doctors seemed to come to the same realization.

"If only we had known," one said softly. "The crystal was here all this time."

"And he used *all* of it!" another gasped.

Jason, equally dumbfounded, stepped back to catch his breath. His chest constricted and his lungs burned. *How did I know what to do?* It was like the time in the Maze when he'd popped his shoulder back into place, but much more intense.

"Jason!" Melanie's voice cried. "How did…"

He shook his head slowly in confusion, feeling lightheaded, then ran out of the room and down the hall. Busting into a vacant room, he stood panting at the window. He was shaky and sweating. He had saved Elken's life, but he had no clue on how he did it. Lifting his head to the night sky, he closed his eyes and took deep breaths. *Air. I need air. My chest…*

Jason placed his hand over his heart to stop the throbbing. So much information, almost too much, flooded his brain. Nausea crept over him. He dropped into a chair, trying to swallow back the acidic taste in his mouth.

"Jason?" asked a voice from behind. "Are you okay?"

He turned to face Melanie, her eyes begging for an explanation. Shaking his head in disbelief, he answered, "Something happened in that room. Like, I could see medicine and anatomy like I never have before. Everything just…made sense."

"Jason…" Melanie walked in front and gripped his shoulders. "That's not something to be afraid of; that was a miracle! You saved Elken's life. The doctors said he's now healing faster every minute."

Jason inhaled deeply, letting it all sink in. "That's why his Abrielstone didn't work. It wanted *me* to save him. It wanted to show me this…ability."

"Are you okay? You're shaking."

Jason took deep breaths. The nausea began to fade, and the tension coiled around his chest loosened. "I feel like I've been punched or something. It's going away now. I'll be fine."

"Jason," Melanie said, sitting in a chair across from him, "something happened to me as well."

Jason listened intently, the dizziness finally subsiding.

"I'm pretty sure I have an ability too."

"You can heal grave lacerations?"

"No, but I can walk through walls."

"What?" Jason scoffed in wonder. "Since when?"

"Seven days ago?" Melanie smirked haplessly.

Jason raised his eyebrows. "Okay, now you've got to show me."

"I would if I knew how it worked." Melanie shook her head with a smile, then sighed. "I'm so happy you're here."

"Me too. Can't imagine where you'd be without me."

Melanie nudged his arm, and for a fleeting moment, the world was normal.

"There you are!" Fallon materialized in the doorway. "We finished speaking with Captain Boliver, and he's arranged rooms for us. I'll take you there."

"Oh, gosh, a *bed*," Melanie said.

"I am absolutely wiped," Jason agreed.

The city sparkled dimly in the moonlight. Melanie and Jason followed the Hündr down the lane about two blocks down from the infirmary to The Silver Lining.

It was not what Melanie had expected from such a medieval world. This was not just an inn, but a hotel. It rose above the nearby buildings by at least ten floors with balconies on each level. Large open windows glowed welcomingly in the night, promises of reviving sleep drifting from the waving curtains.

Fallon led them to their rooms. "Fresh clothes will be here in the morning. Captain Boliver also reserved a room for Elken." She pointed to a door between the siblings' rooms. "The doctors say he will join us within the hour. You have impressed them, Jason." Her golden eyes were wide with admiration.

"Thank you, Fallon."

"I…will leave you to it." The froxil trotted down the hall.

Melanie stepped into her room. A bed stood in the middle, along with a side table, bathtub, and an open balcony behind white breezy curtains. The spacious room, the city view, and fluffy bedding made Melanie wonder if this was one of the city's wealthy areas. Sliding her hand along the edge of the vanity table, she lifted her head and looked at herself in the mirror.

The young woman in the silver glass gazed back with eyes framed in dark circles. Faint trails of old tears cut through the ashy film on her cheeks in dark stripes. Melanie didn't even want to think about her hair. Laughing incredulously, she walked to the bathtub.

After thirty minutes of the most grueling bathing routine ever, Melanie slipped into a silk robe with her hair brushed and towel-fluffed just as a knock came from the door.

"Come in," she said.

The door opened, but she only heard Jason's voice say, "I smell soap or something. You decent?"

Melanie's laugh came out as a sputter. "Yes. I *did* say 'come in.'"

Jason scanned her room, then took in her robe. "I still gotta bathe. I smell unholy."

"Oh…"—Melanie made a face—"lovely." With a laugh, she swatted at Jason with a towel. "Get out of here before you stink up my room! What have you been doing all this time?"

"I was helping Elken move in next door."

Melanie let the towel hang at her side. "Already?"

Jason nodded.

Melanie bit her lip. *What should I do? What can I say? The agony he endured…a simple "sorry" won't cut it.*

"It went right to his ribs, you know," she said softly.

"I know." Jason paused, then added, "Well, it has been a *day* for both of us, and it's ridiculously late, so I'll let you get to bed, Mel."

"Okay. Good night."

"'Night."

The door closed. Melanie walked over to the nightstand and opened one of the drawers to find a white sleeping gown. She changed out of her robe and slid into bed. Melanie immediately fell under the spell of the bed's softness. But as she settled into the mattress, she couldn't shake one thought.

How could Elken ever forgive me?

A soft knock came at the door.

"Melanie?" Elken whispered loudly from the other side.

Barely awake, Melanie stirred in her bed, unsure of where the sound was coming from. A band of light stretched across Melanie's room as the door opened.

"Melanie?" he whispered softly this time. "Are you awake?"

Melanie quickly recognized the voice and, frozen with guilt, pretended to be asleep. She still couldn't accept that she had caused him so much pain. *How can I face him?*

Elken softly entered with no intention of waking her up. Melanie appeared to be asleep. He drew her comforter up to cover her shoulders. When Melanie shifted, Elken leaned in close and whispered, "I forgive you." He kissed her cheek, then left, leaving it once again to the light of the stars.

Through tears of relief, Melanie opened her eyes and smiled.

When morning came, Melanie slipped on a yellow dress with a blue satin waistband and donned her sword. She even had proper shoes. Her old clothes—her last remnants of Earth—lay in a heap in the corner, worn beyond recognition.

With a deep breath, Melanie walked out into the hallway.

"Morning, Mel," Jason said brightly as he exited his suite. "Sleep well?"

"Are you serious?" Melanie laughed. "I don't think I've ever been more in love with a bed."

Jason smiled. "I know, right?"

Briefur stepped out of his own room across the hall. "You had better be well-rested. We still have a massive problem to deal with."

Melanie became aware of her heartlink. It beat warmly, a good sign. So far.

"Is Elken still sleeping?" Melanie asked.

"I think so. We should let him rest," Fallon replied. "He will join us when he wakes."

Passing a window on their walk downstairs to the dining area for breakfast, Melanie marveled at the magnificent architecture of Lakéthion. In the daylight, she could now see the shining, silvery stone with which the city had been built. The city's flag—a blue gem on a white background, surrounded with ornamental flourishes—waved in the calm wind from rooftops. The sun streamed between terraced buildings in golden beams.

"Beautiful," said a voice.

"Elken!" Melanie spun around. "I...I..."

Elken wore Lakéthionic garb, and the change had a positive effect on him. He appeared more relaxed and comfortable. For the first time since Melanie met him, he was clean, and she could see a faint scar stretching from the corner of his right eye to his temple.

"I...I..." Melanie didn't know what to say.

Elken said nothing either, but pulled her into a hug, proving his wound was indeed gone.

Despite hearing his apology last night, Melanie sobbed into his shirt. "I'm so sorry! For everything, my horrible aim, your suffering—please don't lose your trust in me!"

Elken looked into her eyes. "I forgive you, Melanie." He

curled a gentle finger under her chin. "And I've never lost faith in you. Your adamance and courage have reminded me of who I once was. You've been a light in my dark world and a gift I don't deserve."

Melanie blushed.

"Besides," Elken gave his signature dimpled smile, "I refuse to be slaughtered that easily. Least of all by an amateur."

"Oh, that's wonderful to hear," Melanie laughed as she wiped her tears away.

The sound was music to Elken, and he wanted to bring her close to him again. "I suppose that makes us even. I drop you into a volcano and you mortally wound me."

Melanie sniffed, then smiled. "I guess that's fair."

"Hey," Jason interrupted, "you guys are falling behind. And don't think I won't eat your breakfasts, because I can and will!"

The ground floor of The Silver Lining was a large white room with silver chandeliers hanging from the ceiling. Tables crafted from a rich, dark wood paired with the dark crown molding of the space. A fire blazed in the enormous silver hearth, and flecks of crystal speckled in the ivory tiled floor.

As soon as they found seats, blue-vested maids served them porridge topped with an amber syrup and plump purple berries that Melanie didn't recognize.

"Alright," Melanie began, "we need to get Scalaed and free Helnah's child-dragon army. What do we know about Helnah's weaknesses so far?"

"I've been mulling over my stay in the fortress," Jason said, "and from what I gather, she can only be in one of her bodies at a time. The transfer—or however the heck it works—induces a fatiguing episode."

"When I first saw her dragon self, she was completely still, so maybe the body she's not using is left frozen in time, with an impenetrable force field that only *Ilvir* can pierce," Melanie added.

"So you fly in, kill her, and free Scalaed?" Fallon asked, gesturing with a large sausage on her fork.

"It will not be that easy," Elken stated. "Helnah now knows Melanie can harm her. She will have more protection."

"Here's what I don't get." Melanie folded her hands. "If using the dragon is such a drain on Helnah's life, why hasn't she gotten rid of it?"

Elken inhaled. "It's a part of her, in a sense. Both bodies share the same consciousness, so she can't rid herself of it."

"Oh," Briefur said thoughtfully, "so we can destroy both of them at the same time. Kill the dragon, which kills Helnah."

"But she'll be more protected," Jason chimed as he focused on his scrambled eggs.

"We need another distraction." Briefur twirled his knife. "Something so large that Helnah will have no choice but to divert her dragons."

"But those dragons are the kingdom's children," Elken reminded him. "We cannot endanger them. They are the main mission."

No one had noticed the entire place had quieted until a man from another table stood up.

"Forgive my intrusion, but we couldn't help overhear your conversation. You say you know how to kill Helnah of Thornbrill?"

"Yes," Jason replied.

"Helnah stole our children!" another cried out, which caused an uproar as people rose to their feet.

The first man walked up. "We all crave revenge. If it's a distraction you need, we will give you one."

CHAPTER
30

Fire in the Sky

Word spread like wildfire. Crowds grew, and the entire city buzzed with excitement. While citizens volunteered for the attack, to deploy Lakéthion's army was by order of the king alone.

Followed by cheering droves, Melanie and her companions approached King Latthias's palace doors. The two guards stationed there crossed their halberds, understandably looking a little nervous.

"We will wait for your return," the first volunteer said. "Should the king need more convincing, have him look this way."

Melanie straightened, determination pumping through her veins, then walked up to the guards with her companions.

One guard asked, still eyeing the crowds, "Do you have a summons?"

"No, but we bring urgent news of Thornbrill that must reach His Majesty," Elken stated.

The guards exchanged looks and let them pass, but followed close behind. Down a corridor and through a grand pair of doors stood the throne room. Seeing the royal seat vacant, one of the guards excused himself, saying he would alert the king of their visit.

The royal room spanned a shimmering layout of silvery stone and crystal that sparkled in the white light from towering windows. Diamonds and gemstones twinkled from massive chandeliers, shooting flecks of rainbow around the room and speckling the navy blue carpet that stretched to the throne itself.

"Greetings," King Latthias said as he entered.

The five of them bowed, saying in unison, "Your Majesty."

Rising, Melanie straightened her posture. She folded her hands in front of her skirt, but her foot tapped nervously beneath. She cast a quick glance at Jason, who was attempting to keep the same level of formal composure. They were in the presence of a real king.

"I was told you bear urgent news?" Latthias raised his eyebrow.

"Sire." Melanie stepped forward. "We have come to discuss a plan of attack on Thornbrill."

"I applaud the notion and your bravery, dear lady." Latthias turned and sat heavily in his throne. "But I'm afraid a simple plea is not enough for me to condone such an enterprise."

Elken approached the king, unshaken and determined. "My companions and I have found a way to kill Helnah, Your Majesty, but we need Lakéthion's troops to accomplish it."

"My king," Jason pleaded, "this attack would not only bestow fame and glory upon your name, but free your city's children from Helnah's possession! Think of your people, who stand outside your door in high hopes you grant this endeavor not only to free this world of Helnah's scourge, but also to restore their lives!"

"The people have spoken, and something tells me they will march on with or without your consent," Melanie added. "A parent will do anything for their child."

"Your choice is whether or not they march alone," Briefur finished.

King Latthias stood and descended to his audience. "Many kingdoms have tried. All have failed. What makes your plan different than theirs?"

"My king," Elken began, "we have two Indomitable Glass swords which are the only weapons that can kill Helnah. There's a lot to explain, Your Majesty, but not much time. Now is the chance to stop her before she conspires a new way of destroying our kingdoms. Provide your military support, and we can draw Helnah out with that distraction while a smaller team is sent to kill her."

"An army is also needed to take care of the dragons," Jason added. "Once Helnah is dead, her dragon army will disband, and we will need a force to bring them in."

"Bring them in?" Latthias raised an eyebrow.

"Well, Sire," Jason replied, a little nervously, "Helnah has been using your children as weapons. They *are* her dragon army."

King Latthias paled—not in fear or shock, but in wrath. His jaw flexed as his heavy brows lowered on widening eyes. Melanie found the sudden silence chilling.

"So you demand we go to war against our own children?"

he asked, his voice low and eerily calm.

"Helnah controls them with her mind, and we must separate her from their protection," Fallon said.

"There is a way to tell them apart, Your Majesty, so as not to harm them," Jason answered.

"Helnah's forces comprise natural-born dragons and poisoned children," Melanie said. "Wild dragons have four legs while the children have two."

"We had our own confrontation with some of the dragons and found the differentiation effective," Elken confirmed.

"Can they be saved?" King Latthias asked, hiding the emotion that threatened to crack his voice.

"I have faith I can find a cure, Your Majesty," Jason answered. He felt Elken eye him skeptically. "Nonetheless, they will be in better care back with their people than in the unforgiving volcano they've been forced to reside in."

King Latthias looked at each of them carefully, then nodded. "Go," he commanded, "and tear that kingdom down."

While the army assembled, Melanie, Jason, and Elken received Lakéthionic armor. Back in her hotel room, Melanie held the breastplate out in front of her and realized she had no idea how to put it on. She tried to draw ideas from movies she'd watched and hoped she was doing it right. Thankfully, most of the donning was self-explanatory, but she had to improvise in a few areas. She grabbed her sword, preparing to tie it around her waist, when the sudden reality of battle hit her. She stopped and stared at the weapon.

"You won't be alone," said Elken.

Melanie spun around, eyes wide and hand over her heart. "Sneaking up on me?"

Elken stepped inside, smirking. "Apparently so."

"So you've been watching me put this armor on, most likely incorrectly, and you said nothing?" Melanie put her hand on her hip, awaiting his response.

Elken lowered his chin and laughed.

"Look at you, laughing at a poor alien doing her best," Melanie teased. "You clearly know how to do this, look at the awesome job you did!"

Elken wore armor like Melanie's—a steel breastplate emblazoned with Lakéthion's crest and matching plates covering his arms and legs. He looked prouder than before, like a great weight had finally been lifted. He looked ready to fight, and he continued laughing as he walked over to her. "Forgive me, my alien. I will assess the damage."

"Thank you." Melanie held out her arms as Elken tightened and realigned a few straps.

"Consider tying your hair back," he suggested. "Minimize the hazard."

"Or I could cut it, like those female main characters in m—"

"Oh, please don't!" Elken pressed a leather hair tie in her

hand before she could finish. "That would be a tragedy. Your hair is so lovely."

Melanie blushed as she gathered her hair into the tie. "I wasn't serious."

"Then I believe you are ready." Elken stood up and admired her.

"Thank you so much, Elken." Melanie sighed in relief.

"Well, we couldn't very well have you invade Thornbrill falling out of your armor, could we?"

Melanie bent over in laughter.

"Teetering across the battlefield, shedding metal bits… ridiculous!" Elken shook his head as Melanie tried to compose herself, then added, "Oh, I wanted to give you this." He held up a ring with a ruby embedded in the center. "This was my mother's."

Melanie stopped laughing. Her brain seemed to malfunction.

"Let me tell you a story." Elken took her hand, and they sat down on the windowsill. "Many years ago, in the city of Yolderain, lived two girls. Nyvelle and Luciana. They were the best of friends. Inseparable. As a token of their friendship and sisterhood, they gave each other rings. Identical in all ways but the center stone. Luciana's bore a pearl, and Nyvelle's"—Elken held up the ring—"had a ruby. Years passed, and the girls grew up and found husbands. Soon after, Nyvelle gave birth to a strapping baby boy, and the world was perfect."

Melanie narrowed her eyes and smiled. "Was it you?"

"I have no idea what you mean. Now hush." Elken winked.

"As I said, their baby boy was the light of their life, and no one could have been happier."

Melanie smiled as she tried to envision baby Elken, but the expression faded when Elken stopped speaking. His expression darkened, and his voice was grim.

"One day, feral forces of the desert attacked, and the city caught fire. My mother Nyvelle never spoke of it, for it was the last time she ever saw Luciana. Her friend's husband perished, and Luciana was last seen in their burning home, crying out after him."

Melanie softly gasped at the dark turn of the tale.

"Years later, after my parents died, I found this ring and have kept it ever since. It is far too small for me to wear, but perhaps it will fit you."

Melanie smiled sadly as Elken placed the ring in her hand.

"Elken, I…Thank you," she said.

When she looked back up, she found they were much closer than a moment ago.

Elken noticed, too. He stroked her hair behind her ear and caressed her cheek, like he had in the Maze, and the two of them leaned closer. Melanie's lashes fluttered, making Elken's heartbeat thunder. Their noses nearly touched.

Jason barged into the room and froze with an embarrassed wince, and lifted a feeble thumb over his shoulder. "Um…the army is getting ready to leave."

"Right," Melanie stammered, needlessly brushing off her legs.

Elken cleared his throat as he helped Melanie to her feet. "We best be off, then."

They headed for the military stables—an expansive square courtyard next to the castle that was lined with over a hundred stalls. In the middle stood the horse armory, a gray brick building that stored the riding tack and armor. Leading a horse in each hand, a horse master approached Melanie and Elken and assigned them their steeds. Meanwhile Jason approached three laughing guards.

"She won't come down, lad," one guard told Jason.

Poison Ivy was quite content sunbathing atop a tower roof, taunting them with a flick of her tongue. Captain Boliver had notified the city guard to not shoot her down, so she took it as the opportunity to ignore Jason's orders and stalk him through the city from the sky. And she had no interest in coming any closer.

"Pi, get down here, this is really important!" Jason commanded.

The dragon snorted in defiance.

"I have an idea!" A fourth guard approached, swinging a roast chicken on a spear. His comrades laughed harder as he waved the spear at Poison Ivy, who leaped to the ground without hesitation.

"Well done, Aleth," another guard laughed as the four departed for their troop.

Jason shook his head as Poison Ivy shredded her meal. "You're a piece of work, you know that?"

Poison Ivy's only response was swallowing the rest of the

chicken whole.

After fitting Poison Ivy with a saddle, Jason mounted and joined Melanie and Elken in the cavalry. Teams of horses fell in line behind them, pulling what looked like long flatbed trailers. Half were stacked with enormous shields, and the others carried launchers for bolas. With the grave reality of battling their own children, the army stocked up on non-fatal options. But two trailers in the rear creaked with the weight of twelve ballistas. Those were for the wild dragons. Hundreds of hooves clattered on the cobblestone as they marched out of the compound and into the city.

Citizens leaned out their windows shouting goodbyes. Young loves threw their handkerchiefs to their knights. Mothers and sisters threw flowers. Many faces were wet with tears.

"A month is a long time to be gone." Aleth sighed as he pressed his beau's handkerchief to his lips.

Melanie and Jason snapped their heads up.

"I'm sorry, a *month?*" Melanie asked.

Aleth nodded. "With all this weight, and once the infantry joins us at the city gates, it will be a two week march to Thornbrill."

Jason's stomach sank. Poison Ivy and Laena were able to cross the distance in mere hours. He saw Melanie's expression and knew she was thinking the same.

"Scalaed is going to be alone with Helnah for two weeks!" Her voice shook, and the dread seeped into the heartlink. She felt Scalaed's hope deflate. *Be strong, Scalaed!* she told him as the cavalry merged with the infantry at the city gates. A force of three hundred men, one hundred and fifty horses, and five trailers of heavy artillery, the whole army began marching east.

Briefur and Fallon tracked the scent through the Trellin Forest, sniffing the air and a few branches. After marching for three days, they were near enough to Hvitria to summon an Avis Messenger. Briefur sat on his haunches and closed his eyes. Fallon copied him. While they didn't possess telepathy, the telepathic blue jays should be able to hear their thoughts if close enough and appear to receive their message. Telepathy was a guaranteed form of secrecy that no spy could intercept.

A few seconds later, a blue jay landed in front of Briefur's paws.

Hail, Briefur, son of Brefiüll, and Fallon, daughter of Freign! What message can my talents bear in haste?

Briefur replied through the secrecy of his mind. *Send this message to the White Chief: The fall of Thornbrill is at hand, and we request aid to liberate the kingdoms' children.*

The bird bowed. *Truly, this is the greatest message I have ever received. Let there be no doubt, at my glorious speed, it will reach the chief's ears before the next hour ends.*

Thank you, Briefur thought.

The bird asked, *And what shall be my reward for this deed?*

Fallon sighed. *The usual, Ziyar. See my mother for your precious butter.*

Were the nuts plucked in the light of the full moon? Ziyar verified.

Fallon tried to conceal her annoyance. *Yes, yes, and exactly twenty nuts were harvested and only prepared in the rays of dawn, we know.*

Ziyar was quite pleased at this. *It is most important the butter adheres to those rules religiously, for it pours blessings upon me—*

The nut butter has nothing to do with your abilities, Ziyar, and you know it, Briefur growled. *Now deliver this message immediately!*

The blue jay stopped, apologized, and bid them farewell.

The army had been marching for a week. A grim air settled in the compound as they set up camp for the night.

Jason leaned against Poison Ivy, the black gloom of the impending battle weighing him down.

"Are you alright?"

"Geez, Fallon!" Jason flinched. "You scared me, sneaking up like that!"

"I'm sorry!" The froxil reddened and tightened her grip on her satchel. "You just looked so weary."

"I've never been in a real battle before." Jason's gaze was distant. "It's all been games before."

Fallon stood in front of him, a hand on one of her knife hilts. "Would you like me to teach you some fighting techniques?"

"I'm sure I'll lose a hand." Jason managed a small smile.

Fallon returned the smile as she pulled out two wooden poles from her satchel. "We should be safe with these." She handed them to Jason.

Jason moved to Fallon's side as she demonstrated how best to hold the knife and how to find its balance. Adjusting his grip, he followed her directions to strike her. Fallon lifted her own pair of dummy knives and explained the defense. Together, they cycled through attacks from every angle and the correlating defense. The motions came naturally to Jason, and Fallon beamed at her student's aptitude.

Melanie watched from a distance, placing the final basket of potatoes in the cook's tent. Nausea swirled in her stomach. Her brother was going to be in an army, and her dragon lay in a cramped cage in the claws of a monster. Melanie sat on a log and focused on the heartlink in the search of some comfort. Scalaed's heartbeat fluttered happily on the other end.

How are you, buddy? Melanie asked.

The heartlink pulsed in a pattern, explaining how Helnah's dragon form had been dormant for eight days. Scalaed assumed this was from being drained the last time she embodied the dragon. Helnah must be taking a long time to recover, so he had been spared so far. This was a relief to

Melanie. Maybe Helnah would stay weakened by the time they reached the fortress.

The army arrived in Tharretill fifteen days after leaving Lakéthion, and Melanie and Jason sat anxiously among lieutenants and captains in the large blue tent in the center of camp.

Elken entered, accompanied by a man in uniform. He had a hardened look, a prominent chin grayed from stubble, narrow eyes, and streaked hair drawn back in a ponytail. His broad shoulders were held back as he scanned everyone in the tent.

"I am General Lingolm," the man said in a deep voice. "I will be coordinating this diversion. The army will poise itself to strike the fortress. Helnah will dispatch her dragons to attack before we reach the fortress. Two-legged beasts are wyverns. They are also our children. We shoot to *down* the wyverns, not kill. Counterattack with bolas and nets. Four-legged dragons are wild animals. Eliminate them with the ballistas and javelin launchers. While we occupy Helnah, Melanie will infiltrate the Arfire Maze, retrieve her dragon, and kill Helnah's dragon form with the Indomitable Glass sword. The rest of our forces will be on the main front. Once Helnah is dead, we will separate the poisoned children from the natural dragons. Chief Helmir of the Hündr is en route to help us wrangle that task."

Melanie looked around at her companions, agreement written on all their faces.

"Whenever you are ready, Melanie," Lingolm finished.

Melanie couldn't believe it was time already. But the very thought of being reunited with Scalaed fueled her body. The heartlink pounded in anticipation. She took a deep breath as everyone wished her the best of luck.

"I'll be back in time for the finale," she said.

She rustled Jason's hair, much to his embarrassment, and left the tent.

After giving a few more notes on the upcoming battle, General Lingolm called for everyone to move out.

Jason took a deep breath and stood up, his hands shaking. *What if something goes wrong?* The plan seemed solid enough. And they had their Abrielstones. He had no reason to be afraid.

Jason patted his knives which were sheathed on either side of his waist, then walked out. Poison Ivy was tethered outside the tent. She shook her head in greeting.

Jason mounted Poison Ivy and rode her through the forest towards Thornbrill. An ivory horn bounced by his side, and he squeezed it tightly. When he emerged from the treeline, he inhaled deeply, and the Lakéthion army fanned out behind him. Soldiers drew their swords with an echoing whoosh. Horses stomped the ground as their knights hefted lances. Swordsmen were mounted behind them, wielding the great shields to cover the horses from dragon fire. Blue banners were hoisted high, armor shone in the sunlight, and the determined figures of soldiers and horses obscured the entire treeline. The thunderous sound of clanging metal, boots, and hooves shook the trees.

The army stopped with a final thud. Poison Ivy did as well, and she sensed her rider's anxiety. Jason put the horn to his lips and blew. The sound echoed throughout the forest and inside the Fortress of Thornbrill.

Poison Ivy reared and roared loudly with the deafening war cry of the army. Jason kept blowing, hoping this plan would work.

"Helnah!" Thendrell cried as he burst into the throne room without so much as a bow. "Lakéthion is upon us!"

Helnah raised her head from her hand. "Lakéthion dares to approach *us?* Whatever has possessed them?"

"It is beyond me," Thendrell said, "but the boy is with them."

Helnah's mouth warped into a sneer. "Jason…His sister is with him, no doubt, in a feeble attempt to rescue her pet. It matters not. Prepare for battle." Helnah stood from her throne, but collapsed.

Thendrell caught her. "Helnah, you are in no shape to fight! Elthar says you need more time to recover."

"I've already wasted weeks recovering when I should

be breaking that Pyrium Dragon!" Helnah cried. "Time is running out."

"Just stop for a moment!" Thendrell said, forcibly sitting her down. "Whatever you're striving for, you can't do alone."

Helnah locked eyes with his blue ones. *Does he know? There is no way he could.*

"You need help, Helnah," Thendrell pleaded.

Helnah looked out the window at Tildain's Chasm, pondering. *Help...*

"Station the archers," she said, a plan forming in her mind.

Thendrell bowed stiffly and turned around, his blue cape swirling around him. He ran out, leaving Helnah alone in her room once again.

"These aliens have the full support of Lakéthion," she whispered. "No king I know would sacrifice his people for a plan all have tried and all have failed. What are you planning, Jason, you little wretch?"

Meanwhile, Thendrell readied the archers and positioned them all along the parapets, including the watchtowers. Fifty men lined the main floor, their blue capes billowing in the mountain wind. Five more encircled the tops of each tower flanking the fortress.

He shouted to the archers as he walked along the edge, "Shoot straight, show no mercy." He pointed at Keth among the archers. "You...go into the Maze and make sure the girl gets nowhere near that Pyrium."

"Yes, sir," Keth said. "Her mission is futile, if you ask me."

"I didn't," Thendrell said, turning his back on him.

Keth bowed and dashed back inside the fortress.

Thendrell shouted to his archers, "The army of Lakéthion has come to us and will fall like the ones before."

In perfect unison, sixty archers nocked arrows and waited. For a brief moment, there was only the sound of wind and creaking bow limbs. Thendrell pointed at Jason far below. "Kill him."

Arrows descended on Jason and those around him. His breath hitched, and he clutched his Abrielstone, heart pounding. Poison Ivy spewed an arc of fire that incinerated the wave before it hit. Jason could only hope Helnah and her men were solely focused on the army, and that none had seen Melanie.

The archers reloaded their bows. "Fire at will!" Thendrell shouted.

More arrows rained down on the army, but the swordsmen and knights held high their shields in protection.

Elken sat on his horse next to Lingolm. Both drew swords, pointed them towards Thornbrill, and the general shouted, "Lakéthion, attack!"

The horses took off, riders shouting as they charged. Jason's heart pounded in sync with the storm of hooves. This was it. *Come on, Helnah, release the kids. Then you'll meet your doom.*

Helnah watched out her window as the army closed in. *What madness is this?* It would be so simple to set her dragon army upon them. Victory would take mere moments. Scoffing, Helnah returned to her throne. She leaned back into her seat and closed her eyes, reaching out with her mind to the dragons.

Melanie cranked back the lever to open the Iron Gates just as the volcano's peak erupted with hundreds of dragons. Screaming wind from their wings rolled down the mountainside. Roars bellowed overhead, and Melanie watched the steady stream of beasts for only a moment before entering the Arfire Maze. She drew *Ilvir*. She knew where to find Scalaed, but she only had minutes to do it.

"What do we have here?" asked Keth as he entered the light of the gateway.

Melanie planted her feet as she lifted her sword in anticipation.

Keth drew his own sword and sliced it towards Melanie.

To their shock, Melanie parried his blade with a shower of sparks. Keth blinked and tried again but Melanie deflected the blow effortlessly.

A faint voice in Melanie's head said, "Use this." She felt new power flow through her arms and tactics fill her brain. A smile played across her lips, and Keth wavered. She slashed and swung, bringing her blade down with relentless strength. Keth found it impossible to keep up, and every attack significantly damaged his own sword. In desperation, he shoved Melanie toward the wall.

She stumbled and braced to hit it. To her surprise, she simply passed through and landed on her back in the next empty chamber.

It happened again! Melanie thought. She looked at her feet; they were still inside the wall.

Stunned, Keth yelled, "Where have you gone?"

Both fascinated and confused, Melanie reached out to grab the wall. Her hand floated through it like a hologram.

I need to get Scalaed, she reminded herself. Standing up, Melanie stepped out of the wall and shouted, "Hey!"

Taken aback, Keth opened his mouth in alarm. Melanie spun around and, with a flying kick, sent Keth tumbling into the stone wall. He hit his head and lay limply in a heap.

Melanie sheathed *Ilvir.* She had a dragon to find, and fast.

The army of Lakéthion held up their swords and shields, and stood their ground as the dragons descended upon them, mouths blazing. Troops banded together as thick yellow flames rained down on their massive interlocked shields. Smoke and blood stung noses. Bolas twirled through the spark-filled air, entangling wyvern wings and bringing them down with a mighty crash. Ballistas screeched as they launched barbed lances from behind shields, skewering dragon hides. The Thornbrillians atop the parapets eased off their assault to observe the battle with twisted eagerness. Roars and howls, shouts and screams shattered the air. The battle had begun.

CHAPTER
31
Final Attempt

Thendrell entered the throne room once again. He saw Helnah seated in her throne, head bowed and eyes clamped shut. Her nails crunched into the arm rests as her mind grappled with the wills of her dragon army.

"What do you think you're doing, Helnah?" he demanded angrily. "Your strength—"

"Oh, do shut up, Thendrell!" Helnah spat. At that moment, Keth stumbled into the throne room. Seeing his battered state, Helnah stiffened. "Explain yourself."

Keth winced at her words that lashed out like a whip. "I was bested in combat."

"Combat with whom?" Thendrell asked.

Keth flinched. "The girl, sir," he struggled.

Helnah suddenly stood inches from Keth. "And how is this possible?"

"She is a warrior, trained by the best no doubt. A master of invisibility too, it would seem. I did my best!"

Helnah slowly tilted her head, anger radiating from her face. "Your best?"

Keth's mouth dried.

"Your best was not enough if she lived." Nostrils flared,

Helnah leaned into Keth's ear, hissing, "I have no words to express my disappointment."

"Please, forgive—" Keth's plea was cut short as Helnah thrust a knife into his neck.

Thendrell stepped back. "Helnah!" It was the first time her fury resulted in a kill of her own.

She ignored his alarm as she watched Keth's blood trickle down the blade and drip over her fingers. Keth's body dropped to the floor. Expressionless, Helnah wiped her hand on his cloak.

"Our time is up." Helnah lifted her head. "Thendrell, you are in command now." She stormed down the carpet, but Thendrell knew what was going through her mind.

He ran up behind her. "You cannot do this."

"This is the only way to win this battle," she replied calmly.

"Helnah..." Thendrell grasped her shoulder and spun her around. He stared at her square in the eyes. "You barely survived last time. Please, rethink your decision."

"My mind is made up. I will not lose today."

Thendrell watched distantly as she continued to her room.

Helnah slammed the door behind her. She looked around her room, then at her bed. This might be the last time she saw it. Lying down on the mattress, Helnah rested her hands on her stomach. All that she had worked for came down to this. Helnah squeezed her eyes shut and left her human body for good.

Melanie sprinted through the black halls to Helnah's lair. When she peeked in, she saw Scalaed still in his cage, barely visible behind the stone and beneath the frozen bulk of Helnah's dragon body.

Joy exploded through the heartlink, and Scalaed roared with excitement.

"Scalaed!" Melanie cried. She gripped *Ilvir* with both hands and sliced through the thick stone limbs, along with several of Helnah's claws.

Scalaed shook his head and burst out of his cage, colliding into Melanie's embrace.

"Scalaed!" Melanie cried, gasping in relief. "Oh, I missed you so much! I'm here now, it's okay, you're okay."

Scalaed nudged her with his head, whining softly. It really had been so simple for Melanie to free him. And it had only taken mere moments.

When he told this to Melanie, she backed up with an incredulous look. "Did you not see how many dragons were in here? And Elken was dying because of *me*. I had to get him out."

Scalaed snapped. He could have gone with her.

"Now's not the time to talk about this," Melanie said and reoriented the beat-up saddle. "Let's put an end to this monster."

She returned her attention to Helnah and, not moving her gaze, mounted Scalaed. Anger boiled inside her. The massive dragon was still frozen. *Such an easy kill.*

"This is for everything you've done," Melanie hissed as she raised *Ilvir.* "You deserve nothing less than death."

Helnah's eyes blinked. With a shudder, the dragon came alive and screamed at Melanie and Scalaed. Helnah lunged at them, and Scalaed blasted Helnah in the face. Clawing through the air, a frantic Scalaed escaped with Melanie through the top of the volcano, despite Melanie's pleas to go back.

"This mountain cannot hold me!" Helnah shrieked from below. "I will destroy you!"

The sky was ablaze with dragon fire. Columns of smoke and ash burned the air. The sun was setting, and it looked like the sky was burning. A dragon swooped down and breathed fire in Jason's direction. Pi held up her wings to shield him.

"Elken!" Jason screamed. "Is Helnah dead yet?"

"No!" Elken screamed back, "she's still controlling the dragons!"

Jason cursed under his breath. The army of men and horses wavered under the relentless onslaught of dragons and wyverns. The beasts outnumbered Lakéthion two to one and had begun to free the downed wyverns. Formations began to break, and Jason feared all would be lost.

Stamping the ground, Poison Ivy started to take off.

"Pi! No, hey!" Jason shouted. "We have to stay down! Pi, no!" *Where's Scalaed when you need him?*

Poison Ivy bucked Jason off her back. Jason flipped over her head and landed on the ground. Poison Ivy approached him, and she looked angry.

"Oh no," Jason gasped. "Pi, girl, listen, ignore Helnah, please just focus on me. Poison Ivy! Stop!" Jason backed away. "Ivy, stop!" His dragon kept inching closer, her teeth now bared. Jason pleaded, "Ivy, don't! Please!"

Aleth slammed into Poison Ivy, disrupting her approach. Reeling back, she opened her mouth and bit his head off. Then she spread her wings and joined the other dragons.

Jason cursed loudly and flicked out his knives. A gray dragon noticed and careened toward him. Jason shouted in defiance. The beast inhaled and sent a stream of fire in his direction and Jason dove out of the way. He scrambled for a fallen shield, feeling the explosions behind him and the ground vibrating from the impact. Strapping it to his back, he gripped his blades tightly and ran past other soldiers and spooked horses. He could hear the dragon's deep ragged breathing behind him and the screams and neighs from the forces it trampled in its stampede. Jason had to find cover. He felt the heat intensify as the dragon sent blast after blast, intent on his death.

Just when Jason felt like he was escaping the hands of death after all, a red wyvern landed in front of him. Jason screamed and instinctively held up his knives to protect himself on impact. Jason felt his knives sink into the wyvern's flesh and saw them sticking out of a black diamond scar. The wyvern screamed a little boy's cry. Jason's stomach churned, and his fingers let go of his blades.

The gray dragon loomed behind him, flanked by four friends with mouths open and blazing

A blinding blanket of fire far bigger than any before it streaked above him and hit the dragons. Disoriented, and with nowhere else to go, the dragons flew back to the Iron Gates.

Scalaed landed next to Jason with a loud thud. Atop his back, Melanie reached out her hand. "We gotta go! Helnah is coming!"

She pulled him up to sit behind her, and Scalaed roared loudly, shaking Lakéthion's forces around them and grabbing their attention.

"Fall back!" Melanie yelled.

"Regroup!" Jason yelled more loudly. "On the double, let's go!"

Looks of confusion turned to fear as the mountains shook and rumbled the earth beneath their feet.

"It won't take Helnah long to break out of there," Melanie said as Scalaed flew back to camp, Lakéthion's army following suit.

A horn blared throughout the Lakéthion camp.

"Chief Helmir," Briefur said.

The White Chief entered the camp with his Hündr forces and dozens of wagons carrying supplies. Lakéthion was far too busy to greet the Hündr properly. Men rushed around with weapons to sharpen, injuries to tend, and vengeance on their minds. And every passing minute brought a quake signaling Helnah's arrival neared.

Elken galloped up to Scalaed and leaped from his horse, eyes locked onto Melanie. "You found him!"

"Yes, but Helnah's still alive." Melanie slipped off Scalaed's back.

Elken leveled himself with her. "But so are you. And we're going to end this."

Scalaed snorted, demanding a proper introduction, and Melanie obliged.

Amidst the bustle of men falling back into ranks, Brefiüll led Poison Ivy to Jason as he dismounted. "She was searching for you," he explained.

Jason stroked Poison Ivy's nose. She lowered her head, and Jason sensed her remorse. "It wasn't your fault. You were being controlled." Poison Ivy rested her head on Jason's shoulder, and he leaned against her neck. He looked out into Helmir's troops, and someone caught his attention.

"Your dragon wasn't all we found." Helmir turned around.

The chief's wife brought out from under her cloak a little boy around eight with blond hair. Although he wore a pelt vest and britches like the Hündr, he was clearly human. The little boy shyly stepped forward, only to see even more people and slip back and hide inside the chieftainess's cloak.

Jason made a choking sound, and Melanie saw he was a little pale.

"Do you know him?" she asked.

The chieftainess gently pulled the boy to her front and held him close.

Jason nodded. Everything else blurred. The tremors and troops faded, everything but this boy. He remembered him in the dungeons, his little voice. He had been a dragon in the Maze, running around blindly, and had jumped into the lava. The same dragon had jumped in front of Jason during the battle.

"But...how?" He knelt down, staring at the boy's bandage across his chest.

The boy whimpered, and Jason knew he recognized him as the one who stabbed him. "I know, I know, and I'm so sorry." The child was probably scared of him.

The boy sniffed and scratched his bandage. A little tear dropped onto his nose as he whispered, "I'm not scared." Then, he held out his little arms and hugged Jason as he began to cry. "Thank you."

Jason wrapped his arms around the boy and, unable to find a response, felt tears fill his own eyes.

Elken recognized the boy and was equally as shocked as Jason.

"What's going on?" Melanie asked him softly.

Elken whispered back, "He was...he used to be a dragon."

Melanie watched Jason say something to the boy, who hugged Jason more tightly. Standing with the boy in his arms, Jason explained, "Wren doesn't know how he changed back, but I promised to take him home after the battle."

A stronger quake rocked the camp, and Jason hastily handed the boy to a nurse. "Keep him safe, understand?"

Chief Helmir approached Elken. "Hvitria will provide relief for the other children once we free them."

"Thank you, my friend." Elken shook his hand.

Lingolm ran up to them from the medical tent, blood-streaked and wild-eyed. "If Helnah is coming, our weapons will do nothing."

"He's right." Melanie looked around at the sea of anxious faces. "Elken and I have the only weapons that can kill her. It's no use joining us if you can't hurt her."

The quakes quickened, and shouts of alarm rose from the compound.

"What of our children?" a soldier cried, others calling out in support.

"Plans change!" Lingolm snapped. "We can do nothing so long as they are enslaved. Killing Helnah is our only course of action."

"You will get your kids back, I promise!" Jason assured them.

Another earthquake shook the earth, and the sound of splitting rock echoed from a distance, and everyone fell to the ground. A cold gust of wind blew through the army, carrying the scent of death.

"She's here," Melanie breathed.

A deafening roar blared throughout the forest, and Melanie and Jason looked at each other.

No longer curled in her cave, Helnah was far larger than anyone had expected. Her ashy black body loomed over the forest, standing tall and terrifying. Her eyes glowed white and her wings stretched over the treetops.

Helnah's eyes latched onto Melanie with murderous intent. Her mouth glowed white-hot with liquid light streaming from her jaws. With a wrathful roar, she dove towards Melanie.

"No!" Without hesitation, Elken stepped between the monster and Melanie and hurled *Clavnir*.

The sword sparkled as it spun straight into Helnah's chest. She roared so loudly that all present covered their ears. Helnah whipped her tail around, scattering the army and sending Melanie and Scalaed tumbling across the battlefield, separating them. Helnah shoved her head in Elken's direction, and he retreated for the cover of the trees.

A huge explosion blasted on Helnah's head. When the smoke cleared, Elken saw Scalaed and Poison Ivy rain fire upon Helnah. Circling the monstrous dragon, Scalaed and his new ally sent stream after stream of fire. With Helnah distracted, Scalaed swooped down and pulled Melanie onto his back.

"Get me close to her," Melanie ordered as she poised to strike.

Scalaed dove toward Helnah, and Melanie drove her sword as hard as she could into Helnah's heart. Now two Indomitable Glass swords were sunk to their hilts, sliding down, cutting open the wound like it was melting wax.

Helnah spun around, wailing, and in a final attempt, clawed for Elken loading his bow under a tree and swept him off his feet. Melanie's heart stopped as he flipped through the air and vanished over the edge of Tildain's Chasm.

With a bloodcurdling shriek, Helnah dropped dead. Her body thudded against the ground, vibrating the earth. Her dragon body twisted and deflated in coils of smoke and sludge.

Ignoring the fallen dragon, Melanie screamed and ran to the edge of the cliff, "Elken! No!"

The cliff was a hundred-foot drop. Mist and fog blanketed the bottom, veiling any sign of Elken. Melanie crumpled, losing all feeling in her limbs, and screamed into the earth.

When Melanie looked back up in a daze, she felt disconnected from the world around her, oblivious to how much time had passed. Someone helped her to her feet. She heard nothing. She said nothing. She felt nothing. Everything was a haze. She found herself walking alongside Hündr as she was guided back to camp. Melanie barely noticed Jason when he rushed to her side, asking questions she could not hear and holding hands she could not feel. She saw his face, and a tear trickled down her cheek. Melanie felt herself being lifted up and carried. Jason brought her to a large tent and laid her delicately on a bed. She stared at the ceiling, her world spinning as it fell apart, for Elken was gone.

CHAPTER
32

The Visitor

No one bothered Melanie unless they had to. Jason watched her sit on the edge of her bed, staring at a ring. When he asked her about it, Melanie simply gave him a sad look, and Jason realized it was from Elken.

"He proposed?" he asked, shocked.

Then he was kicked out. Apparently, that was the wrong thing to ask.

The army remained stationed in the forest. Lingolm said that it was only a matter of time before news of Helnah's death reached the Thornbrillians' ears. Without a leader, they would be forced to surrender. And without Helnah, the dragon children were free. So Lakéthion waited.

Being bored was one of Jason's least favorite activities. So he walked into Melanie's tent with a tray of food. "Mel?" he asked.

She didn't look up from her hands or say anything. She didn't even acknowledge his presence. Jason continued anyway, placing the food next to her. "Melanie, you have to eat something. You haven't eaten since yesterday morning before the battle. That's one breakfast, two lunches, and soon to be two dinners you will have missed. Please, eat something!"

Melanie's eyes crept toward the food, then back to her hands.

Jason groaned, "Melanie! Elken wouldn't want you to sulk in a dingy tent. That won't help you or anyone else."

A tear dropped from Melanie's cheek.

Shaking his head, Jason plopped down next to her. After a long silence, he put his hand on Melanie's shoulder. "Please eat, Mel. Elken wouldn't want you to wither away to nothing."

Melanie looked at the plate, then reluctantly took an apple.

Jason bit his lip and left the tent with, "He was wearing his Abrielstone, right? So maybe there's hope."

Melanie watched him walk to his own tent as the familiar fingers of distrust dug into her heart. *Then why haven't they found him?* She bit into her apple and lay back on her bed. The memory of Elken sitting with her by the window made her eyes burn with tears. His soft caress...the kiss that never came... Lifting her hand, she extended her fingers and watched her ring glitter in the light of the flickering candle by her bedside. It was all she had left of Elken.

Melanie hadn't realized she'd fallen asleep until she woke up from rolling off her cot. The quiet darkness of night filled her tent. Her candle had burned to a stump, and was already starting to fade as it ran out of wick.

Melanie stood up and peeked outside her tent. Scalaed snoozed outside the doorway, and guards were stationed around the perimeter of the camp on the lookout for any Thornbrillians riding in with a white flag.

Melanie crept behind the tent, avoiding Scalaed, and scurried past an unsuspecting guard. She was alone in the forest with the stars. Quickening her pace, Melanie broke into a run. She felt sobs rising, constricting her throat, and she ran blindly through the woods until she unexpectedly arrived at Tildain's Chasm. She fell to her knees, but her cries were no more than suffocated chokes in the darkness.

A soft hand stroked her hair. Melanie looked over her shoulder and saw Empress Elethýna. She seemed to glow, lighting up the air around her. The Empress smiled with such purity and warmth, yet Melanie could see in her eyes sympathy and sadness. Extending her arms, Elethýna beckoned for her.

Melanie stood, and the Empress's presence cast a wave of calm over her. Elethýna gently held Melanie's chin and said sweetly, "My dear, set it free."

Something inside Melanie released. All her pain and her tears poured forth, and she surrendered to Elethýna's embrace.

Both sank to the ground as Melanie cried. Not quiet, shaky sobs, but loud, messy cries filled with pain, anger, and sorrow. Cries that made her weak and her face hot. Cries that had built up and been held back for far too long.

Enveloped in overwhelming comfort, Melanie felt like she had known Elethýna for years. She felt safe and loved.

Cries turned to sniffling, and Melanie felt herself coming back to life. She breathed in deeply, and the mental suffocation lifted. Her sadness remained, but Melanie now bore it more easily. Standing, she wiped her eyes and looked up at Elethýna. The Empress smiled again, and Melanie whispered, "Thank you."

"Your tears were not made to be stifled." Elethýna combed back Melanie's hair. "They must be released before you drown." Rising, Elethýna helped Melanie to her feet.

"Why are you here?" Melanie asked her.

"You needed closure, my dear one, and it pains me to see you in sorrow."

"The one time I finally let down all my walls…" Melanie sniffed, "…the one time I actually allow myself to trust, to fall in love, Elken is taken away from me. Why? Why did he have to die?"

"Everything that happens is for a reason. There is always something good that blooms from it."

"What good things? How can something good come from someone's death? From someone's suffering?"

"Faith," Elethýna replied. "Faith forged in the face of adversity conquers all. Faith in knowing good triumphs over evil, and that the forces of good are the most powerful. You shall find this faith, my dear, but for now you must focus on your place in the task at hand."

"And what exactly *is* the task at hand?"

The Empress answered, "When I sent Scalaed to your world, I knew he would return with the Descendant of Light.

The one who is foretold in the Spire's Scroll."

"But Scalaed brought two: me and Jason. Which one of us is it?"

"You both have powers," Elethýna said, "abilities granted to you by someone you will soon meet. The answer to your question lies in the Spire's Scroll."

Melanie looked at her quizzically. "Where is it? And what do you call everything we just did? Sounds like we already saved the day."

Elethýna caressed Melanie's face and smiled. "Go to Endlewood. The next step of your journey begins."

With that, Melanie was transported back to outside her tent, once again alone with the stars. Elethýna had gone.

CHAPTER
33
Amends

Thendrell waited by Helnah's bedside for a long time. Taking on her dragon form would have sucked out whatever life remained in her. *The stubbornness of this woman!*

So, when Helnah suddenly opened her eyes and gasped for air, Thendrell nearly fell out of his chair.

Helnah looked around wildly. Then her eyes shut, and she sunk into her bed again.

"Helnah…?" Thendrell couldn't believe she'd actually survived.

"Thend…" Helnah began, her voice barely audible.

"How are you here?"

Helnah replied weakly, "I don't know, but I feel…free."

"Thank the Celestials you are still with us." Thendrell sighed and leaned in closer. "Your plan can still work. I know what is really coming."

Helnah shoved her hand in his face. "Stop!"

Thendrell held her hand. "It's alright, I've known for years. It was why I joined you from the beginning. That and–"

Helnah gasped. "You are not supposed to know!"

"Why not? Tindoria must prepare for this grave danger."

"Silence, Thendrell!" Helnah cried out. Thendrell obeyed,

and Helnah pulled him closer. "His spies are *everywhere*. It isn't safe for *anyone* to know my plan but me and me alone. You are never to speak of this again."

Helnah took a ragged breath, and Thendrell put his hand on her forehead. She was burning, and she slipped from consciousness. Thendrell brushed aside Helnah's hair, which had always veiled the ashy black scales and white eye. But now, he saw the scales had begun to flake off. He brushed them gently, and a mucus-like residue squeezed through them as he wiped them off her face, leaving just scars behind.

Thendrell knew that without Helnah, Tindoria was doomed. Rising from his seat, he left the room, preparing what he would tell the men. Surrender was the only way to avoid annihilation. He met Helketh, who knelt over Keth's body still in the throne room.

"It was only a matter of time before he got himself killed," Helketh said, his voice hollow in the large empty room. Unfolding the sheet that lay in his lap, he draped it over the body.

"Helnah has been defeated," Thendrell said.

Rising to his feet, Helketh sighed. "So we both lost someone today."

"We must surrender, so you are coming with me to sign the treaty."

Helketh crossed his arms. "I will not be a prisoner of war."

Thendrell took a step closer, his blue eyes glaring. "Prison is merciful. We'll be lucky they don't execute us all. Drafting a treaty gives us a chance."

Helketh took a deep breath and finally nodded. "So be it."

"We set out overmorrow," Thendrell finished grimly.

Jason was talking to Wren when the camp's horn blew. Lakéthionic soldiers and knights jumped to their feet. A horseman galloped into camp and cried, "Three Thornbrillians approaching!"

"Three?" asked Lingolm.

"Yes, sir. It's a surrender delegation."

Everyone looked at each other, excited that a surrender was finally happening.

Helketh rode a tarothyl, and he raised an iron pole with a long white banner. On his left rode Thendrell who clutched a scroll of parchment. Lingolm and Jason walked up to them.

"Thornbrill surrenders," Thendrell said.

"A wise decision, because, you know, Helnah's gone," Jason quipped.

They think Helnah is dead, Thendrell thought. *If they know she's still alive, they'll attack again.*

Thendrell handed General Lingolm a scroll. When he unrolled it, he read the terms on which Thornbrill was to surrender.

"Come with us," Lingolm instructed the three men and showed them to his tent. Melanie, Jason, Briefur, and Fallon followed.

Thendrell explained, "With Helnah no longer with us, we cannot control her dragon army, and thus cannot withstand a second attack. I wish to surrender before any more of my men's lives are lost."

Melanie was fuming. They deserved no mercy after Helnah killed Elken. They deserved to be wiped out for the atrocities they committed under her rule. She slid the treaty around so she could read it. Lakéthion would take custody of all their weapons, soldiers, and coin, but Thendrell would stay behind in the fortress. He would agree to random inspections to further prove he had no sinister intention other than to live in solitude, and would surrender any equipment necessary to ensure their trust.

Melanie's hands tightened to fists. Punching the table as she stood, she shouted, "Elken died! Helnah killed him! You're very lucky there's a table between us—"

Jason pulled her back from Thendrell and apologized to Lingolm. "Forgive my sister. She hasn't eaten or slept, and she's half-mad with grief." He escorted Melanie from the tent, telling her to cool down before she blew it, then came back and sat down.

Thendrell asked, "Were they close?"

Jason was about to answer when Lingolm held up his hand and took over. "That is irrelevant. As I recall, we were discussing the terms of your surrender."

Their conversation continued back and forth until all representatives signed the contract. Jason, who couldn't quite follow their decisions nor their tactics of negotiation, took his leave to visit Wren. The boy sat in the medical tent, fiddling with a tiny wooden bird.

Jason walked in and said, "Hey, buddy." He sat down and asked, "What's that?"

Wren held it up. "The chieftainess gave it to me." He spoke with the same accent as Laena.

"You ready to go home?" Jason asked.

"Now?" Wren's eyes widened in disbelief.

"Yeah!" Jason said. "Come on, let's go."

Jason picked up Wren and gave him a piggy-back ride to Poison Ivy's post.

"Here you go, bud," Jason said as he lifted Wren onto Poison Ivy's back. He mounted behind Wren and held onto him. "Okay, Pi, fly."

With a shake of her head, Poison Ivy took off. Jason and Wren looked around. They could see for miles. Mountain ranges rose above the clouds.

"Where do you live, Wren?" Jason asked above the wind.

"Endlewood."

"Well..." Jason scratched his head, "I don't know where that is or how to get there."

"My home is to the west. It's very green."

Poison Ivy hovered in place and sniffed the air. With her dragon senses, she knew where west was, and she flew off in that direction.

Jason bundled Wren in his cloak against the cold wind. Wren told Jason about the day he was stolen from his home by a dragon during an attack. After the poison injection, his heart had never rested. It had been a constant pounding that kept him awake during those long, lonely nights. Sharp pains stabbed at every part of his body as he transformed. He had never felt more worthless.

The battle where he met Jason was his first, and he barely remembered any of it. He remembered waking up with no clothes, covered in blood, and surrounded in smoke. He ran off only to be intercepted by the Hündr, who took him in. Wren grew quiet as the horrors replayed in his mind. Sensing his distress, Jason held the boy closer, and they flew the rest of the flight in silence.

Wren was asleep when Jason spotted the city. A collection of green towers and spires, it must have been twice the size of Lakéthion. But what else would Jason expect? From what he'd heard, this was the capital of Tindoria.

Pi beat her wings, and they plummeted towards the city. Jason shook Wren awake as he marveled. This was no city. This was a medieval metropolis.

Huge buildings rose in glittering towers of green stone. Many levels of huge archways soared between them. The wide streets were filled with such bustle that Jason wondered how they could function so smoothly without stoplights or traffic control. There were streets and sidewalks for people and wider highways for horses and carriages. And at the center of the city was the castle, a magnificent architectural wonder. The spanning structure contained stained glass windows several stories tall, towers as wide as his house, and countless graceful staircases.

As the kingdom's walls neared, horns sounded an alarm.

"Dragon attack!" a guard shouted, loading a ballista.

Jason maneuvered Pi onto the turret and said, "No, no, stop!"

The guard looked like he was about to wet his pants when he saw Jason on Poison Ivy.

Jason continued, "I'm just here to take this boy home, okay? Cool? Alright, now tell your troops 'false alarm' and go have breakfast or something. Ciao!"

Jason cruised Pi through the city, asking Wren where he lived and if any place looked familiar. Not knowing what to expect from an eight-year-old, Jason continued to hope they would find at least someplace or someone Wren knew. The cityscape lessened as Poison Ivy carried them into the neighborhood sectors.

"Wait!" Wren grabbed Jason's hand. "That street! I know that painting."

Poison Ivy swooped right, passing the mural, and glided over the people below, causing a commotion among the unsuspecting citizens. Poison Ivy landed in a quiet neighborhood lane.

Dismounting, Wren pulled Jason along when he saw his house. "Faster, Jason! Come on!"

Running behind the boy, Jason tugged Ivy into a trot.

"Mother!" Wren squealed, approaching a young woman watering her flowers.

She whipped her head around in shock. "Wren? Oh, my

darling!" She grasped his shoulders and studied his face. "My precious son, is it you?"

Wren nodded enthusiastically. "Yes, Mother!" He hugged her, and she began to weep. When Wren's mother looked up from her son, she saw Jason.

"Jason saved me, Mother," Wren explained, "and he brought me back."

"Oh, thank you, thank you so much!" she sobbed. "Jason, how can we ever repay you?"

"Oh, there's no need." In reality, Jason had no idea what to ask for.

The woman shook her head adamantly. "There is no greater pain than a mother losing her son, yet no greater joy when she is reunited. There must be some way, please."

Jason thought for a while before giving her his decision. "You can spread the news that Thornbrill has surrendered and Helnah is dead."

Wren's mother stared at Jason with wide eyes and a hand over her pounding heart. "Is that true?"

Jason nodded. "I witnessed it all."

Wren's mother looked Jason up and down with deep admiration and gratitude for this brave, young knight. She knelt before him and said softly, "You surely must be the one in the Scroll, for only a great man of courage and power could achieve such a victory."

Jason lifted her to her feet and said, "Well, I would say your son has twice the bravery."

Wren's mother wiped her tears and pulled Wren close.

"I hope we meet again." Jason mounted his dragon.

"I will spread this news so all may know!"

With a final wave to Wren and his mother, Jason flew away. He looked back one last time and saw a man run towards them, embracing them in a huge hug.

Jason and Poison Ivy flew out of the city, which drew screams from terrified citizens, but as he moved on, they changed to shrieks and cheers. Before he exited the city walls, a guard called out to him from a parapet. Jason landed Poison Ivy.

The guard fell on one knee. "His Majesty King Eldrain wishes an audience with you and any companions you have at the soonest moment you find. Bear this message with haste and return, for all of Endlewood will be gathered to see."

"Oh. Okay," Jason replied, not quite grasping the significance of the news, and took to the air. During the silence, Jason had time to entertain his many thoughts—the most prominent one being he had cured Wren somehow. Somehow Jason found the cure. Replaying the last moments of the battle over and over, he tried to think of anything that might have caused the reversal of the poison.

When Jason and Poison Ivy returned to camp later that afternoon, there were one hundred and ten new men;

all prisoners from Thornbrill. Shackles bound their wrists as Lakéthionic soldiers stripped them of any weapons. The Thornbrillian's heads hung low and grumbles flitted among them as they were loaded into large prison wagons. They would be sentenced for aiding in abducting children and plundering the kingdoms.

Suddenly, a hand pulled Jason and swung him behind a tent. He found himself facing Fallon and Briefur.

"There you guys are! What are you doing?" Jason asked. "By the way, there's got to be a less painful way to get my attention," he added, massaging his wrist.

"I overheard the surrender treaty," Fallon said, "and Thendrell said he wished to stay behind in Thornbrill."

"Without weapons and without guards, mind you," Briefur added.

"So?" Jason shrugged. "He said he was taking the isolation as punishment."

"You don't really believe that," Fallon frowned. "Don't you think it strange that he'll be the only one in that huge fortress?"

"Maybe just a little bit," Jason answered.

"I'm going to send my sister Bareth to spy," Briefur said. "She's better at espionage than anyone else I know."

"I don't know." Jason shifted his weight. "If she's discovered, that breaks—"

"She won't be," Briefur said with certainty.

"Now that Thornbrill has surrendered, we shouldn't do or say anything to mess this up. That includes complaining about the treaty, okay?"

Fallon and Briefur nodded.

"Oh, Briefur!" Jason exclaimed, shooting finger guns at the now very confused trarewolf. "A while ago, Melanie told me you got cured by some medicine. You wouldn't happen to have any left would you?"

"Yes, why?"

"I want to examine it," Jason replied, "I think I know how to save the rest of the dragon kids."

"What is this stuff?" asked Jason. He stood in the medical tent, looking through a magnifying scope. It was made of brass and reminiscent of a spyglass, and it was attached to a tabletop base by a brass arm, allowing hands-free use. Jason had taken a drop of the medicine that cured Briefur, and was examining it on a plate through the scope's many layers of crystal lenses. He moved aside and pivoted the device for Briefur to see.

"I don't believe it!" Briefur gasped.

"What?"

"I see traces of Yelnight crystal in this medicine."

"Which is...what exactly?"

Briefur stood back from the scope and explained, "Yelnight crystal is very rare, and extremely valuable for its healing properties. Only a very small amount is ever used at any given time. This small dosage sustained me for several days after being severely wounded. But I suspect if one were given a stronger dose, they could be cured instantly. "

"So"—Jason looked back into the scope—"you think this stuff cured Wren?"

Briefur shrugged. "Possibly, but…" He looked at Jason. "…did you have Yelnight crystal with you?"

Jason shook his head. "I don't—wait!" Jason unsheathed one of his knives and placed it under the scope. He looked through the scope and cried, "I knew it!"

Briefur pushed him out of the way and looked, too. "What?" Little specks of crystal sparkled on Jason's blade.

"How did you get Yelnight crystal on your knife?" Briefur asked.

"When I helped Elken in Lakéthion. I spilled some of it, and…" Jason grabbed a piece of parchment, detached his scabbard, and tipped it upside down. Pure, shimmering crystal trickled onto the paper. "…some of it got into my scabbard, essentially coating my weapon each time it was sheathed."

Briefur crossed his arms. "That is a lot of crystal."

"Which is awesome!" Jason took the parchment paper and delicately poured the powder into a black pouch. Jason left the equipment to be packed and headed over to Poison Ivy, who was tethered to a tree at the edge of the compound.

"Jason!" Fallon ran after him. "Where are you going?"

"I'm gonna save those kids."

"We're coming with you."

Jason nodded and mounted his dragon and took off

towards the Iron Gates. Poison Ivy zoomed over the trees, Briefur and Fallon below, and landed in front of the Gates. They were unhinged and battered.

"Whoa whoa whoa," Jason studied the open doors. "What is this?"

"The dragons must have knocked them down when they returned," Briefur guessed as he inspected the damage.

"Yeah, and with nowhere to go, I can only hope they stayed in here." Jason walked into the entrance, the shadows swallowing him. A wyvern swooped down, chomping the air before landing gracelessly with a thud. Jason drew his knives, Fallon doing the same behind him.

When the wyvern turned around, Jason cried out, "Laena!"

The dragon froze, blinked a few times, then stumbled back. Laena squinted her eyes, as if to make sure Jason was actually there. She cautiously walked over to him, then her eyes widened.

"I told you I'd find you!" Jason said, reaching out for her. "And I was hoping you'd be here because, guess what? I think I can cure you!"

Laena straightened and tried to speak.

"Sorry, but I don't understand what you're saying," Jason said. "Just lie down, and I'll have you fixed in no time."

Laena did as she was told, and Jason knelt next to her, one knife still drawn. The wyvern eyed it and squirmed.

"It's okay," Jason soothed. "This shouldn't hurt a whole lot." He took his knife and made a tiny puncture in her black scar on her chest—the same mark of poison Wren had—with the tip of his knife. Laena barked as Jason drove it a little further into her chest. "I have to get to your bloodstream," he explained. Pulling out his black pouch, he carefully pressed the crystal sand into Laena's cut. "Just give it time," Jason instructed as the cut began to glow beneath his hands.

Jason felt a tingling in his hands that spread over his body. He closed his eyes to concentrate. The crystal bubbled in clear jelly, and through Jason's magical vision, he saw it seeping through veins and arteries, soaking up a black substance. Jason began to sweat as his whole body heated like a furnace.

Seconds later, Laena started to shrink. Her scaly skin slipped off in sheets, and a wet, stringy substance leaked out underneath. Her wings wilted and withered off her arms.

That was when Jason made a face. "Ooh…" He watched Laena slowly transform back into her old self, but told Briefur, "Could you guys step aside for a few minutes?"

Briefur grabbed his cousin and left without question.

Jason hurriedly unclasped his cloak and wrapped the half-conscious Laena in it before leaving.

When Laena finally made sense of what happened, she sat up. She was perfectly human and perfectly naked. Seeing her own arms again, she choked on a sob. Laena spun around, searching for Jason, but he was gone. She wiped off the mysterious residue and wrapped the cloak more tightly as she ran out of the Maze calling, "Jason!"

She found him outside sitting on the ground and taking deep breaths. Approaching quietly, she asked softly, "Jason?"

Quickly wiping his brow, he turned around and smiled

in relief. "Laena! Hi…! Um, I just wanted to give you some privacy since—"

Laena smiled, which Jason had never seen before, and threw her arms around him, crying.

"Hey, don't cry," he said.

"Thank you!" Laena sobbed, then pulled away and wiped her eyes. "Oh, thank you! I never thought…"

Jason nodded in understanding.

Tears still streamed down her face, and Jason softly wiped them away. "Well, you're back now."

Laena laughed through the tears and nodded. "Yes."

Jason looked toward the cave and said, "Those kids are gonna need some clothes. They seriously outgrew their old ones."

Laena smirked. "Let me see to it. It's the least I can do." Hearing her own voice made her want to cry all over again.

Briefur and Fallon approached, excitement written on their faces at Laena's successful recovery.

"My people have extra clothes for you," Fallon told her. "We can't have you walking around in naught but your skin!"

When they reached camp, Laena did not go unnoticed. She caught the attention of some of the soldiers who began whispering in confusion. A strange girl wrapped in fur was sure to raise questions.

Jason dismounted and helped Laena off.

"Where are we going?" she asked as Jason brought her to General Lingolm's tent.

"General!" Jason announced as he entered.

Startled at the unscheduled visit, Lingolm demanded why he was there.

"Sir, I found the cure," Jason gestured to Laena. "To save the rest, I need Yelnight crystal on a large scale."

Lingolm scanned Laena, his voice soft. "I have a nephew who was taken. How many of you are there? How much crystal do you need?"

"We have a central nest in the heart of the volcano." Laena took a deep breath. "I must have seen over a hundred. You'll need a chest's worth to tend to everyone."

Lingolm nodded. "Consider it done. I'll dispatch troops to the other kingdoms."

"Oh speaking of, King Eldrain wants to see us at his palace immediately," Jason added, then muttered, "Almost forgot about that..."

"I'll arrange our departure then."

"You're coming with us to Endlewood, right?"

"My duty lies with my men, and I wish to see them home safely."

The Lakéthion army began packing, giving Melanie a chance to actually do something. She helped take down tents, saddle horses, and load luggage. Jason thought that was good; it might help Melanie get her mind off her heartache.

Scalaed was never far from her, watching her like a guardian and occasionally stroking her with his nose to make sure she was okay. She smiled a little more, talked a little more, and Jason saw her eyes were less sad.

"You guys can ride with us if you want," Melanie told Briefur and Fallon as she mounted Scalaed. "That way you don't have to run the distance."

General Lingolm passed the two dragons, and Jason asked, "You sure you don't want to come with us? You've got to have a second-in-command to take your place, right?"

"I won't be missed. In any way, I must return home our wounded and dead. Then I will do my best to collect your Yelnight crystal."

"Thank you, sir." Jason turned to Laena seated behind him. "Hold on," he told her.

She immediately wrapped her arms around him, squeezing him.

Jason gasped. "Not that tight!"

"Sorry."

The dragons leaped into the air and started to fly towards Endlewood.

"Excuse us," Jason said as he shuffled through crowds of people. Laena held onto his hand, determined not to lose him.

He chose to stay with Laena as the rest of his companions had gone on ahead. He wanted to see her returned safely to her family.

Some people who saw Jason started screaming and cheering and made way for him. One older woman said, "Helnah of Thornbrill is dead! Thank the Celestials for you, young man!"

Suddenly, Laena let go of his hand and started running towards a broad, richly dressed man. His hair color matched his daughter's.

"Father!" Laena shrieked, and the man spun around.

Eyes wide in disbelief, he held out his arms. "Laena!"

She ran into them and buried her face in his mountainous fur cloak.

Jason decided now would be a good time to slip away. He already had people chanting his name behind him, and that was plenty of praise for the moment.

With some help from the palace guards, Jason disappeared behind the doors to the palace and just stood there. The clamor of people dulled behind the castle walls, and Jason rubbed his head wearily before walking down the hallway. Melanie rammed into him from around the corner.

"Oof!" Jason grunted as he fell to the ground. "Ugh, Mel...whoa."

Melanie wore an orange silk ballgown. Her sleeves rested on the sides of her arms, and intricately stitched flowers spilled down the side of her dress.

"Hey, you look gorgeous!" Jason complimented.

Melanie smiled. "Thanks! My hair is really soft, too. I think I'm gonna take one of those brushes back home with me; I swear they're magic."

Jason raised an eyebrow, but smiled back. It was nice to hear her make a joke.

"We're going to be on the balcony with King Eldrain as he thanks us publicly."

"Oh wow, okay."

"You need to change," Melanie ordered. "Follow me or you'll be late!"

The crowd went wild as King Eldrain appeared on the balcony with Melanie and the rest behind him. Teetering from nerves on her high heels, Melanie hoped she wouldn't have to say anything to all these people.

Jason held his hands behind his back so no one could see him twiddling his thumbs. Every city square and building window was packed with cheering subjects, and soldiers waved the city's flag from the towers.

Jason felt Fallon's tail brush against his leg. He looked over at her with amusement, and she scooted more to her right. Fallon's tail still twitched from underneath her orange pelt dress. While looking stiff in his fur and leather trench coat, Briefur stood beside Melanie, whose eyes were fixed on the king. In the space behind them, Scalaed and Poison Ivy sat on their haunches.

When the crowd silenced themselves, King Eldrain began his speech. "With Helnah and Thornbrill defeated and their army in chains, the kingdoms of Tindoria can once more live in peace. We owe our lives to those who made this victory possible." He gestured behind him. "If it were not for them and their sacrifice"—Melanie's heart sank as she thought of Elken—"our cities would ultimately be in ruins, and our legacies in ashes. Let all kingdoms know of their greatness and celebrate a time of peace!"

The people down below cheered again, and the soldiers on the towers fired flaming arrows into the sky. They exploded in rainbow sparks.

The king ushered the heroes to the front of the balcony, and the crowd cheered even more loudly, which Melanie hadn't thought possible. She looked at the overjoyed crowd, the fireworks, and began to smile. Lifting her arm, she waved to Endlewood. *We did it. We saved Tindoria! We can go home.*

Melanie was whisked into a great ballroom where a huge feast had been laid out on a long table. Couples danced on the floor, and she stiffened. *Elken could have been here...with me.*

"I may not be Elken, but may I have this dance?" Jason held out his hand.

Melanie melted as she took it. "You can't dance, goof."

"Neither can you! We're a match made in heaven." Jason twirled her out, her dress spreading like a blooming flower. While those around them performed tidy, choreographed steps, Melanie and Jason danced to their own rhythm. Jason kept Melanie spinning, and he dipped her as often as needed to finally make her laugh. Her hairdo was coming undone, but she was smiling.

Then the music slowed, and the two saw one another for who they were in the moment. Siblings. Adrift on another planet. Inseparable.

Melanie leaned her head on Jason's shoulder as they waltzed.

"Love you, Sis," Jason said, patting her head.

"I love you, too."

They waltzed through a cloud of delicious aromas, and they wandered off the dance floor towards a food display. There they saw a familiar face.

"Baraden?"

He turned around and gave a huge smile. "My friends! The whole world is indebted to you and your companions."

"Wow, word travels really fast," Melanie remarked.

"Probably those birds," Jason scoffed into his cream-filled pastry.

"I look forward to what else you achieve while here."

Melanie's breath caught. "'What else?' No, no, we already saved the world."

"Well, I've decided to stay behind to help now that I found a cure for the poison." Jason gestured as he reached for seconds. "You were probably too depressed to remember."

"But, Helnah's death," Melanie stammered, "the scroll… we fulfilled it!"

Baraden raised his eyebrows. "Whatever do you mean? You have not even read it. Which is why I'm here. There is more to the Scroll than you realize, and even more to your destinies."

Melanie froze and whipped her head to Jason, who slowed his eating. "Wait, we don't get to go home after rescuing the kids?" Jason met Melanie's wide eyes.

"Oh, no, Melanie and Jason," Baraden said. "Tomorrow you will read the Scroll yourselves. Your purpose here has only just begun."

Acknowledgments

This book has had quite the tumultuous origin. Over fourteen years, *Prisoners of Thornbrill* has seen major rewrites, sat in limbo for years, and was even published then unpublished! But here it is, finally in your hands, so I'd love to thank you, reader, for giving my story a chance!

I also wouldn't be here without my alpha readers: my incredible parents. My mom caught plotholes and was always brimming with amazing new ideas on how to fix them. My dad taught me the importance and impact of saying much with little. There were so many words trimmed from that first draft!

Thank you to my favorite teacher of all time, Andrew Pudewa, who taught creative writing with such passion it spurred my own efforts to write and complete a novel; I miss being your student! I always think of you whenever I write participle phrase sentence openers. "The thing after the comma is the thing doing the -inging" will forever be ingrained in my brain!

When I joined the instagram book community, my mind was blown by the ways I really should have launched my book. After a ton of prayer, I unpublished the first edition and met many new friends who gave wise advice on self-publishing and how to grow a reader base. All these amazing authors are a huge inspiration, have incredible books, and I'm so grateful I got to know them!

So off my book went to my beta readers. Elissa, Sam, Heather, and Hannah, I can't thank you enough for your time and insight, and for finally helping me understand "show don't tell." You guys rock!

And Victoria, you are a light in the indie author community, and I thank you for your prayers and help with the first "new" draft. You are a joy to talk to!

Another *huge* thank you to Addison! I have never been more excited while reading an editor's notes. Every comment and recommendation inflamed my love for my story even more. You asked the right questions, pressed for more details, and showed me the importance of story structure and meaning. With every suggestion, I felt my story growing stronger. I devoured your edits and knowledge with hungry obsession!

Renee, you blew through this book so fast, which stunned me! Thank you for your final set of eyes and speedy turnaround time.

Of course, I thank my Lord God for creating me with this fantasy-driven imagination of mine. This story is His as much as it is mine. Dear Holy Spirit, thank you for infusing me with perseverance on days I wanted to give up. I also thank Jesus my Savior for being by my side and talking about what direction to take my book. May It Happen Press is a tribute to You and your holy mother's words of submission to the Divine Will. Heavenly Father, may Your Will always be done in my life and works. May I strive to be who You made me to be. All praise and glory are Yours, forever and ever.

Kickstarter Acknowledgments

Thank you to every single person who backed my Kickstarter campaign! It is because of these generous people that *Prisoners of Thornbrill* was brought to life.

Wes Adam
The Bickfords
George Carpenter
Chris Cox
Taylor Fleming
Heather Fletcher
Olivia Gratehouse
Sterling Jaquith
Dmytro Kocherhan
Krystle

Victoria Lynn
Miranda Markley
Christine Pennington
Nathan Pennington
Andrew Pudewa
Maria Snow
Lexi Spencer
Lauren Straus
Francesco Tehrani
Adrian J. Whitaker

About the Author

Hannah has been writing stories since she was seven. From stapling together hand-written and illustrated stories to give her siblings on Christmas, to a fantasy collab with her best friend where they alternated writing chapters and put them in each other's mailboxes, to Star Wars: Clone Wars fanfiction, which featured her first original character: a bug-eyed alien named Chihuahua Huffus.

When Hannah was eleven, the beginning foundations of what would later become The Tindoria Chronicles began to form in her imagination. Thus began the very first draft. At first, it was simply a pastime she enjoyed, and she was mainly writing for herself. As her world and story grew, however, she realized she had something really special and dreamed of sharing it with the world. So she began to tackle her writing journey with a new end goal in mind of being a real author. While it took her over ten years to finish Prisoners of Thornbrill (book 1), it was all in God's perfect timing, and Hannah couldn't be happier than where she is now.

She is a proud support of the #ProtectCleanFiction movement, and strives to spread awareness alongside other like-minded authors of the psychological effects from reading explicit sensual content. Visit www.protectcleanfiction.com for more information.

To follow Hannah on her author journey and receive exclusive news and content about upcoming projects, be sure to subscribe to her free monthly email newsletter: www.hannahpenningtonauthor.com/subscribe

Instagram: @hannahpennington.author
Facebook: @hannahpennington.author
www.hannahpenningtonauthor.com

www.ingramcontent.com/pod-product-compliance
Lightning Source LLC
Chambersburg PA
CBHW030130310726
48970CB00005B/1372